Praise for **ALWAYS**

"[Sarah] Jio's novel is a fantastic read that explores the world of lost love in a poignant and beautiful way, while still being light and easy to digest. The protagonist is one whom readers can relate to. . . . Jio's tale also beautifully blends stories from both the past and the present. . . . It's a great read and comes with high recommendations."

—RT Book Reviews

"Jio's . . . newest novel explores intersections of past and present and the complexities of love. . . . [Kailey] must confront her own past as she tries to figure out what she really wants. . . . Fans of Jio's work will still find her signature emotional depth."

—Publishers Weekly

"A heartwarming story of personal growth and the power of nostalgia . . . Fans of Elin Hilderbrand and Emily Giffin should enjoy this warm and compassionate novel."

—Booklist

"Perfect for fireside reading."

—PopSugar

"When it comes down to it, Always isn't just one love story. It's layers of love stories to which everyone can relate. Choices, sacrifices, actions, reactions. All lead to true love."

—Fort Worth Star-Telegram

"This quick beach read will appeal to those seeking a clean romance as well as to fans of Elin Hilderbrand and Karen White."

—Library Journal

"A beautiful combination of heartfelt struggles, deep connections and social issues that should not be ignored . . . Five stars indeed!"

—Winter Haven Books

ALWAYS

Always

A NOVEL

SARAH JIO

BALLANTINE BOOKS
NEW YORK

2018 Ballantine Trade Paperback Edition

Copyright © 2016 by Sarah Jio
Reading group guide copyright 2018 by Penguin Random House LLC

Published in the United States by Ballantine Books, an imprint of Random House, a division of Penguin Random House LLC, New York.

BALLANTINE and the HOUSE colophon are registered trademarks of Penguin Random House LLC.

RANDOM HOUSE READER'S CIRCLE & Design is a registered trademark of Penguin Random House LLC.

Originally published in hardcover in the United States by Ballantine Books, an imprint of Random House, a division of Penguin Random House LLC, in 2016.

LIBRARY OF CONGRESS CATALOGING-IN-PUBLICATION DATA
Names: Jio, Sarah, author.
Title: Always: a novel / Sarah Jio.
Description: First edition. | New York : Ballantine Books, 2017.
Identifiers: LCCN 2016032331 (print) | LCCN 2016039989 (ebook) |
ISBN 9781101885048 (paperback) | ISBN 9781101885031 (ebook)
Subjects: LCSH: Triangles (Interpersonal relations)—Fiction. | Man–woman
relationships—Fiction. | Mate selection—Fiction. | BISAC: FICTION / Contemporary
Women. | FICTION / Romance / Contemporary. | FICTION / Sagas. |
GSAFD: Love stories.
Classification: LCC PS3610.I6 A79 2017 (print) | LCC PS3610.I6 (ebook) |
DDC 813/.6—dc23
LC record available at https://lccn.loc.gov/2016032331

Hardcover ISBN 978-1-101-88502-4
International edition ISBN 978-1-101-96604-4
Ebook ISBN 978-1-101-88503-1

Printed in the United States of America

randomhousebooks.com
randomhousereaderscircle.com

2 4 6 8 9 7 5 3

Book design by Susan Turner

To old love and new, but most of all, to the kind that lasts, always

*Have enough courage to trust love one more time
and always one more time.*

—Maya Angelou

ALWAYS

one

"Oh no, why do I *always* do that?" I say to my fiancé, Ryan, as we walk into the restaurant.

"Do what, baby?"

"Leave my purse in the car."

We've just valet-parked, and as we look out the window, Ryan's white BMW is being driven off. "I'll go get it, my forgetful one," he says, kissing my cheek. "You grab our table. I'll be back in a sec."

Four years ago, we had our first date at Le Marche, the French restaurant on Fourth Avenue with a waiting list five months out. Somehow Ryan was able to get us a table, just like he got us one tonight. My fiancé, it seems, can move mountains.

"I want you to have a perfect night," he said when he surprised me with the reservation. He reached for my hand as if he never wanted to let go, the diamond, much larger than I wanted, sparkling on my ring finger. We're getting married in July, at the Fairmont.

"Do you have a reservation?" the host asks as I check my coat.

"Yes," I say. "Two. Under Winston." It's hard to believe, but in a matter of months I'll be Mrs. Ryan Winston; that is, if I take Ryan's name. He wants me to, and part of me does, as well. I mean, this is the *Winston* family, confidants of the Gateses and the Nordstroms. This is a family name one doesn't eschew.

But I've always been Kailey Crain. *KC,* although no one has really called me that since, well, the sixth grade. Still, it's hard to just let that go. I close my eyes tightly, then open them again, trying to banish a memory that's fighting its way to the surface.

"Right this way," the host says, leading me to an intimate table by the window. I peer through the glass, noticing the way the raindrops make the lights outside look like gemstones. Seattle may be an old gray lady, but she still sparkles under cloud cover. I tug nervously at the right sleeve of my dress, pulling it higher on my arm, the way I do when I'm mingling with the type of people Ryan grew up with. He isn't a big fan of the tattoo on my shoulder, and I suppose I'm not either. Skin inked a decade prior is a glaring reminder of a past that didn't become a future, of the dreams that evaporated into thin air. I couldn't hold on to them, and yet the word *toujours,* French for "always," remains branded on my skin. I rub my shoulder, wishing for a magic eraser.

I sit down, place my cellphone on the table, and watch as couples stroll by outside, hovering under hoods and shared umbrellas. A woman in her twenties clutches her boyfriend or husband, and they laugh as they precariously dodge a mud puddle. The scene transports me back to age twenty-two, to the year Tracy and I moved to Seattle. Back then, we were wide-eyed and idealistic. We believed in true love and happy endings.

Funny how things turn out.

I catch my reflection in the window. My shoulder-length brown hair is showing signs of frizz, rendering the time I spent flat-ironing my thick, naturally wavy locks a veritable waste of time. But what did it matter—wasn't Ryan always telling me he liked my natural curls? My green eyes? My nose dusted with freckles? I smile to myself. My life is full now, with my job at the *Herald,* making plans to remodel the Craftsman in Wallingford, the one I bought with . . . Ryan, of course.

I smile as he walks into the restaurant with my purse in hand.

"It's a monsoon out there," he says, handing me the black Michael Kors bag he bought me for Christmas last year, then smoothing his rain-soaked hair. *Handsome* is the best word to describe him. Classically handsome. Tracy's initial impression, whispered in the bathroom of a restaurant the night I first introduced them, was that he resembled a strapping Disney prince come to life. He did, and he does. Tall and toned with a thick head of dark hair: Give him a shield and white horse and Ryan is the spitting image of the cartoon prince who swept Cinderella off her feet. I'm lucky.

He reaches for my hand across the table. "I called earlier and made sure they had your favorite Bordeaux. Remember, our perfect night is just beginning."

I grin as he pulls my hand to his lips.

"Every detail counts," he says with a sweet smile. "You've seemed a little distracted, and I want to be there for you."

I tug on my engagement ring and nod. He's always been able to read me, perhaps better than I can read myself. "It's been hell at work since I've added the business beat to my ongoing reporting on life in Seattle," I reply. "I've been crunching to get that series about Pioneer Square written."

The first of three pieces was published today. I'm certain Ryan has read it, but we've agreed to disagree on the areas where our professional interests diverge. He's a smart man, sharp enough to know that his taking issue with my article would ruin the night before it has even begun.

He bends the rules by steering the conversation to other people's opinions, people who are not present at this cozy table for two. "You know, a lot of my colleagues think they should dynamite that six-block radius."

I shake my head. "Is that you talking or your risk-management team?"

"It's difficult to ignore the fact that there isn't much down there but addicts and vagrants. You can barely walk two feet without stepping in human excrement."

"Well," I say, weighing the satisfaction of making my case against Ryan's romantic plans for the evening, "the people there need help, and the Hope Gospel Mission is the only organization doing anything about it. The way I see it, the vitality of a nonprofit is a crucial measure of neighborhood longevity. You can't blame me for wanting to help them keep their doors open."

The sommelier arrives and uncorks Ryan's preselected bottle of red before pouring us each a glass.

"Honey," Ryan says tenderly as I take a sip of my wine. "You have the biggest heart of anyone I know. How could I ever blame you? For anything?"

I think of the sensitive content of the series, how hard I have to work not to let emotion cloud the impartiality that being a good reporter demands. Earlier today, I spent the afternoon interviewing the mission's director, a heavyset woman named Melissa. She looked into my eyes and practically begged me to protect the organization from the very developers Ryan works with—builders hungry to throw up cheap apartment buildings, displacing the lifelines for hundreds of homeless people in the process.

True, Seattle's Pioneer Square neighborhood is a bit on the seedier side, and development could bring new life to its streets, but Ryan painted a grim picture of a place I loved so long ago and still do. Anyone with a heart for the down-and-out could see that the plan to overhaul the neighborhood would not only close the doors of the Hope Gospel Mission, it would entail demolishing thousands of low-income units and two shelters. As such, property developers, many of whose financial outlooks Ryan manages, remained in gridlock with the city of Seattle.

"I guess I just like it the way it is," I say. "The neighborhood has an old Seattle feel. It's gritty, I know. But it's real. And it's home to so many people."

"Didn't you used to live down there?"

His question is one I would rather not answer, so I busy myself refolding the napkin in my lap.

"No," I finally say. "But I used to know someone who did."

I don't tell him that over the years my curiosity about that *someone* has gotten the better of me, eaten at me like a cancer at times. I squeezed the marrow out of Google. *Cade,* it seemed, had not only left me but had possibly left the face of the earth. But that is all in the past.

Ryan raises a suspicious eyebrow. "And who is this someone?"

"No one," I say, eager to change the subject. I'm as uninterested in speaking about my past love life as I am in hearing about his, especially the woman he dated before me: Vanessa, the Southern belle whose father and Ryan's were blue-blooded best friends and real-estate moguls with connections on the East and West Coasts. She was a shoo-in to be Mrs. Ryan Winston until I stumbled into his life and ruined their collective plans. Imagine the look on their faces: "Mom, Dad, this is Kailey. I love her. And she has a tattoo!"

When I tried to wrap my head around the situation early on in our relationship, Ryan was direct. "You know as well as I do that Vanessa and I were best suited as friends," he said. "We grew up together."

"And she's still in love with you," I replied without missing a beat. Ryan shook his head. "No, she's not."

"Ryan," I said. "I'm a woman. I saw the way she looked at you in West Virginia." She had been with her family at the Greenbrier for the annual extravaganza Ryan and his family and friends have taken part in for generations. The men golf, and the women lunch. I survived the ordeal by conning a sympathetic waiter into spiking my sweet tea with bourbon.

Ghosts, as Tracy calls these youthful loves. We must not let them haunt.

I look over at my handsome fiancé as he straightens in his chair. Yes, we come from different places and see the world in different ways. He challenges me, and I wouldn't have it any other way. But what informs our past stays there. Ryan is my present. I am grateful that our once-separate paths have converged, brought us here together. Tonight. Forever. Always.

"I love you so much," I whisper, sliding my arm across the white tablecloth to hold his hand.

"I love you, too," he says with an intensity that I swear I can feel in my soul.

As he speaks, rain splatters the window. A full moon shines behind a tiny patch of clearing in the sky, trying desperately to emerge from its cloudy cloak. A supermoon, Tracy said. A physician with a quirky penchant for the mystical, she has talked nonstop about some astrological eclipse that is apparently taking place tonight. And though I have no interest in astrology, I secretly love her daily reports. Somehow I can stomach the woo-woo when carefully curated and sifted by my best friend.

And now I wonder if Ryan's edginess can be blamed on the metaphysical. The thought lingers as I take another sip of wine, silky and peppery at the same time. I hear the telltale crackle inside the glass and a memory surfaces. Like always, I tuck it away, far away, where it belongs. I've long since stopped feeling the ache in my heart that I lived with for so long.

I may not have had closure, but I have tasted wisdom. Anyone who has ever had their heart broken, or even just bruised, has learned that there's finality in the facts. He left. And I've realized that when someone wants to leave, you let him go.

Ryan refills my wineglass and begins telling me about his day. He modestly recounts an incident when a coworker fell asleep during a meeting with the company president. Events could have turned dire, until Ryan surreptitiously set off his cellphone alarm, waking his sleeping colleague in the nick of time. My eyes crinkle with emotion at his kindness. My face melts into a smile.

"I'm happy," I say unprompted. The words leap from my mouth, or maybe my heart. I can't keep them in. "You make me so happy."

"Me too, baby," he says.

My cellphone buzzes, alerting me to a new voicemail, but rather than check it I tuck it into my purse.

Ryan winks and waves his hand to summon the waitress; she appears at our table a moment later. "Can I get a negroni?"

"Yes, sir," she says, turning back to the bar.

We share the salmon and duck-fat potatoes and an order of the prawns. "They're a little spicy," Ryan says, taking a bite, "don't you think?"

Ryan has an adventurous palate, a necessity for the fiancé of a food enthusiast, and yet unlike me he doesn't tolerate the taste of heat. I swear I nearly gave him a third-degree burn on his tongue the first time I made him breakfast. The Tabasco I'd whisked in with the eggs for an added kick didn't go over so well. Lesson learned.

"Want to order something else?" I suggest, but Ryan tells me he's happy to watch me enjoy the food. We talk about the wedding. Our gazes drift off to separate corners of the restaurant during the occasional lull in conversation as each of us pauses in turn to consider a key detail that would never have occurred to the other. We're a complementary pair. It's comfortable and nice, the way life is with Ryan, the way it will be for a lifetime. I finish another glass of wine, drinking in the feeling of contentment.

Ryan pays the bill, and we collect our coats. "Why don't you wait here while I get the car," he asks as I button my black wool coat and take what's left of pre-wedding cake, a gift from the chef that our waitress has carefully boxed up.

It's stopped raining, but the temperature has plummeted. "You're so thoughtful," I say. "Thanks, honey."

I watch him walk up the block in his perfectly tailored suit. I'm lucky, I know. This man, with these good looks. He's successful and funny and has eyes only for me. Ryan has it all. I take a deep breath and nod to myself.

Outside the window, a bearded homeless man approaches a couple also waiting for their car. Visibly annoyed, they turn and walk in a different direction as he shrinks back and sits cross-legged on the sidewalk.

The host shakes his head. "Sorry about that," he says. "Once they start loitering, it's hard to get rid of them."

"Maybe he's just hungry," I say. "Do you have any leftovers in the kitchen for him?"

The man shakes his head. "With all due respect, miss, we're not a soup kitchen. Besides, they usually just want money, probably for drugs."

I know from my reporting that this remark is a generalization. Homelessness cannot be singularly blamed on substance abuse. There are hundreds of other reasons why people find themselves on the streets. But I can do more by engaging this kind of thinking in print than in an impromptu confrontation.

I exit to the sidewalk, where I cast a cautious glance at the homeless man. His frame is thin, painfully thin, and his clothes hang from his limbs. I remember the bag of leftover food in my hand and I take a step closer. If only I had more than sugar to offer, but eggs are ingredients in cake.

"Excuse me?" I say. He doesn't seem to hear me, so I repeat myself, a bit louder. "Excuse me, I have some food here. Would you . . . like it?"

He looks up as I approach, and when our eyes meet, I am overcome with a feeling of familiarity that I cannot place. I lose hold of the bag, and it drops from my grasp to the rain-kissed sidewalk at my feet. My brain's circuits fire, and the contents of my memories flood out like an overturned file cabinet. If this man recognizes me, his eyes don't show it. Headlights strobe ahead, and I hear the sound of tires rolling to a stop. I look behind me and see Ryan pulling his car up. Just then the man reaches his bony hand toward the bag and pulls out the box of food. He looks at it for a moment before tentatively opening the container. I can see the hunger in his eyes, and then his hands grab for the cake and he crams it into his mouth, crumbs sticking to his beard.

Ryan rolls down his window. "Kailey, is everything okay?"

I nod and take a step back, then numbly walk to the car, get in.

I don't tell Ryan that I am not okay.

I don't tell Ryan that I know this man.

I don't tell him that his name is *Cade* and he used to be the love of my life.

two

"Do you believe in soulmates?" Tracy asks, book in hand, looking up from the futon in the Seattle apartment we share. With its one wall of exposed brick and floor-to-ceiling windows, we instantly fell in love with the space, even if it was smaller than my childhood bedroom. Two people should not inhabit a 380-foot shoebox of a studio, but recent college graduates who want to live in the coolest building on First Avenue, with a view overlooking Elliott Bay, have to make concessions. Thankfully Tracy doesn't snore.

"No," I say to Tracy, observing the deft flick of her wrist as she rubber-bands her long dark hair into a loose ponytail. Effortlessly beautiful, she has the kind of high cheekbones, lithe frame, and inherent style that would make her a lot of money as a model, except she'd rather gouge her eyes out than pose for a camera.

We were college roommates in Chicago, and after graduation we both took a good long look at a map of the U.S. and pointed to Seattle.

A week later, we packed all of our belongings into the back of her dad's old Subaru with the broken stereo and drove across the country (singing for hours on the long stretches, terribly out of key) to the rainiest city in America. That month, I got a job as a junior reporter for the *Seattle Herald;* Tracy spent her days studying for the MCAT exam. We were living our fledgling dreams.

"Staying home every night is *not* how you do it, my dear," Tracy says, setting her book down and pushing her glasses higher on her nose.

I pour a cup from the Mr. Coffee machine that Grandma bought me at Target on that shopping trip the week before I left for college and plop down in the threadbare red egg-shaped IKEA chair by the window. We're an advertisement for IKEA, the two of us.

"Have you read your horoscope?" Tracy asks.

"Trace, you know I don't believe in that stuff."

"Well," she says, "I'll read it for you, then." She picks up the newspaper from the coffee table, turns a few pages, then reads in silence for a minute. "Aha," she finally says. "New love is in your future." She nods. "But it says, 'You have to open yourself up to it. Instead of staying home, do something spontaneous and unexpected. You never know who you might meet.'"

I roll my eyes.

"Come out with us tonight!" Tracy exclaims.

She's dating a guy named Mark who's doing his surgical residency at the University of Washington. He's tall, with thinning hair and a loud laugh. Whenever they have a free night together, which is rare, he takes her to concerts or plays, or on walks around Green Lake. Sometimes I think I need a Mark in my life. Sometimes I think I'd like someone to take me to the theater or the farmers market or a symphony. "Mark got tickets to Mazzy Star at the Crocodile."

"By agreeing to this," I say, raising my left eyebrow, "am I walking into a blind date?"

"Well," Tracy says mischievously, "his friend Eric *is* coming."

"I don't know," I say, watching the slow path of a ferry leaving the bay.

"Just come," Tracy says, "if only because you love Mazzy Star."

"I do love Mazzy Star," I say with a grin.

She nods. "Good. All settled."

It's just begun to rain, and Tracy, Mark, and I huddle under an awning in front of the club, where a tattooed woman with short bangs and a nose ring takes our tickets. It's dark inside, and some moody music I don't recognize seeps through the overhead speakers. The air is smoky, and every third person around us sports a pair of weathered Doc Martens. I love Seattle.

"Eric will be here in a few," Mark says. "Can I get you girls something to drink?"

"I'll have a vodka soda," Tracy says.

"The same," I add as Mark dutifully approaches the bar.

Tracy elbows me. "Mark says that Eric is one of the top surgical residents at the hospital."

I shrug.

Tracy smiles. "Just have fun. Who knows, you may really like him. Besides—"

I take a step back when someone bumps into me. He's holding a camera with a huge lens, and after the flash goes off, he lowers it to his side. "Oh, I'm sorry," he says, smiling. "I didn't see you standing there." He's a little older than me, with dark hair and a trace of stubble around his chin. His boots and faded plaid shirt hint at his association with the music scene, and yet there's something entirely unique about him. I can't tell by the way he smiles if he's confident or cocky. Or both.

"How great does the stage look under these lights?" He lifts the camera to his eye again, and flashes go off in rapid succession. "Hope has one of the most haunting voices," he says. "But she's humble, you know? She's not one of those diva singers who believes she's God's gift to music."

My eyes narrow. "You talk as if you know her."

"I do," he says, smiling only at me.

Definitely cocky.

"I signed her to my label five years ago," he says. "Just a solo album, but I like to think that it gave her some traction."

"Your label?"

He winks. "I'm in the music biz."

Biz.

"You should have heard her demo tape," he continues. "Pure magic." He taps his chest lightly. "The kind you can feel."

"What do you mean?" I ask cautiously, intrigued.

He takes a step closer to me. "Good music *moves* you. It *changes you,* even." He reaches for my hand and presses it against my chest as the skin on my arms erupts with goosebumps. "Right there. A gifted artist can create music that hits the heart." He lets go of my hand, but I keep it pressed against my chest. "Anyway, that is the type of artist I'm always searching for."

Mark returns with the drinks, and I return my arm to my side.

"I'm Cade," he says, eyes fixed on mine. When he extends his hand, I feel like we're the only two people in the club.

I take it limply. "Kailey Crain."

"KC," he says, grinning.

Mark clears his throat, and I notice that there's a tallish guy with curly brown hair standing beside him. He's wearing a dress shirt tucked into his jeans, which are about an inch too short. "Kailey, this is *Eric.*"

"Well," Cade says with a smile and a quick false bow, "it's been a pleasure. Enjoy the show."

I feel Eric's eyes on me. "So . . . Mark tells me you're a writer," he says eagerly.

"Yeah," I say, taking a sip of my drink. It's stiff and smells like rubbing alcohol; I shudder a little as it goes down. "I report for the *Herald,* but food is my favorite topic."

Involuntarily my gaze wanders across the room to where Cade now has his hand on the shoulder of an attractive blonde. "How about you?" I say, willing my eyes back to Eric's face. "What's your surgical specialty?"

"Feet," he says.

I begin to laugh, then immediately stop when I notice that his expression remains unchanged, not even the hint of a smile.

"Oh, you mean you're not joking? You're really specializing in"— I pause to collect myself—"feet?"

"Yes," he says, straight-faced. "I may be biased, but I think that toes, ankles, heels are, well, some of the most amazing parts of the body. Don't you agree?"

"Well," I say, trying very hard not to laugh, "I guess I really haven't put much thought into, er . . . feet. But I suppose they're . . . pretty great? They do take us where we need to go."

He glances down at my feet just as the opening band walks on-stage and begins playing a song I don't recognize. The crowd erupts in applause. After two songs, the foot doctor leans in closer to me. "This may sound a little forward," he says with a smile, "but I bet you have really beautiful feet." He raises an eyebrow. "I'd love to see them sometime."

I nearly choke on my drink. "You know," I say, edging to the left, "I think I need another cocktail."

"Let me get you one," the foot doctor says.

"No, no," I say quickly. "There's a huge line. I'll . . . just . . . go."

He nods and takes a swig of the beer he's been nursing, then turns to say something to Mark, who I want to murder at this very moment. Tracy too. I make my way to the bar and order another vodka soda, this time a double.

"I'll have the same," Cade says, appearing out of nowhere beside me.

I give him a nervous smile and turn my gaze to the stage.

"So how's your date going?"

"I'm *not* on a date," I protest.

"Oh c'mon, you two have first date written all over you," he says with an amused smile.

"Well," I concede, "if you must know, it's a very unfortunate setup that I did not agree to."

"So you escaped to the bar."

"I did."

"What does the dude do?"

"He's a doctor who specializes in"—I pause and grin—"feet."

"No way."

"Way," I say. "He asked to see mine!"

"Tragic."

"Truly."

The bartender returns with two vodka sodas, and before I can protest, Cade tells him to put it on his tab.

"Hey," he says, taking a sip. "I have an idea."

"What?" I ask curiously.

"Why don't you let me sabotage your date?"

I raise an eyebrow.

"I mean, your nondate." He smiles. "Want to escape backstage?"

"Backstage?"

"Yeah," he says. "You can watch the rest of the show from the best seats in the house and avoid more banter with Dr. Short Pants."

"His pants *were* short, weren't they?"

"Seriously. They're probably illegal in some countries," he adds.

I laugh.

"Come on, what do you say?"

I give him a cautious smile. "Why not," I finally say.

He reaches for my hand and leads me through the crowd to a dark door that blends in with the black walls. We walk down a long hall and find a seat on a couch at the side of the stage.

"Not bad, huh?" After a few more songs, Mazzy Star takes the stage and begins the opening to "Fade into You."

"I love this song," I say.

"Me too," Cade says.

He moves his hands together to the beat of the music, as if he's holding an imaginary instrument. "The tambourine," he continues. "That was a brilliant addition."

"I can hardly imagine Mazzy Star without it," I say. "It's their sound."

He nods, then lifts his hand just as the piano begins, as if to cue it into motion. "Best transition, right there," he says.

"You must be a musician, then?" I ask.

He shakes his head. "No, I can't read a note. I just know music." He pats his heart. "Just like I told you earlier, I feel it." He pauses for a second, then says, "Right here."

I should be watching the band, but I can't take my eyes off him.

"Listen to that line," he says softly. "'I want to hold the hand inside you.' Such a beautiful lyric. Gets me every time."

I nod. "I discovered this song in college. I'd play the song over and over again."

"What does it mean to you?"

I pause, feeling light and floaty from my second drink. I close my eyes, remembering for a tiny moment my naïve imaginings of love.

"I think it speaks to wanting to be entirely united with someone you love. Like the idea of being one room away from someone and missing them, or sitting right beside someone yet feeling this powerful desire to . . ."

"Be even closer," we both say in unison.

I smile and look away. Cade's eyes return to the stage. He reaches for my hand. I let him take it.

three

My heart beats furiously as the phone rings. I stare at the kitchen clock: 11:34 P.M. *Tracy, you'd better be awake. Wake up. Wake up. Wake up.*

"Hello?" She sounds groggy and grumpy.

"Thank God you picked up," I whisper.

"Kailey," she says, her voice robotic and annoyed. "This had *better* be important. I've been on call for a week straight. I *just* closed my eyes."

"Sorry," I say.

"Wait, why are you whispering?"

"I don't want to wake up Ryan. You wouldn't believe who I saw tonight."

She yawns. "I give up."

"Tracy, listen. I saw *Cade.*"

"*Cade* Cade?"

"Yes, Cade. Cade."

"Are you sure?"

I hear a creak at the top of the stairs, so I tiptoe around the corner to see if Ryan's woken up. He hasn't. It's only Eddie, my aging black Lab, on the landing. He's eleven but still a puppy at heart.

"Yes, I'm sure," I whisper. "But, Trace, he wasn't himself. He . . . he didn't even know me."

"What do you mean?"

"Outside of the restaurant tonight, he was . . . he was . . ." I pause for a moment. I almost can't say the word. "He was . . . homeless."

"I don't understand," Tracy replies.

"I hardly recognized him under the beard," I continue. "And his clothes were dirty, rags. I didn't know what to do or say, after all these years. After he just vanished. I thought for sure he'd moved somewhere crazy like Australia, or got married, or *something*." Tears sting my eyes. "But I think he got into some real trouble, Tracy. I think something terrible happened to him."

"Wow," she says. "Does Ryan know?"

"No," I reply. "Not yet. I was so stunned. I just . . . couldn't."

"What are you going to do?"

"I have to help him," I whisper, shaking my head at the enormity of the situation.

"How, Kailey? What if he's on drugs? What if he's dangerous? What if . . . ?"

I shake my head. "No," I say. "Cade could never be dangerous."

Tracy is silent for a moment. "Do you want me to come with you?"

"Yes," I say, wiping a tear from my cheek. "Could you?"

"I can," Tracy says.

"I loved him, Trace," I whisper. "I loved him so much."

"I know you did, honey. I remember. I remember everything."

As I wake, light streams in the window; I roll over and bury my face in the pillow.

"Morning, you," Ryan says sweetly from the bathroom. He has a towel wrapped around his waist. Water droplets glisten on his muscular chest.

"What time is it?" I ask groggily.

"Nine-thirty," he replies. "You haven't slept like that in ages. I'm glad. You needed the rest."

I stretch, which is when the fog lifts and the events of last night come back into focus. I saw Cade outside the restaurant. I sit up in bed nervously as Ryan slips into a pair of jeans and a T-shirt and flops down beside me. "What's on tap for today, soon-to-be Mrs. Winston?"

I crinkle my nose. "Ryan, you know I haven't decided yet about changing my name."

He looks momentarily wounded but quickly recovers. "I know this is one of the most important choices you'll ever make. I'm proud of you, and I want us to share a name as a sign that we've chosen each other."

"When you put it that way," I say, marveling anew at his romanticism, "how can I refuse? I promise I'll decide soon."

He rubs my neck for a moment. "Want to get breakfast?"

"There is nothing I enjoy more than your company on a lazy Sunday morning," I say, "but I have too much on my mind to relax. The second piece in the series is due soon, and I don't even have the background research finished. The business angle is new to me, and I can't afford to make any rookie mistakes." It isn't so much a lie as a half-truth. I planned to interview some of the regulars in Occidental Park.

"All right," he says. "Want me to bring you back something?"

"Nah," I say. "To be honest, I'm still full from dinner. And I have to get some Tracy time in at some point. I'm sure she'll insist on caffeine at the very least."

He nods, kisses my forehead, heads for the doorway. When his footsteps quiet and I hear the front door close, I reach for my cellphone and call Tracy.

"Can you come over?"

She groans. "Can I at least sleep another hour?"

"No," I say urgently, in the way that only good friends can speak to each other. "I need you, Tracy."

"Okay," she says, letting out a long yawn. "Let me get dressed and maybe inject some coffee into my veins. I'll be there in a half hour."

"Thanks," I say.

"Kailey, you don't sound like yourself."

"I'm not," I say honestly. "My life just got turned upside down."

I push down the filter of my French press, pour myself an extra-large mug, walk despondently to the living room, and sink into the couch. Eddie sidles up beside me, leaning his head on my lap the way he did as a puppy so many years ago. The way he did with Cade. I look up when I hear the creak of the door.

"Kailey?"

"Come in," I say. "Thank God you're here."

She doesn't waste any time. "Tell me everything."

"Well," I say, setting my coffee mug down. "Like I said, I was at Le Marche with Ryan, and there he was, right outside the restaurant."

Tracy nods. "And you're sure it was him?"

"I'm positive," I say. "At least I think I am."

"It's been a long time, Kailey," she says. "Maybe he just looked like Cade? Or he's been on your mind and you had some sort of transference? Like you saw his face in this homeless guy's face. That's a thing, you know. Psychics talk about that stuff."

I sigh. "I don't know."

"What are the chances that he's been living, unrecognizable, under our noses all these years?" Tracy continues.

"I know it seems impossible," I say. "But I saw his eyes. I know those eyes."

Tracy nods. "All right, let's go downtown and see what we can do."

"What can we do?"

"Get him some help, social services, that sort of thing."

I nod, thinking of all the connections I've made in my reporting on Pioneer Square, and yet part of me feels paralyzed, too. "Trace, I hardly know where to begin with this."

"First off," Tracy says, "we'll talk to him. See what he says. See if he wants our help."

"And if he doesn't?"

"Then that's his choice. We can only offer."

I bury my head in my hands. "What do you think happened to him?"

She shrugs. "It's hard to say why people fall into homelessness, and I'm just a humble pulmonologist. But it's pretty well accepted that mental illness is the number one culprit."

I shake my head. "Cade had his challenges, but mental illness wasn't one."

"Then it might have been something else," Tracy says in her clinical voice, one that I so rarely hear.

"Like what?"

"There are countless possibilities. He might have had some sort of accident that left him with acute amnesia. Some people never recover."

"So you don't think there's any chance for him, then?"

"No, no," she says. "I'm not saying that at all. We wouldn't be able to accurately assess his condition without a thorough examination, brain scans. And, frankly, I'm not convinced this guy you saw is even Cade."

I clear my throat, unable to accept her doubts. "And if he recovers . . . ," I say, pausing for a moment, feeling the weight of it all. All these years, I thought he'd gone away for good. And now he might be back. "Tracy . . . I'm getting *married*."

"I know, honey," she says, her face softening. "This has to feel very heavy. But let's not jump to conclusions. Don't worry just yet. We'll find him. If it *is* him, then you can proceed from there." She squeezes my hand. "A lot of time has passed. We're not even the same people anymore."

I let her words marinate for a moment. Eddie licks my hand, and I reward his affection with a scratch on the sensitive spot behind his right ear.

"Maybe you're right," I say, looking around at the beautiful home I share with my fiancé. The mantel is punctuated with little objects we've found together on our travels. The paintings on the walls he commissioned from a favorite artist. The dining room table where we've entertained dozens of friends, and so many more to come. My life is seemingly perfect now. How can I let my past tarnish the carefully curated present I've worked so hard for? I wince inwardly.

"Speaking of past lives," Tracy says, flipping through a magazine on my coffee table, the latest issue of *Dwell*. I've dog-eared a few pages to show Ryan for our remodel. "You know who I ran into at the grocery store the other day?"

"Who?"

"A cheerleader from my high school," she continues. "Chrissie Gearheart." She shakes her head in awe. "She lives in Seattle with her husband and two kids. And I will admit that I do take comfort in knowing that the prettiest girl in school has officially let herself go. Chrissie Gearheart. Every boy's dream."

"Funny," I say, chuckling, "why is it that everybody can always remember cheerleaders' first and last names?"

"You know, you're right," Tracy replies. "I can't even tell you the last names of the girls I sat with at lunch all through the ninth grade, but *Chrissie Gearheart* just rolls off the tongue."

"Sheena Thompson," I add. "Roosevelt High School's it girl with pom-poms."

"Weird how the past gets embedded," Tracy says, standing as she tosses the magazine onto the coffee table beside a stack of bridal magazines that I keep telling myself I'm going to find time to browse through. She buttons up her coat and takes a deep breath. "You ready to face the present?"

I nod, giving Eddie a final nuzzle before I stand up. "I think so."

four

Tracy and I sling our bags of laundry over our shoulders and step out of our apartment in pursuit of Sit & Spin. There are other closer laundromats, of course, but none with that certain cachet of the iconic café on Fourth Avenue, where you can sip coffee while your clothes tumble in the dryer.

"Look," Tracy says as we round the corner to a street lined with cherry trees, all with stunning pink blossoms.

"They're beautiful," I say.

"Yeah," Tracy says, "but I mean, that." She points to a tree branch as we walk closer. Above our heads is a single red ribbon tied to an upper branch.

"What do you think that is?"

I shrug.

"Maybe it's like those yellow ribbons people tie onto trees to remember soldiers at war," she says. "But this is the long-lost-love version."

"Trace," I say. "You crack me up."

"No, really," she says. "I bet it's a thing. Like, tie a red ribbon around a tree branch for your one true love."

I roll my eyes as we walk into Sit & Spin. The air smells of laundry detergent and coffee grounds. Tracy and I find a table in the corner and scope out a couple of empty washing machines. Tracy pulls a textbook out of her bag. Anatomy. Not exactly pleasure reading, but it's what you do when you're cramming for the MCAT exams. I slide into an orange chair and take a sip of my foamy macadamia nut latte in a gigantic orange teacup. Only here could a gritty laundromat-café combo have so much appeal.

"I think that's the guy from Soundgarden," Tracy whispers.

I peer shamelessly over my shoulder and spot a bearded Kim Thayil having a beer with an equally burly-looking man.

"Mark loves Soundgarden," she says dreamily. "I don't know. I guess I do, too. But I'd really flip if I saw Eddie Vedder in here."

I take a sip of my latte. "If I ever get a dog, I'm naming him Eddie."

Tracy grins. "Look at you, you've been a Seattleite for barely a year and you're already naming your imaginary dog after the city's most beloved rocker."

"Eddie," I say, nodding. "A golden retriever—no, a black Lab." I lift up my laundry basket and a pair of panties with a visible hole in the backside falls to the ground.

"Man, I need to go shopping," I say.

Suddenly Tracy's eyes widen. "Don't look now," she says, pushing her book aside and turning her attention to her latte, "but I think that guy from the Mazzy Star show just walked in."

Without my permission, my heart begins to beat faster. Even though I scrawled my number on a napkin that night at the Crocodile, it has been a whole month, and I haven't heard a peep from Cade. *Did he lose my number? Did I connect more with him than he did with me? Was it just a fleeting Seattle moment?* I'm not sure.

"You should go talk to him," Tracy whispers.

"No way," I say, playing it cool, though the truth is, I had hoped to run into him by now, and even peered into the Crocodile one night after a work dinner to see if he might be in view.

"Wait," she continues, returning to her book, which she pretends to read, "he just looked this way."

"Did he?" I'm instantly aware that I'm wearing my rattiest T-shirt and haven't a speck of makeup on. Of all the days to reunite with Cade, this is not the moment.

I quickly smooth my bangs into place and wish I'd at least put on some mascara.

"Kailey?"

"Oh, hi," I say, as my eyes meet his. "It's Cade, right?"

Tracy almost chokes on her latte.

"Right," he says. "It's good to see you." His eyes are kind and confident.

"You too," I say, glancing down at the laundry in front of me and feeling a sense of panic when I realize that my holey panties are at the top of the stack.

"No better place to do laundry in Seattle," he says, grinning. *He saw them. He totally saw them.*

"Can you imagine seeing Kurt Cobain folding his boxers in here before he was famous?" Tracy asks. Though over two years have passed since the tragic loss of the local great, all of Seattle continues to mourn him actively.

"Well," Cade says with a respectful pause, "I actually did."

Tracy clears her throat. "No way."

Cade nods and points to where an anemic-looking ficus tree wallows in the corner. "He was standing right there, next to a big pile of laundry, putting a quarter in the jukebox. That was way before Nirvana even played their first show." He shrugs. "He changed a lot after that. Fame really sucked the joy out of him, and he knew it. It's sad, but it happens to a lot of artists."

A hip-looking red-haired woman, barely twenty if that, approaches our table before I can respond. "Excuse me," she says to Tracy and me with a nervous smile before turning to Cade. "Are you . . . *Cade McAl-lister* from Element Records?"

"I am," he replies with a quick smile.

"Wow," she says, gushing. "I'm such a fan. Such a fan. I love all of your bands. I mean, your record label is probably the reason I'm alive today. The music you put out got me through some hard times. You know? I mean, wow. It's so good to meet you."

"Thank you," Cade says casually, and somehow I have the feeling that this kind of thing happens all the time.

"I'm Jenna," she continues, touching her heart. "Thank *you*." She looks back at me. "Sorry, I just had to say hi. I'll let you get back to your conversation now."

After she's gone, my eyes meet Cade's. "So, it seems you're kind of a big deal."

He shrugs. "I'm just a lucky guy who gets to do what he loves. So what's your passion, Kailey? I know it can't be laundry." He winks in the direction of my basket.

"She'd spend her last dollar on the rarest goat cheese at Pike Place Market," Tracy says.

"So will you make me dinner sometime?"

Tracy pretends to be focused on her book, but if there was a thought bubble over her head, it would be littered with exclamation marks.

"Uh, well . . ." I fumble with my words.

"Sorry, was that presumptuous of me?"

I grin. "Well, maybe a tad."

"How about this," he continues. "I take you out for dinner, and if you have a good time, then you make me dinner one night? Deal?"

I smile coyly, prolonging the moment until I say yes. "Deal."

"Good," he continues, turning to the door. He waves at a guy with a beard and a sleeve of tattoos who's just walked in, before turning back to me once more. "Speaking of laundry, you wrote your number on a napkin the night we met. I put it in my pocket and then, in tragic form, accidentally washed those jeans." He grins. "So, well, can I get it again?"

"Sure," I say, grinning back. I dig through my purse and find a pen.

Cade extends his hand. "This time, you better write it on my hand. Safer."

"Okay," I say with a laugh, taking his hand in mine. I print my name and number on his palm. "Now, don't wash it off."

"I promise," he says with a wink.

Tracy catches my eye after Cade is gone. "You know what I think?"

"What?"

"That one," she says, shaking her head, "is going to get under your skin."

I don't tell her that he already has.

Later that night, I'm in the kitchen, gently folding batter for a cinnamon coffee cake. "My grandma used to always say that cinnamon is the scent of a happy home," I say to Tracy, smiling. "I always liked that."

"Cinnamon?" Tracy says, looking up from the coffee table, where books and notebooks are splayed out.

"Yeah," I say. "It was this quirky theory she had, that the more cinnamon a person consumed, the more love in her life." I pour the batter into a Bundt pan, then lick the edge of the wooden spoon. "Cute, huh?"

Tracy nods. "The world was more romantic in our grandparents' time. Remember, mine got married two weeks after they met. Two weeks!"

I smile. "My grandparents met at a wartime dance hall. My grandpa asked my grandma to dance, and that was that. Love, to the tune of Glenn Miller."

Tracy holds her hand to her heart in dramatic fashion. "'Moonlight Serenade,'" she says with a swoony look, just as the phone rings. She answers it as I tuck the cake pan into the oven.

"Hello," Tracy says, pausing for a moment, smiling. "Yes, she's here. Just a sec." She points to the phone and mouths the words "It's him!"

My heart beats fast as I wipe my hands on a towel, then run over to take the phone. "Hello," I say, intending to sound breathy and effortless. Instead, the word comes out like a squeak.

"Hi, it's Cade." His voice is somehow deeper on the phone than it was in person. I like it, and my stomach feels fluttery.

"Hi," I say.

"It was good running into you today," he continues. "I was thinking that maybe we could get together on Saturday for dinner. I mean, if you're free."

"I'd like that," I say.

"Ever been to Wild Ginger?"

"No," I say. "But my editor raves about it. I've been meaning to check it out."

"Good," he says. "Meet me there at seven?"

Tracy is frantically waving at me, but I ignore her.

"Sure," I reply, catching Tracy's eye.

"Ask him what his sign is," she whispers.

"No," I mouth back.

"Seriously," she says. "For me. I have to know."

"Tracy!" I whisper.

"Please?" she asks, grinning.

"Um, so," I say into the phone. "My best friend is a nut and she wants to know what your sign is."

"My *sign*?" He chuckles.

I roll my eyes at Tracy, wishing I'd kept my mouth shut. "She loves astrology. I don't. But I love her."

Cade laughs some more. "I don't know anything about all of that, but I do know that I'm a Taurus."

"A Taurus," I say, as Tracy nods in approval.

"Tell her I'd love to hear my horoscope someday," he says.

I grin. "Really, it's best not to encourage her."

"Okay," he says, laughing. "See you Saturday."

"See you then," I say, grinning as I hang up.

Tracy squeals as I sink into the couch beside her. "Someone has a date."

I can't help but smile. "I do."

"And he's a *Taurus*," she adds in a dreamy voice.

I shrug.

"That's good, Kailey. *Really*. Tauruses are lucky in love. They're ruled by Venus, which is known for beauty and pleasure." She smiles to herself. "Just make him one of your fabulous meals and you're golden."

I smile. "That simple, huh?"

"I think so." She brushes a bit of flour from my shirt. "Told you this is the beginning of something big."

A ferry streams across Elliott Bay in the night, and I think maybe, just maybe, she might be right.

five

NOVEMBER 16, 2008

Rain splatters the windshield of Tracy's car as we whiz down I-5. The wipers squeak back and forth frantically in time with the beat of my heart.

"I remember your first date with him," Tracy says a little nostalgically.

"You do?" I ask, turning to her.

"You were so nervous. You tried on a thousand outfits before you left."

"Wild Ginger," I say, my brain spitting out memories in rapid fire. "We went to Wild Ginger."

"And I almost called the cops because you, always the homebody, didn't come home until two A.M. You nearly gave me a heart attack."

Tracy takes the James Street exit and winds her way down to Fourth Avenue. "We can park here, then walk around a bit. See if we find him by the restaurant."

"Okay," I say nervously.

When we pass a café, Tracy stops. "Coffee first."

"Someone should make T-shirts with that phrase," I say.

"I'd buy one," Tracy says.

I follow her in, and we each order a double Americano, then Tracy changes hers to a triple at the last minute. "Remember the lattes we used to drink?" she says with a laugh.

"All that sugar," I reply. "I think I drank a macadamia nut latte for at least a year straight."

"I had a thing for toasted marshmallow," she says. "Remember that?" I nod.

Her eyes light up. "And tiramisu." She laughs. "What were we thinking?"

I laugh, but it's hollow, and lonely. A laugh filled with regret and longing for the way things used to be. Those bottles of Torani syrups, like the two wide-eyed twenty-two-year-olds we once were, are distant memories now.

We sip our no-frills coffee and begin our search. My eyes dart right and left as we make our way down Fourth, and then to Third. I scour every alley, every dumpster, every crevice along the way. The rain is falling harder now, so I pull the hood of my jacket over my head as Tracy ducks under the eave of a building.

"Le Marche is just up the way," I say. "It's closed now, but maybe he's there again."

Tracy nods and follows me down the next block and up a side street. "At this point, it's probably our best bet."

We walk in silence for two more blocks, and I toss my coffee cup into a garbage can. I can't speak. I can't even really think. All I can do is put one foot in front of the other, heart pounding.

I see the green awning of Le Marche in the distance. I'm so distracted crossing the street that I don't notice an SUV to my right, and the driver honks in annoyance as I jaywalk.

The restaurant is dark as I peer through the windows, then scan the exterior.

"He's not here," I say, crestfallen.

Tracy pulls her phone out of her pocket and steps under the awning to answer it while I walk a few steps to look down the alley beside
the restaurant, which is empty, save for a dumpster and a waterlogged
cardboard box.

We wait for a few minutes, then I suggest we walk up to Fifth.
"There's a homeless shelter up there," I say, recalling an article I wrote
last year, a piece about a hotshot chef in town who had teamed up with
a benefactor—off the radar, until the meal preparations somehow
ended up as a Food Network special—to cook for the homeless.
Thanks to their efforts, soggy grilled cheese sandwiches were replaced
with salmon en croute and endive salad with candied walnuts. I'd like
to think that my local coverage—more than the onetime TV exposure—
led to it becoming a yearly event for charity.

"We could see if . . ." My voice trails off. I still can't believe Cade's
plight. That I could possibly walk into a shelter and find him there
lying on some urine-stained cot.

Tracy pats my arm. "Don't be scared," she says. "You can do this."

I nod, and together we make our way up the next block to a brick
building with peeling black paint on its door. A toothless woman with
stringy gray hair stands on the sidewalk, drinking from a bottle wrapped
in a brown paper bag.

"You cops?" she asks in a deep, raspy voice, taking a step back.

"No," Tracy says. "We're not."

The woman nods and lifts the bottle to her lips once more. I notice
an open wound on her left arm, festering and red; I shudder inwardly
as Tracy places her hand on the doorknob. "Maybe we'll get lucky," she
whispers to me.

I follow my friend inside to a lobby, where a middle-aged man
with a goatee and a receding hairline sits at a desk. The air smells of
body odor, damp carpeting, and stale cigarettes, but also of sadness,
dashed dreams.

"Howdy," the man says, looking up. His face is familiar, and I immediately remember the unexpectedly cheerful tenor of his voice. He
must remember me, too. "Are you the reporter from the *Herald*?"

"Yes," I say. "Kailey Crain." It's been at least a year since I interviewed him. "Forgive me, you'll have to remind me of your name."

"Abe Farrell," he says, extending his hand. "I figured the two of you weren't looking for a room for the night." He laughs to himself, but Tracy and I are too stunned to respond to his attempt at humor. We just stare blankly. "What can I do you for?"

"We're looking for someone," I say quickly, taking a step forward. "A man."

"Got a name?"

I look at Tracy, then back at Abe. "Yes, his name is Cade McAllister."

Abe shakes his head. "Don't think we have anyone by that name, but with our clientele, you never know. Some of them don't even know their own names."

I nod. "He's about six foot. Thin. He has a beard. He was wearing an army-green jacket yesterday, boots." The image of him sitting on the sidewalk, now burned into my mind, lingers. I feel unsettled thinking about his eyes—so sad, so lost. "His jeans had holes"—I point to my shins—"right along here."

"Sorry, miss," the man says, smiling again. "That about describes every man in this place."

I let out a defeated sigh.

He shrugs. "If you'd like to show me a picture, maybe I could be of more help."

I reach for my wallet and pull out a faded snapshot of Cade and me together, in Big Sur, at a scenic outlook along Highway 1. I smile to myself, remembering the trip in vivid detail. We rented a convertible, and I wrapped a beige scarf around my head Grace Kelly–style. By the time we'd reached that little overlook, each of us was green from car sickness after navigating one too many twists and turns, but you couldn't tell from the photo.

"This is him," I say, holding the picture out to Abe, who squints, then shrugs.

"I'm afraid there's no one like that around here," he says after a few moments. "But if you'd like, I can take you in and you can have a look for yourself."

"Thanks," I say, looking at Tracy, then back at him. "I'd appreciate that."

We follow him, a bit warily, down a small hallway and through a doorway to a large room, where bunks line the walls. Three men sit at a central table, immersed in a game of cards. A few others appear to be asleep or passed out in their bunks. Another is muttering to himself in the corner. None of them is Cade.

"No," I say with a sigh. "He's not here."

"Sorry," Abe says. "This man, is he your . . . boyfriend?"

I shake my head. "No, no," I say, rubbing my engagement ring. "He's just an old friend."

"Well," he says. "This old friend of yours is lucky to have someone like you looking for him." He smiles. "I hope you find him."

"Me too," I say.

As he turns to the door, I place my hand on my right shoulder. "Wait," I say, taking off my jacket and lifting up the sleeve of my T-shirt. "This tattoo—he has one just like it. Does it look familiar to you?"

"No, I'm afraid I haven't seen any tattoos like that one."

Just then I notice that one of the men who's playing cards, older and with a long gray beard, is looking up at me.

"All right," I say dejectedly, slipping my arms into my jacket as the bearded man stands up from the table.

"Excuse me," he says, walking toward me, a fan of cards in his right hand. I notice the ace of spades, and I think of the time I taught Cade to play Thirty-One, my grandparents' favorite card game. Cade won. "That tattoo. It looks like . . . Mitchell's."

I shake my head. "Mitchell?"

"Yeah, he's a strange one. Doesn't speak. He's in and out of here, but he spends most of his time up on Fourth by that fancy Frenchy place, what's it called—"

"Le Marche?" I ask eagerly.

"Yeah, that's the one."

My eyes widen. "Are you sure you recognize the tattoo?" I slip my jacket off again to show him.

"Yes, ma'am," he says, peering closer.

"Please tell me. Why do you call him Mitchell?"

He shrugs. "Hell if I know. Mitchell is what's printed on that army jacket he always wears. I guess everyone just assumed that's his name. Maybe it is; maybe it isn't." He chuckles to himself. "My name's Frank, but everyone calls me Mad Dog."

"Mad Dog," I say. "Well, thank you."

He nods and begins to walk back to the card game; I think about Cade, wearing an army jacket with the name MITCHELL stamped over his heart. *How did this happen?*

"Pardon me for being nosy," Mad Dog says, turning to face me once more. "But how's it that someone like you and someone like him have the same tattoo?"

Tears sting my eyes. I take a deep breath, my lower lip trembling a little. "He and I are not different. We are the same. And I once loved him, very much."

I feel Tracy's hand on my arm. "C'mon, honey, let's go."

Numbly I walk out behind her to the street.

The rain has picked up again, and when we make it back to the sidewalk in front of Le Marche, Tracy and I duck under the awning.

"What next?" she asks.

"I think I'll stay here for a while," I say. "See if he comes back."

Tracy nods as she reaches into her pocket to pull out her ringing phone. I wander a few steps ahead and have another look down the alley beside the restaurant. Vacant, aside from a pigeon pecking at the pavement in the distance.

"That was the hospital," Tracy says, walking toward me a moment later. "Patient crisis. I'm so sorry; I have to go."

"I'll be okay on my own," I say as the pigeon startles and flies off farther into the alley, desolate and gray.

I stand on the sidewalk for a few minutes, then begin walking up the block to a Starbucks, where I order another coffee and slide into a chair by the window. It's raining harder now, and the window is foggy, like my mind. I use the sleeve of my jacket to clear away a spot so I can see the passersby. Any of them could be Cade, but none is.

I leave the café. An hour passes, and then two. Ryan calls, and I tell him I'm doing some field research. Another white lie. He asks if I can make risotto for dinner. I say yes, and ask him to pick up Arborio rice at Whole Foods. Our conversation is easy, effortless. It ebbs and flows as if each of us has a script. But right now, I don't love the script. I hate that I am talking about Arborio rice and Whole Foods when Cade is somewhere in the city, cold, probably hungry, perhaps slumped over in some alley in the rain. I hate it all. The rice and the rain and the way life has unfolded.

I lean against the brick wall of the restaurant, which has just opened for Sunday lunch. Through the windows, I notice an attractive couple at the bar. She's wearing a flouncy ivory linen dress, straight off the rack of Free People. She twirls her long brunette hair and leans in flirtatiously toward her date, a clean-shaven man with dark-rimmed glasses. I imagine their conversation.

"I love oysters," she is saying.

"Me too!" he replies.

"But not mussels," she adds, daintily sipping her chilled rosé.

"Never mussels," he says in instant agreement. "Those are the questionable mollusks."

She laughs, taking another slow sip of her wine, which is the color of the MAC blush she applied to her cheeks earlier. She wonders if she's put on too much. And whether she's met her soulmate.

A car speeds by and I narrowly miss the spray from a mud puddle. I clutch the gold chain around my neck, letting my fingers trace the familiar path to the locket at its base, gold, with my initials engraved on the back. It was a gift from my grandparents for my tenth birthday, and I've worn it ever since.

"What are you going to put inside?" Grandma asked me when I first slipped it on.

"I don't know yet," I said, imagining that the object I'd choose above all others would have to be very special.

That very day, Grandpa pulled out an aged cigar box and sorted through old coins, photographs with scalloped edges, postcards, and yellowed snippets of paper until he'd selected a tiny object, which he held in his hand.

"The prettiest shell, for the prettiest girl," he said, planting a kiss on my forehead.

I turned it over and over in my hand, beaming.

"Would you like to hear the story of how I found it?" he asked.

I nodded, keeping my eyes on my new prized possession. I had always loved Grandpa's stories.

"It was August 1944, and we'd all but liberated France," he recounted. "It was hot, I remember that. Muggy. A few of my buddies wanted to go down to the beach for a swim. We'd listened to Eisenhower on the radio that morning. Everyone was in a good mood, so the commander didn't bat an eye when we left camp for the beach, though we'd been warned to be careful of land mines and holdover enemy troops hiding in caves or in the homes of villagers. Still, we wanted to go to the beach. And what a beach it was. We wandered up past Omaha, where all the fighting had gone on, to a little cove along a rocky bluff lined with beach grass, cypress trees, and a few old craggy-looking apple trees, where Captain Raines and I picked and ate every last piece of fruit." He stopped talking, showed me a smile. "It's funny, whenever I sink my teeth into an apple, even now, I'm back on that beach." Grandpa's eyes were distant.

"And then we kept walking," he continued. "The surf got heavier down that stretch of beach. There was a dangerous riptide. Raines nearly got swept out by it." He chuckled to himself. "I just sat there on the shore as the waves rolled in and out. And that's when I noticed something wash up. At first I thought it was a rock, but when I inched closer I could see that it was a shell. But not just any shell. This one glistened in the sun. It was the color of jade, iridescent, unlike anything I'd ever seen.

"When Raines sat down beside me, I showed it to him. 'That's a special one,' he said. 'How do you know?' I asked. He went on to tell me that he'd met a French girl with a shell just like this one attached to a necklace. Apparently they're rare and only wash up on that beach once in a blue moon, and only on *that* beach. The locals say that if you find one, you're lucky, that it's a good omen, a sign of love, happiness, and protection." He smiled again. "I've kept it all these years, and you know, I have had a happy life. A wonderful one, in fact. And now you get to keep it."

I couldn't believe my good fortune, and I proudly kept Grandpa's shell on my bedside table, until my friend's annoying little sister took it one day, and in a scuffle on the sidewalk it slipped from her hands and hit the pavement, shattering into a dozen pieces.

I cried; sobbed, really. I mourned that shell more than I'd mourned the day my best friend had moved away in the second grade. How could I face Grandpa? How could I tell him that in my care, the shell had been destroyed, his treasured memories shattered, all with the flick of the wrist by a thoughtless neighbor kid? But I did tell him, and he forgave me, as I knew he would.

I saved the largest shard of the shell in the top drawer of my dresser, beside my Wonder Woman underwear and rainbow-striped bikini with the ruffles on the front, until I tucked it inside my locket, where it remains today. I pat it, thinking of Grandpa, who passed away two days after my twenty-sixth birthday. "Do you still have your shell?" he asked me the last time I saw him.

"I do," I said.

"Good girl."

I look up, jarred from my thoughts, when I hear a male voice ahead. "Don't you listen?" he says sternly.

It's a man from the restaurant in a white half-apron, tied at the waist. He's obscuring the person on the receiving end of his interrogation, so I strain my neck to make out the scene.

"I've told you before that you need to go," he continues. My heart beats faster. Could it be . . . ?

"Wait!" I call out as a man slowly strides away. I can only see his back, and his *army-green jacket*. "Please wait."

The man from the restaurant clears his throat. "Please accept my apologies if that man was bothering you."

I don't respond, and race ahead to the next block, following the man in the army-green jacket as he turns the corner. I run faster, but when I round the block I see that he has slipped into the plaza in front of Westlake Center. It's thick with people—mothers and daughters holding umbrellas over Nordstrom shopping bags, college kids with earbuds attached to iPhones. A street violinist plays "Happy Birthday" in the distance. And then I catch a glimpse of army green.

"Cade!" I call out. He's a few hundred feet away, and I know he hears me because he immediately stops and looks right, then left.

"Cade!" I say again, slowly walking closer. I'm fearful that if I move too quickly, I might frighten him. So I take careful, measured steps, the way one might when trying to lure a scared, injured puppy into safety. *Just a few more steps.* "Cade, it's Kailey," I say.

He turns around to face me. When our eyes meet, it's as if the world, once a rushing waterfall, has slowed to a trickle. I do not hear the buzz of conversation around me. I do not see the people fluttering by. I do not feel the rain on my face. There is only Cade. And he sees me.

six

"How do I look?" I ask Tracy, twirling in our apartment's kitchen so she can get the full effect of my dress. Blue, with crocheted edging on the hem and sleeves. I picked it up at The Bon on my lunch hour. "Is it too much?"

"No," Tracy says, "it says 'I'm a professional, but also secretly a beguiling artist.'"

I scrunch my nose. "Beguiling artist?"

"Yeah, the artsy mysterious type," she says. "Men love intrigue."

"Hmm," I say, tugging at the waistline and trying to make out my reflection in the glass of the microwave. "I'm not so sure."

"Don't worry," she continues. "He's going to love it. But not if you don't cut this tag off." She reaches for a pair of scissors on the kitchen counter. "Here, let me help you."

I shrug. "Man, I hate dating."

"Everyone hates dating."

"Why do we put ourselves through all of this, then?"

Tracy smiles. "Well, despite that armor you put up, you're an Aquarius, and that heart of yours secretly idealizes love, believes in soulmates, the whole nine."

"Well," I say in a sober voice, "even though he asked me to dinner, I'm committing for one drink, and maybe an appetizer. If it's weird, I'm out."

I reach for a black cardigan as Tracy rummages through her bag. "Here," she says, handing me a quarter.

I give her a confused look.

"Tuck it in your purse," she says. "If you need reinforcements, find a pay phone and call me."

I smile. "All right."

I sit at the bar at Wild Ginger, where I nervously stab my straw into the lime in my vodka soda. He's late. Just ten minutes, but still.

"Care to see the menu?" a sympathetic bartender says, looking my way.

"No," I reply. "I'm waiting for someone."

"First date?"

My cheeks redden. "Yeah."

He nods. "I kind of thought so."

"How can you tell?"

He smiles. "Occupational hazard."

I exhale. "I admit, I'm a bit nervous."

"Why?"

Before I can respond, I feel a tap on my shoulder and turn toward it.

"Sorry I'm late," Cade says, stepping in to face me. "Staff meeting ran over, and of course I got into it with my business partner, for the thirty-seventh time this week." He rubs his forehead. "A little tip: Never go into business with your best friend."

"Noted," I say, unable to stop grinning.

"Hi," he says, smiling.

"Hi right back," I say. He's wearing jeans, a gray sweater, and a pair of well-worn Converse high-tops. He's just as I remembered from that night at the Crocodile. A little random, a little irreverent, completely fascinating.

"I hope you won't hold my tardiness against me." He grins as though he knows I won't.

The bartender winks at me as the hostess leads us to our window table toward the back of the dining room. We both sit down.

"I like your dress," he says.

I glance down at my lap and smooth an imaginary wrinkle. "Do you?"

"Yeah," he continues. "It's sort of Stevie Nicks–esque."

I laugh and take a sip of my drink.

"Do you like Fleetwood Mac?" he asks.

"I do," I say. "'Gypsy' is one of my all-time favorite songs. My mom was an old hippie."

The waiter hands Cade a menu, and he grins at me, then orders a martini with cheese-stuffed olives.

"You know how I can tell if a restaurant is any good?" he asks, setting the menu down.

"How?"

He points toward the bar. "Cheese-stuffed olives."

I give him a confused look. "I'm not sure I understand."

"Most places don't have them at all, even the high-end spots. But the key is whether they offer to *make* them for you. A good restaurant will always make them."

"Interesting," I say.

He winks. "If you ever do a story about restaurants, you should add that little gem."

"We'll have to see about that," I say with a grin.

"So tell me more about your work."

I nod. "I think I told you that I'm a reporter for the *Herald*."

"Yes, that's right," he says. "I'm impressed."

"Don't be. I'm very junior."

"Oh, come on," he says. "Obviously your job is a lot more exciting than you're letting on."

"Well, I do love the work," I say. "And I have a great editor who is letting me take on subjects that interest me."

"Like what?"

"Well," I say, squirming in my seat a little. "Politics, poverty, profiles of people making a difference."

"Wow. Heavy stuff."

"Stuff that matters," I continue. "At least to me."

Cade stares at me for a long moment until I feel my cheeks redden and look away. "You have a big heart, you know."

I smile. "Or maybe I just didn't want to get stuck on the fashion beat."

The waiter returns with a martini, in which floats a cocktail skewer punctuated with cheese-stuffed olives. Cade plunks one into his mouth, then takes a sip. "Have you always loved to cook?"

"Always," I say. "I grew up cooking with my grandmother in Iowa."

"And I've always loved music." He takes another sip of his drink. "Funny how we're born with certain passions that never fade."

I nod. "If I didn't love my work so much, I might have become a chef."

"Tell me about Iowa."

"Yeah, I moved there after my parents passed away."

"I'm sorry," Cade says.

I shrug. "I was five. They died in a head-on collision on the way to a Grateful Dead concert."

"What do you remember of them?" Cade asks, leaning forward.

"My mom's voice," I say. "She used to sing that song from *Porgy and Bess* to me every night."

"'Summertime'?"

"You know it?"

He nods.

"Yeah," I say, trying to remember the tune, and then in an instant I begin humming the chorus. "So hush little baby . . . ," I sing softly.

"Don't you cry," Cade continues, finishing the line for me, and when he does, I feel goosebumps on my arms.

I smile to myself over the confession I'm about to make. "I had a weepy moment the other day at work. For some reason, I was struck with the memory of a dress my mom used to wear. It was rust-colored and had blue embroidery on the front."

"My parents died, too," Cade says. "My aunt took me in when I was seven."

"Wow," I say, stunned. "I've never met anyone else whose parents died at a young age. I always felt like I was the weird girl with dead parents."

"A couple of orphans, the two of us," Cade says with a grin.

"Tell me what happened to your family," I continue.

"So, the story goes: My mom died of cancer. I remember the idea of her, as if I can somehow recall her spirit, if that makes any sense." He pauses. "She gave me the music gene, though it took a few years to emerge."

"Of course she did," I say. "I recently read that children who are separated from their mothers, even at birth, can grow up and still pick them out of a lineup. It's a connection that's never severed."

He nods. "She died the week after my second birthday and spent months before that in the hospital, so I know it seems impossible that I could have any real memories of her. But I do. And I can't really explain it."

"I get that," I say. "I think our brains are forming memories, and cataloging them, before we're even aware."

Cade blinks hard. "Once, in junior high, the mom of one of my friends gave me a hug, and there was something so incredibly familiar about her perfume. It sounds crazy, but I swear I could smell my mother in that moment."

I feel a twinge inside, remembering when Grandma let me try on some of my mom's old dresses. The way I felt, it was like an excavator had come through my heart and dredged up memories I didn't even know I had.

"I feel that way all the time," I say. "It's like déjà vu, but more intense."

Cade nods. "My dad never got over Mom's death."

"How did he pass?"

"Suicide," he says. "Exhaust in the garage. Late at night. The next morning I was looking for my lunch box, but I found his body. I was in second grade."

"Wow," I say. "You must have been terrified."

He shrugs. "So after that, I lived with my aunt Fay, my mom's sister."

"Was she good to you?"

"Very," he says. "She bought me my first record player when I turned ten and lent me and my best friend, James, fifteen thousand dollars to start Element Records. We both left college a year early to launch the business. Even though we really had no idea what we were doing, Fay believed in us. And because she did, we turned that little dream into a company that's sold more than twenty million records and employs seventeen people."

"That's incredible," I say.

"Yeah, I guess," he says. "The fulfillment of a dream, for sure. But it hasn't always been easy."

"So working with your best friend has had its challenges?"

Cade exhales deeply. "It's the sad truth, yes. We went to high school together. He played guitar. I played bass. We were a couple of nerdy band guys the cheerleaders wouldn't talk to." He places his hand on his heart. "But, boy, did I ever have a crush on Stacy Rios."

I smile.

"So, yeah, we started the label, and things were great for a while. Insane but great. I was on a plane every week, to New York, L.A., Miami—wherever there were new bands to see, I'd be there."

"And James, too?"

"Yes and no," he says. "At first we traveled a lot together, but we realized that it made sense for him to hold down the fort at the Seattle office, so we divided and conquered that way."

"How did you come up with the name Element Records?"

"After one too many drinks," he says, grinning. "But there's meaning in it, at least for me."

"How so?"

"It's the way I look at music," he says. "When I'm in the presence of a band I know is destined for greatness, there's a feeling that comes with that. Senses are heightened. The music moves you in a way you can feel. Just like when I stopped on a corner in Nashville and listened to a street performer; just a guy with this dog, singing and playing his guitar. People were throwing money in his case. I offered him a record contract and he's now a platinum artist."

"Wow," I say.

"That's what I call being *in the element*." He grins. "James wanted to name the label Bonsai Records."

I scrunch my nose. "Bonsai?"

Cade shrugs. "We really have different ideas about how to run the company, and at times that can be difficult. If I said the success of the label hasn't hurt our friendship, I'd be lying."

He takes a long sip of his drink and his face appears strained and suddenly serious. I can tell that the subject of James pains him more than he's letting on.

"How about this," he says, quick to change the subject. "It's a nice night. Why don't we have another drink, order a few snacks, and take a walk? Remind me, how long have you been living in Seattle?"

"About a year," I say.

"Then you need a proper tour," he replies with a grin. "I'll show you *my* Seattle. All the places that mean something to me. What do you say?"

My eyes are wide. I love his confidence. "Yes," I reply. And he reaches for my hand.

• • •

A couple of men in expensive-looking suits pass us as we walk out of the restaurant to the sidewalk. One of them is talking about the NASDAQ.

"I could never be like them," Cade says a moment later.

My eyes meet his. "What do you mean?"

"The suits, the daily eight-to-five grind. Endless meetings about company profits and losses, bottom lines. Working for the Man."

I nod. "You're a born entrepreneur, I see that."

Together we walk down the block.

"Magic hour," Cade says, gazing up to the sky. The sun has just set, and an orange glow lingers on the horizon. It's not yet night and no longer day, but some whimsical in-between, which I suppose is where Cade and I are. Suspended between two places.

The flutter in my stomach that I felt when we first met returns, and I smile when he pretends to be holding a microphone.

"I'd like to thank you, ma'am, for coming out for this exclusive tour of Seattle." He clears his throat in a very official manner. "Allow me to introduce myself, your tour guide, Cade McAllister." I can't help but laugh. "Here on our left, we're coming upon one of Seattle's best-kept secrets: Zig Zag. For years, the bartenders of this establishment have been shaking cocktails for Seattle's music elite." He lowers his voice to a hush. "And if you'd like to get a proper look at Duff 'Rose' McKagan from Guns N' Roses, come by on a Thursday, just after eight o'clock. He sits on the right side of the bar."

"I'll tell Tracy," I say. "She'd kill me if she knew I told you this, but as a kid she was actually in a Guns N' Roses fan club."

He stops suddenly. "And what about you? What singer would you flip out over seeing?"

"Oh, I don't know," I say, playing coy.

"Come on," he says. "Don't hold back on me."

"Well," I say a little shyly. "It might be a weird response."

"I love learning about people's eclectic musical tastes, and I'm especially interested in yours."

"Okay," I say cautiously. "So, as a kid, I gravitated to a lot of the music my parents loved, before they died. While my girlfriends were rocking out to the eighties hits, I loved the Mamas and the Papas; Crosby, Stills, and Nash; Neil Young, that kind of sound."

He grins. "And the singer you'd go nuts over seeing?"

"You know that song 'Happy Together' by the Turtles?"

"I do," he says.

"The lead singer is Howard Kaylan," I continue. "My mom loved that song. She had the record, and we used to sing along together. It's one of my few memories of her. Of course, he's probably a bearded old washed-up hippie now, but his voice, that song, well, it's like it's been sewn into my heart, right there where my mother resides. Someday I'd like to meet him and tell him that story."

"That would be a beautiful moment," Cade says.

"Is this the end of the tour?" I ask.

Cade shakes his head. "Next stop is the scene of an embarrassing first date with a radio DJ whose name shall go unmentioned." He points to a pay phone. "I really liked her, at least I wanted to, but our date coincided with the closing on a huge new deal with a band that James wanted me to sign. I promised her I'd only be five minutes, and unfortunately, the call ran a half hour. By the time I returned she was gone, though she had ordered a drink for everyone at the bar and left me with the tab."

I cringe on his behalf. "So rude!"

"Well, I did leave her there. Let's just say, I never heard from her after that night, and I definitely learned my lesson."

He produces the imaginary microphone again, and I can't wait to hear what he's going to say next. I slide my hand up his forearm, bending my elbow into his. Grins plastered on each of our faces, we step in sync as we round the next block.

"Next up, the first office of Element Records, right here on the left," he says, pointing to a door with gray peeling paint beside a Chinese restaurant. "Never mind the rat problem, and the fact that not one employee will ever again be able to stomach chicken chow mein, we did put out several platinum records from this little hole in the wall."

I peer into the window and imagine Cade beginning his business inside. I know at once that I am in the presence of a very rare soul. Creative, perhaps ingeniously so, and confident, but with an unexplainable vulnerability. He's standing close to me, and yet I have the desire to be even closer.

"See that streetlamp right there," he continues, "the one that's flickering a little?"

"Yeah," I say.

"That's where Pearl Jam began."

I shake my head. "Right there?"

"Right there," he says. "Everybody thinks Eddie Vedder sent the guitarist Mike McCready a demo tape. And he did. Mike passed on it. But then Eddie moved to Seattle, and Mike heard him singing under that lamppost." He pauses and points ahead. "He was drunker than the devil, but he sang like an angel. The rest is history."

It's darker now, and I inch closer to Cade as a homeless man approaches. His clothes hang from him like rags, and he exudes a pungent smell of urine and grit.

"Spare some change?" he mutters, eyeing me. I instinctively shake my head and take a step back.

"Sure, man," Cade says, suddenly reaching into his pocket. He pulls out a few ones and a handful of loose coins. "Here you go."

"Thank you very much," the man mutters. "God bless you."

"Take care of yourself," Cade says as we walk on.

"What you did back there," I say a moment later, "it was nice."

He shrugs. "What, give some spare change to a homeless guy?"

"Yeah," I say. "Most people don't."

"Well, more people should."

I nod. "But don't most of them spend the money on drugs?"

"Maybe," he says. "But they're people just like us. And for whatever reason, life didn't turn out the way they planned. Maybe because they screwed up. Maybe because someone else screwed up. Who knows. But I think homelessness is less of an individual problem and more of a collective problem. More people should help when they can."

"I like that," I say.

We walk in silence for the next few blocks. For so long, I have felt lost, like a balloon floating aimlessly. And then this man reached up and plucked me down, tying the string around his wrist.

"The Element Records office is right up there," he says, pointing to a handsome-looking brick building. We own it now, James and I. I just put a pool table on the top floor."

"A boss who prioritizes fun," I say. "I love that."

He stops suddenly. "What time will you turn into a pumpkin to-night?" he asks with a slow smile.

I glance at my watch. It's not quite ten. "I guess I could stay out a bit later."

"Good," he says. "Because I think we should have another drink." He pauses for a moment. "My apartment is just around the block."

"I don't know," I say, hesitating. Are you supposed to go to a guy's house on the first date? Probably not.

"Just one drink," he says. "No shenanigans."

"Okay," I say, after a pause. "Just one more."

We walk ahead to an ivy-covered brick building and stop in front of a door right off the sidewalk. Cade slips in his key, and I follow him inside.

"Home sweet home," he says, walking to the record player on a side table. "Do you know the Breeders?"

"No," I say.

He nods and pulls a record from its sleeve, setting it on the turn-table with master precision, then catching my eye again. "You'll love them."

I lean against the wall and listen as a catchy bass line seeps through the speakers.

"Kim was in the Pixies," he says. "This was only supposed to be an experiment, a side project. But they ended up creating one of the most raw and unpredictable sounds in rock, at least from my humble per-spective."

"I like them," I say.

He smiles. "There's so much music I want to share with you."

His words make me feel fluttery inside, and just as he wants to teach me, I want to learn.

"Do you hear that?" he asks, taking my hand and tapping it against the side table to the drumbeat.

"Right there," he says, closing his eyes, continuing the repetition with his hand on mine.

"Yeah," I say. I'm grateful the lights are dim, because I feel my cheeks reddening.

"That's some solid drum work," he says, letting go of my hand and turning to the kitchen. "Can I make you a drink?"

"Sure," I say.

"Vodka soda?"

I nod as I let my eyes wander his condo. It has an open, loftlike floor plan, with exposed brick and one of those cool, quirky wrought-iron spiral staircases, which leads to the bedroom, above.

"Shoot," he says. "I'm out of vodka. Do you want to walk over to the liquor store with me?"

"Sure," I say as he grabs his keys.

He locks the door behind us as I slowly walk ahead.

"It's just around the corner," he says. "I think it should still be open."

I nod, looking up at the building beside Cade's, which must be under construction; it's surrounded by scaffolding, part of which extends over the sidewalk.

"Oh, is this the site of the new homeless shelter?" I ask, remembering some of the discussions among reporters in the newsroom. A non-profit organization's generous donation to build the shelter had been met with disdain from property developers who had hoped to turn the lot into a high-rise.

"Yeah," Cade says.

"How do you feel about it?"

"Feel about what?" he asks, shaking his head.

"Well, I know the project has been controversial," I say.

"What's controversial about helping the needy?"

"Nothing," I say with a smile.

"To be perfectly honest," he continues, "I'd take a shelter for a next-door neighbor over another sterile, overpriced condo building filled with pretentious people and their spoiled dogs."

I laugh. "You make a good point."

"Think about it," he says. "First the condo building goes up, then come the chain restaurants. Before you know it, my favorite café on Main will be a Gap." He pauses for a moment, catching my eyes under the streetlight. "You're so beautiful," he says suddenly.

My cheeks feel hot as I smile, then look away.

"You are," he says, squeezing my hand.

After finding what we need at the liquor store, we walk back to the apartment. Cade makes us drinks and we both sink into his sofa. I rest my head on his shoulder, quietly nestling into him. My eyelids are heavy, and when they flutter I don't fight to keep them open.

Disoriented, and what feels like hours later, I open my eyes and sit up frantically. "What time is it?"

Cade is awake beside me. "It's almost two in the morning. I couldn't bear to wake you. You looked so peaceful."

I smile. "I should go."

"I know," he says. "Let me call you a cab."

I fumble to button my cardigan sweater as he makes the call. And for a moment, I wish I could stay. Tonight and the next night. And the night after. Always.

Cade walks me to the sidewalk and pulls me into an embrace. He holds me like that for a long moment before letting his lips find mine. We kiss as the cab approaches and makes a U-turn to circle back to me.

I remember the quarter Tracy gave me earlier. Before I wave good night to Cade, I reach into my pocket and toss it into the hat of a homeless man sitting beside his dog on the sidewalk nearby.

seven

C
ade. He saw me, he recognized me. I saw a flicker in his eyes. "I'll come back," I promised him. "I'm going to help you."

My heart pounds as I pull out my phone and frantically search for James's number. Keatley. James Keatley. Element Records has long since closed its doors, but I know that James started a successful venture-capital group downtown, and its portfolio of start-ups is impressive. Apparently he and his partners have made millions, or at least that was the insinuation of the article in *The Wall Street Journal* I came across six years ago. At the time, I called to congratulate him. I casually asked if he knew how Cade was doing, but he said, like everyone else from the past, that he'd lost touch with his old friend. Part of me was glad. At least I wasn't the only person Cade had cut out of his life. Another part of me grieved. He was really gone from the face of the earth, it seemed.

I remember being struck then by how quickly life can move on.

James shut down the record label, married his girlfriend, Alexis, and had a few children. One chapter closed, another begun. A life too full to wonder about an estranged friend who slipped off the grid. But now? My fingers race through my phone's address book to find his name. I have to tell him that Cade is in Seattle, that he's been under our noses perhaps the entire time.

"There," I say to myself, pulling up his contact information. *James Keatley.* I hit the call button.

"You've reached the offices of Keatley, Brown, and Sloane," croons a male receptionist on the other end of the line. It's Sunday, and I'm surprised to hear a live voice.

"Yes—hello—I'm calling for James Keatley," I stammer. A weekend receptionist. He really must have made it big. "It's very important."

"Who may I say is calling?"

"Kailey Crain."

"I'm sorry," he says after a brief hold. "Mr. Keatley is busy."

"No, you don't understand. Please tell *Mr. Keatley* that this is an emergency. I need to speak to him now, either on the phone or in person. Your office is not far from Westlake Center, is it? I'll come by."

"I'm afraid that won't be possible," he replies. "We're normally not open on the weekends. Mr. Keatley is not taking any meetings. I'll pass along the message that you called."

Sunday or not, James is in his office, and I'm undeterred. I hang up the phone and immediately hail a cab. "Take me to the Fourth and Pike Building, please," I say to the driver.

A gust of wind whips my hair into my eyes as I struggle to open the heavy brass door. I'm grateful to see the security desk empty as I find my way to the elevator, which takes me to the seventh floor. To the left is a law office suite, so I turn right. At the end of the hallway, a gold placard with James's name on it is affixed to the door. I take a deep breath and walk inside.

"I'm here to see James," I say, peering past the reception area into the mass of empty cubicles.

"Wait, you have to—" the man behind the counter begins to say.

He wears a suit, a cobalt-blue bow tie, and the sort of dark-rimmed glasses that have the air of being for style, not vision correction.

I set my sights on James's office and walk ahead, clearing my throat as I walk into his open doorway.

James's eyes widen as he looks up from his computer. "Kailey?" His voice is just as I recall: urgent, abrupt, with a touch of jovial sportscaster that rounds out the edges. "What's going on?"

"Hi," I say. There's a dusting of gray at his temples; he's aged more than I imagined.

"It's been a long time," he says, standing up and waving away the guy from the front desk, who is hovering like a pit bull puppy. James clasps his hands awkwardly, as if he doesn't know what to do with them.

His office looks like a page from the latest issue of *Dwell,* with a desk made of iron and reclaimed wood and a space-age swivel chair. I eye the photos on the wall, all in matching black frames: babies, a big happy family posing barefoot in front of palm trees by the beach, Hawaii, maybe; James with band members from Element Records, at shows; and one of him and Alexis standing on a yacht called *Stella May.* None of Cade.

"You look good, Kailey, the years have been—"

"I found him," I say, no interest in small talk. Not now.

"You what?"

"I found Cade."

"What do you mean, you found him?"

"Here in Seattle," I say. "Right under our noses."

"Well, I didn't realize he was lost," he says, shaking his head with a strained smile.

I sit down. "I didn't either, at first. But when he left, when he never came back, part of me worried that something had happened. I guess I've always worried that. And, James, something *did* happen. He's on the streets. Homeless."

"Homeless?"

I nod solemnly. "I saw him outside Le Marche last night. I was too stunned to know what to do, but I decided to come downtown this morning to try to find him. And I did. I saw him at Westlake Center. James, he looks terrible. He's in rags." I exhale deeply. "I don't even know if he knows *himself*."

James clasps his hands together once again. "Are you sure it was him?"

"Absolutely sure."

"Perhaps it was just someone who looked like Cade."

"No," I say, pulling up the sleeve of my shirt to reveal my tattoo. "A man at the homeless shelter recognized it. It's Cade, James. It's really him."

I hear the hinges of the door behind me, and I turn around.

"Oh, hi, sweetie."

Alexis, now with a baby on her hip, is just as I remember her: dark curly hair, a little round; big, wide-set eyes. After Cade's disappearance, she reached out on numerous occasions to see how I was, offering to have lunch or coffee. As much as I appreciated the gesture, I was too raw to discuss the past, and by then I'd moved to New York.

"Hi, Alexis," I say.

"Kailey!" she exclaims, rushing over to lean in and give me a one-armed hug. The baby, a little boy with blond hair, smiles as she jostles him higher on her hip. Alexis flashes James a quick glance. "It's been . . . such a long time. You look great!"

"You too," I say, though I notice bags under her eyes. Age has snuck up on her, or perhaps just the stress of parenting.

"Lex, Kailey is here because she believes she saw Cade downtown," he says, raising an eyebrow.

Alexis looks stunned. "You're kidding?" They exchange a knowing look before her gaze returns to me. "Cade's back? That's . . . wonderful." She looks at her husband again, then back at me. "How is he?"

"Not well," I say. "As I was just telling James, he's living on the streets. Something happened to him."

"That's terrible," Alexis says, shocked. "James, can we do anything to help him?"

James sighs and runs his hand through his hair. I try to remember

Alexis in the nineties, but the images that rise to the surface of my mind's eye are blurry and incomplete. She was there, all along, of course, working alongside Cade, at all the parties, all the concerts, and yet there was something oddly unmemorable about her, something vacant about her presence. I watch her tenderly rock the small child in her arms and wonder if she's happy, if motherhood is the path she's been on all along. The baby coos at me, and I feel a twinge in my heart. I look away.

"It's been years," Alexis continues. "But it's never too late to come home. He must have changed his mind about the new life he started somewhere else. He always talked about France, remember, Kailey?"

I close my eyes tightly, then open them again. *We* talked about France, specifically that little seaside town in Normandy I'd visited once as a child with my grandparents. Coincidentally, Cade had traveled there, too, that very summer, with his aunt. We laughed about how we probably saw each other on the train. After Cade disappeared, it crossed my mind that he might have moved to France. The very idea of it sent shock waves through my beleaguered heart.

James turns in his chair to face the window. How strange it seems, suddenly, to see how life unfolds. Once a record label executive in Vans and jeans, he's become one of the masses. A businessman, in a bland office building, with a chair that swivels.

"Cade's out there," I say, looking out at Seattle in all her gray glory beyond the window. "Right now."

A moment later, he spins his chair around and nods like a doctor who has deliberated and settled on a diagnosis. "Alexis has always been sentimental, and, Kailey, you used to live with your head in the clouds. But I see your byline on the business pages these days. You've joined the real world. And the reality is that when it comes to Cade, it's his life, not ours. If he wants to live on the streets, that's his prerogative."

I shake my head. "James, no one chooses to live on the streets. Something happened to him, I know it. He's not well. He needs help."

He shakes his head. "Kailey, I helped Cade so much at the end. You remember what it was like then. You remember how bad it was."

I don't want to remember, but I do. The accusations James made.

The way everything spiraled out of control. I had Cade's back until . . . well, until I couldn't any longer. And even then I wondered if I'd gotten it all wrong. Wondered if I'd misread the situation. Wondered if I would have stayed, for just another hour, just one more conversation, if life would have turned out differently for me, for Cade, for all of us.

"It's no longer my job to help him," he says.

Alexis walks closer to her husband. "But, James—"

"I've moved on," he says, disregarding her. "I have a new business to run, and"—he points to his wife—"a family to think of. What if he's on drugs?"

"James," I say, shaking my head.

His eyes narrow. "There was a lot he kept from us," he says. "A lot he kept from you."

I close my eyes tightly, then reopen them.

"I think we both know that."

I search James's eyes. They're void of any love, any bond, any loyalty he might have once had for Cade. Did it wither and die over the years? Was it missing all along? "But, James," I say, almost pleading. "He was your best friend."

James stands up. "When I was a kid," he says, straightening the collar of his oxford shirt, cuffs embellished with custom gold links. "But somewhere along the way, I grew up. Obviously he didn't."

Alexis gives me a sympathetic look as James reaches for the baby in his wife's arms.

"I'm sorry, Kailey," he says, kissing the child's forehead. "You have our sympathy, and I do hope you're able to get him the help he needs. We all make our choices. Cade made his."

"Right," I say, walking out the door.

My heart sinks lower in the elevator with each descending floor.

If Cade is going to be saved, I'll have to do it myself.

I walk back to Westlake Center and sit on a bench, numbly watching the passersby. A child with a yellow balloon skips past, a few paces behind his mother. An older couple with matching white hair hold hands as they take slow steps across the brick cobblestones.

I pull my phone from my purse and call my grandma. She met Cade once, when she and Grandpa flew to Seattle to visit. They loved him, and he them. "Marry this one," Grandma whispered to me the night after our dinner at the Space Needle, which Grandpa had last visited in the 1960s at the World's Fair. I was always grateful that he got to see it once more before his heart attack. And always grateful that he got to meet Cade.

"Oh, honey, I've missed you," Grandma says. She's always seemed young to me. In fact, when I was in school, she often passed as a mom who had children later in life. People rarely thought of her as my grandmother. But now her voice sounds weak and unsteady, and it troubles me.

"Grandma," I say, unable to stop the tears from coming.

"What is it, love?" she asks tenderly. I'm at once eleven years old again, in the old Craftsman in Iowa, lying on my stomach in the room my mother grew up in, on that old red-and-blue quilt with loops of soft white yarn in every corner. Grandma is patting my back and I can taste the salt of my tears as they find their way down my freckle-dusted cheeks to the corners of my mouth. A batch of chocolate-chip cookies is baking, and the comforting smell of butter and sugar wafts in the air.

"It's Cade," I say.

"Your old boyfriend? I thought he'd . . ."

"Disappeared? Left the country? I did too. But he's here, Grandma. He's here in Seattle. And he's . . . homeless. I saw him yesterday and today, bearded and skinny."

"Oh dear," she says.

"And his best friend won't help him," I continue. "I just went to see him." I wipe away a tear. "Grandma, what am I supposed to do? I'm getting married soon. How am I supposed to deal with this?"

She's silent for a moment as she always is when she's gathering information, when she's on the verge of saying something wise.

"He barely recognizes me," I say. "He's not himself. Something must have happened to him. Something awful. I know it."

"But he's out there," she says. "Your guy is out there."

I shake my head. I know her memory has faded in the past years. Perhaps she's forgotten momentarily that I'm engaged to Ryan. "Grandma, he's not my guy anymore. *Ryan* is. I'm marrying Ryan. Cade left so long ago. I never knew why. I had to mourn him. I had to move on. And I did. I finally did."

She's miles away, but I can see Grandma's face in my mind's eye: soft and freshly powdered, kind pastel-blue eyes, skin that smells of rose soap.

She's silent, as if considering what I've just told her, remembering the man I pledged myself to, back when the door to the past was closed, when things were simpler.

"I don't know what I'm supposed to do."

"Maybe you don't now," she says. "But in time, you will."

"What do you mean?"

"Your heart will guide you, dear," she says.

"I don't know," I say, discouraged.

"It's okay not to know," she continues. "Your path is not an easy one."

"I love Ryan," I say. "I really do, Grandma. I want to marry him. I want a life with him."

"Yes," she says. "And you may very well have that. But you must sort out your past first, and that means facing it head-on."

"Yes," I say. "You're right."

"Sweetheart," Grandma adds, "no matter what has happened or will happen, one thing is certain."

"What?"

"You told me that Cade saved your life once," she continues.

"Yes," I mutter. Her words ping my heart, twisting like an acupuncturist's needle in a way that hurts as much as it feels good and right.

"Now it's your turn to save his."

eight

"*F*or you," Cade says, standing in the doorway of my apartment.

"They're beautiful," I say, receiving the large bouquet of flowers from Pike Place Market. Tulips, hydrangeas, and stock wrapped in white paper. I press my nose to a lavender-colored blossom, which makes me think of home. Stock was always my Grandma's favorite flower—her garden was lined with white and pink varieties. On warm summer mornings, their soft floral scent would waft into my bedroom window.

"Nice apartment," Cade says, looking around.

"It's not much," I say. "But it does have a killer view, and Tracy's a great roommate. We each have an uncanny ability to know when the other person needs her space. She's at her boyfriend's house tonight." I smile. "Are you hungry?"

"Starving," he says.

"Good," I say, glancing at the clock. "Dinner won't be ready until about five of eight. I hope that's okay."

He grins at me.

"What?"

"I like the way you speak."

"The way I speak?"

His smile widens. "Five of eight. No one ever says that kind of thing."

"Oh," I say with a grin. "Well, when you're raised by your grandparents, you do. Dinner was 'supper,' the couch was a 'davenport.'" I laugh. "I can go on and on."

"It's cute," Cade says.

"Well," I reply, opening the oven to have a peek, "it's less cute when you say 'Oh fiddlesticks' on the playground in the sixth grade and every kid in school teases you about it for the rest of the year."

He looks amused. "'Oh fiddlesticks,' huh?"

"Yep."

He takes off his jacket and hangs it on a hook by the door. I select a few leaves of basil from the fridge as Cade nestles into a chair at the table, and suddenly I feel ill-prepared to pull off this meal. *What if I oversalted the meat? Is the romaine in the salad a bit wilted?*

I realize that I've forgotten to pour the wine. "Here," I say, reaching for a bottle of Bordeaux. "I'm not sure how good this is. It was a gift."

He eyes the label confidently. "I guess we'll find out."

I find a corkscrew and do my best to carefully wind it into the bottle, but when I tug it upward, the cork cracks and then breaks. "Darn," I say, stepping back. "I think I messed this one up."

"I can fix it," he says. "Any chance you have a toothpick?"

"A toothpick?"

"Yeah," he says. "My aunt taught me the trick to salvaging any cork conundrum."

I smile, digging through the utensil drawer until I find a box of toothpicks, left over from Tracy's failed attempt at making mini-meatballs for a party last month. I hand him the box.

"Great," he says, getting to work. "So here's how you do it: While the corkscrew is still in, you wedge in a toothpick at a forty-five-degree angle." His hands work with expert precision. "You tug at the corkscrew really carefully, and then"—he lifts the cork, miraculously intact, out of the bottle—"voilà."

"Amazing," I say with a smile, pouring two glasses and handing him one.

He holds the glass to his ear. "This is a good wine."

"Are you listening to it?" I ask, a little confused.

"Yeah," he says. "I know nothing about wine. But one of my friends who works in the industry told me that a good wine, especially a French red, will crackle a little after it's poured."

I hold the glass up to my ear and smile. "You know, I can actually hear it," I say. "I never in my life knew there was such a thing as that."

"Snap, crackle, pop . . . grenache blend."

"You're funny."

He winks. "Stick with me, kid, and I'll keep you in stitches."

I grin, pulling two dinner plates from the cupboard. Part of me thinks: *Who is this guy, and, more pressingly, who does he think he is?* And another part of me wonders where he's been all my life.

Cade takes a sip of his wine and walks to the window. "I never get tired of watching the ferries," I say. "They each have personalities, you know."

He turns to me and grins. "Oh?"

"Yeah," I say, pointing to the vessel streaming through the water at a slug's pace ahead. "That's Bertha," I say. "She's bossy."

Cade chuckles. "Oh, is she?"

"Maeve is sweet," I say, squinting to make out another ferry in the distance. "And Eleanor is sassy."

Cade looks at me as if I've said something either hilarious or bizarre, or both.

He makes me want to confide in him. "I love Puget Sound. The salt water, the seagulls, the islands."

"I do too," Cade says. "I don't know that I could be happy without saltwater nearby."

"Me too," I say.

"Let's go to the island sometime."

"Would you want to?"

"Sure," he says. "Let's make a day of it. Ferry, beach, dinner—the works."

"Okay," I say, smiling, topping off each of our glasses. I flip on the radio, and a band I don't recognize is playing.

Cade rolls his eyes. "Soulstreet Underground," he says. "We signed them to Element two years ago, and they've been the most difficult artists to work with." He rubs his forehead.

"How so?"

"Their tour bus wasn't big enough. Their album cover took eleven thousand go-rounds to get right. The lead singer refuses to perform unless a certain type of bottled water from France is waiting for him before a show. That kind of stuff."

I shake my head. "Seriously?"

He shrugs. "It's bad. And then we found out that someone from *SNL* was a fan, and they were this close to being booked for one of the spring shows last year, but the lead singer claimed he hated *SNL,* so that fell through."

I throw up my arms. "Who hates *SNL?*"

"Right? Anyway, the music business is filled with big personalities," he says. "It was one part of the job I didn't bargain for. I'm in it for the music, not the drama." He takes a long sip of wine. "James handles most of it. He doesn't let it get to him the way it gets to me."

"So you're more of the visionary and he's the operations guy?"

"I guess you could say that," he says. "I'll introduce you to him sometime."

"I'd like that," I say with a smile, just as the smoke alarm begins to sound. I rush to the oven, where smoke is billowing out of the door. "Oh no!"

Cade leaps up and attempts to disarm the smoke alarm, but after a few tries it continues to let out an ear-piercing sound. "Damn, this thing is wired in."

"Can you just yank it out?" I ask, reaching for an oven mitt, then pulling our now-charred dinner out of the oven.

"Should I?" he asks, laughing.

"Anything to make that sound stop," I say, fanning the smoke away before opening the window and letting in some fresh air.

"Okay," he says. "Here goes." With a single tug, he breaks the smoke alarm free from its place in the wall. Severed wires dangle from the ceiling. We look at each other and laugh.

"Sorry," I say.

"And you call yourself a food enthusiast," he jokes.

"It was going to be good, too," I say. "Melanzane."

He closes his eyes and places his hand on his heart dramatically. "Don't torture me with what might have been."

The smoke alarm suddenly lets out a single chirp from where it sits on the kitchen counter.

"I thought we killed this thing," Cade says.

We both hover over the device as if it quite possibly has a brain of its own.

"It's not even battery-powered," I say.

Cade nods. "It could be an alien."

It chirps again, and we both laugh.

"Maybe it's like when someone loses a limb, but they can still feel the pain."

"A phantom limb," Cade says.

I nod. "A phantom chirp."

"You're funny," he says, chuckling.

"How do we get rid of this thing?"

He looks around. "We could stuff it under the couch cushions."

"Or put it out in the hallway," I say.

We laugh again, and I pause to mourn our dinner, then shake my head. "I promise, I really can cook."

He surveys the seared disaster in the nine-by-eleven dish on the stove. "Sure you can," he says teasingly before taking my hand. "Hey, why don't we just go out for Thai."

"Okay," I say with a laugh.

As I slip on a sweater and sling my purse over my shoulder, he grabs his coat and the chirping smoke alarm. "We have a nice home for you, little fella," he says. "And it's called a dumpster."

Twenty minutes later, we're seated at a corner table at Jai Thai, two blocks away, both sinking our forks into pad Thai.

"Do you ever wonder what your parents would think of you now, all grown up?" Cade asks.

"Yeah," I say, twisting an uncooperative noodle around my fork for the third time. "I wonder if they'd be proud of me, I guess."

"Me too," he says. "I mean, I'm almost thirty, and yet in some ways I still feel like the kid who's looking for his parents' approval."

I nod. "I still feel like a kid."

"Do you think we always will?"

"I don't know," I say. "Maybe. Maybe some people always remain young at heart."

"I hope I'm one."

"I think you are," I say, watching a pair of teenagers saunter by on the sidewalk outside the window. The girl stops so her boyfriend can light her cigarette. She takes a long drag, then flips her hair behind her shoulder the way every girl does when she is sixteen.

"Did you ever smoke?" I ask.

"Nah," he says. "But I tried. Didn't we all?"

I grin. "My first cigarette was a—"

He holds out his hand. "Wait, let me guess, a—"

"Clove," we both say in unison before laughing.

He reaches for another spring roll, and the humor in his eyes drifts away. "It's funny to think that our parents did all the same things we did. Smoked cloves. Got in trouble. Felt lost."

"Yeah," I say. "Isn't that the great realization of adulthood?"

He nods. "Exactly, that our parents didn't have it figured out, nor do we. Maybe no one does."

"Exactly," I say. "I still can't believe my byline's in the newspaper."

He grins. "And how could a kid who refused to take piano lessons and could barely pick out a few notes on the bass end up running a record label?"

"Your parents would be proud," I say with confidence. "So proud."

He looks away, and I wonder if my comment has found a pathway straight to his heart. He purses his lips for a moment, then turns back to me. "How did your parents meet?"

"In Big Sur," I say.

"Big Sur?"

"Yeah, they were hippies. Mom and her best friend were driving up Highway One in a Volkswagen bus, and my dad and his friend were hitchhiking on the road."

"No way," he says, smiling.

"They hit it off immediately, and ended up spending a weekend in Big Sur at some campground overlooking the ocean. It always sounded magical to me, at least in the way my grandmother described it."

"I've never been," Cade says.

"I've always wanted to go," I say, "to retrace the steps of my parents' love story." I pause for a moment, remembering the stories my grandmother would tell of that dreamy time in my parents' lives. Mom was beautiful, with golden hair, olive skin, and eyes the color of the sea. Dad was handsome for any decade, but particularly in 1971, with strong arms, a warm smile, and dark hair tied back in a ponytail. He wooed Mom with his passion for life, his dreams for the future, and his skill with the guitar (apparently he played her favorite Joan Baez song upon request and knew all the words). "They were soulmates," I continue a little wistfully. "If you believe in that sort of thing."

Cade shrugs. "I don't know if I do," he says. "I mean, I *want* to believe that each person gets to have one true love, someone who completes them." He shakes his head. "But is that really the case?"

"Have you ever had your heart broken?" I ask, instead of giving him an answer.

"Yes," he says simply.

I don't press him for details, but I wonder about this girl who broke his heart. Was she beautiful? A musician? Someone who's still in his life? And while I mourned a college breakup for longer than I care to admit, I don't know that I can say whether I've ever had my heart broken in the true sense of the term. My heart has hurt, yes. But it hasn't broken, not really.

"What are you keeping close to your heart?" he asks, pointing at my locket as a waitress refills our water glasses.

I immediately raise my hand to my neck and look down at the little locket I've worn all these years. I so rarely open it and, frankly, can't even remember the last time I did. But it feels natural somehow to open it now, and so I finger the clasp until it releases; the tiny shell fragment, still the color of milk jade, falls into my palm, which I hold out to Cade.

"My grandfather found this shell on a beach in Normandy during the war," I explain. "It broke, but I've always kept a little piece of it with me, for luck."

"I love that," Cade says, his eyes flashing. "I've been to Normandy."

"Really?"

He nods. "My mom always wanted to see the north of France. She never got to go, so my aunt took me for her. Even though she couldn't afford it, she put the whole thing on her credit card and we flew to Paris." He pauses for a long moment. "Seeing my aunt cry one day at the beach." He sighs. "It was something else."

"Wow," I say. "Have you been back?"

"No," he says. "Not since then. But I'd like to." He grins. "Maybe we could go back together and get you another one of those shells."

I feel warm all over.

"How about this," he continues. "Let's make a pact that we'll go there together, for the memories." He touches my arm lightly. "What do you say?"

"I say yes."

nine

"Hi," I say to Ryan, setting my keys down on the kitchen counter.

"Hi," he says, leaning in to place a kiss on my cheek. "How did the research go?"

"Good," I say distractedly.

"Educate me. Tell me something about our city that I don't already know. That will surprise me."

"Over dinner, I promise. My thoughts are scattered now," I say, sidestepping the truth—the surprise I got at Westlake Center.

He looks at me for a long moment. I avoid his gaze.

"I hope our children get your nose," he says. "It's so darn cute."

I bite my lip. "Ryan, I'm not sure if I—"

"I know, I know," he continues, his grin melting away. "You don't know if you're ready for a family. I get it. I'll be patient. I promise."

I nod, grateful to tuck the subject away once again, not ready to discuss it. Not yet.

"Is there something bothering you, baby?" he asks like a mind reader, tucking his hand in mine.

"No, no," I lie.

"You and Trace didn't get into a fight or anything, did you?"

"No," I say.

"You're stressed," he says. "I can tell. Is it the feature? Are you getting any interview resistance? Because I can help. I can make some calls—"

"No, it's not that," I say. "I'm just overwhelmed, that's all."

"All right," he says, nestling in closer to me. "You just say the word, and I'll do what you need."

"You're wonderful, you know," I say as he kisses my cheek lightly. And he is, this man I'm going to marry this summer. He's wonderful in every way; I feel a pang of guilt rise in my chest.

"Hey," he says, reaching for an old Converse shoebox beside the bar. "My parents are coming to visit next weekend, so I thought I'd better get the guest room in shape. Anyway, I found this."

I reach for the box filled with old postcards and letters I've saved over the years. I intend to sort through and dispose of them, the same way I mean to spend quality time with those bridal magazines. Buried at the bottom is a black-and-white photo I thought was lost ages ago. I lift it out, and the hair on my arms stand on end.

"Wow," Ryan says, leaning over my shoulders. "I know you're camera-shy, but I wish I had more pictures of you. You look gorgeous. We should have it blown up and frame it. Maybe hang it over there by the—"

"No," I say quickly, turning the photo over. "No, I'd rather not."

"Oh," Ryan says, a bit injured. "Why not? It's a great picture from a composition standpoint."

I blink hard, remembering how I stood on the edge of the ferry, leaning up against that kelly-green railing, wind blowing sideways against my cheek, whipping my hair this way and that. Still, I was smiling. I didn't feel the cold. I wasn't bothered by the wind. Cade was in front of me, his camera clicking. I look at Ryan again, his face expectant, eyes filled with love.

He tucks a wayward strand of my hair behind my left ear. "Was this taken in Seattle?"

I nod.

"You're so quiet about that time in your past," he says.

"It feels like a lifetime ago," I say with an exaggerated shrug.

"Kailey," Ryan says, locking his eyes to mine. "I want to believe that. I really do. But sometimes, in moments like this, I feel like there's a part of your heart that I haven't yet been given access to." He squeezes my hand. "Tell me you'll let me in. Because I—"

"I *have* let you in," I say quickly.

"Someday I want to meet the girl in that photo," he says with a sigh, returning to the kitchen, where he pulls the dishwasher open and begins unloading the glasses into the upper cabinet by the window.

"You know that Ryan is a rare specimen," Tracy told me after I started dating him four years ago. "An anomaly in the sea of men." And she was, and is, right. Of every woman I know, none of their husbands or boyfriends helps out around the house, and yet Ryan insists on changing the sheets, folding laundry, and keeping the sink free of dishes.

"So, I thought that when my parents are here next weekend, we could take them to the Fairmont, show them the ballroom where the reception will be."

"Sure," I say absentmindedly.

"My mom would love that," Ryan continues. "She asked me the color of the walls." He gives me a knowing grin. "You know how she loves to color-coordinate."

I force a smile. "Then let's do it."

Part of me is envious of Ryan, with his loving parents who are interested in their children's lives. And yet, I suppose I'm ultimately jealous of *anyone* who has parents. As much as I've always been eager to gain a set of parents when I say "I do," from day one there's been something forced about the relationship with my soon-to-be in-laws. Ryan's dad, Bennett, a banker who spends almost all of his free time at the country club, is nice enough, but I struggle to connect with him on any real level. Ryan's mom, Melinda, is perpetually manicured and coiffed, clad in overpriced designer outfits she'll wear only once to the lunches and galas that litter her schedule. High-maintenance, with the emphasis on *high*.

"I know my parents can be a little much," he says, closing the dishwasher door. "But it's just for a few days."

"They're always welcome in our home," I reassure him.

"They love you, you know," he continues. "They've always wanted to have a daughter, and now they're getting the very best one."

I smile as I reach for a pan from the pot rack. "I promised you risotto. Are you hungry?"

He shrugs. "Not very. Are you?"

"Not starving, but you should eat something."

"I won't argue," he says. "You know there's nothing you could make that I wouldn't devour."

"Just as long as it's not spicy," I say with a smile, noticing a bottle of Tabasco as I open the refrigerator. Although I might normally have enjoyed the challenge of putting together a last-minute meal, I don't feel like cooking tonight. "You know," I say, "I'm pretty tired. How would you feel about just getting some takeout?"

"Sure," he says. "Indian? Thai? Something else?"

"Thai sounds great," I say quietly.

Ryan nods and picks up his phone. "I'll call it in."

As I stand in my kitchen, my heart churns. I love this man I'm about to marry. I love how he places the water glasses rim-side down in the cabinet and thinks I look like a goddess with my hair up, even though I've never felt I had the face for it. I love how he kisses me in the morning and at night. Mostly I love how he loves me, so freely, so all-encompassingly.

In a burst of inspiration, I turn on the oven. *Cinnamon. The scent of a happy home.* I can bake Ryan some breakfast rolls for a fresh start tomorrow, to show him how much I adore him every day.

Suddenly the smoke alarm sounds. I intended to clean up the burned drippings from dinner two nights ago, but I forgot, and now my plan is ruined.

Ryan leaps to his feet. "I'll get that," he says, reaching up to the offending smoke alarm on the ceiling.

"There," he says, removing the batteries.

I turn off the heat and open the kitchen window to let some of the smoke out, and at once I'm transported back to that little apartment overlooking Elliott Bay. Cade is standing beside me. I have burned our dinner, and we are laughing about a chirping smoke alarm that seems to have a mind of its own.

But Cade has been gone for so long. He left me, and I never knew why. And Ryan is here now. Ryan is beside me, and he loves me.

I pull my fiancé toward me fiercely. Last night and this morning have been intense. It's true, I want to help Cade; I want to know what happened to him. But the world turned, and somewhere along the way I had to move on, and I did. And now I am Ryan's and he is mine. I tell myself this over and over again until it is burned on my heart. I am Ryan's and he is mine.

"I love you, you know," I whisper into his ear.

He kisses me, and I feel the familiar hunger well up in my body. "Take me upstairs," I say, running my hands along his chest. "I need you."

He lifts me into his arms.

The next morning, I open my eyes. Ryan is dressed, and he sits beside me where I lie in bed. He's wearing the blue tie I bought for him last month. "Morning," he says, running his hand lightly across my shoulder. I feel goosebumps erupt on my skin as I pull him toward me.

"I can't," he says. "I'll miss my train."

"That's right," I say, having forgotten about his business trip to Portland. This particular venture falls into the no-discussion zone we've set up around potential conflicts of interest. To further the development of Seattle's Pioneer Square, Ryan envisions forging a partnership with Portland's Pioneer Courthouse Square. Success for him spells displacement for the homeless, and disappointment—personal and professional—for me.

"I have to devote two business days to this phase of the project," he reassures me. "KGW NewsChannel Eight's HD Studio on the Square is set to open next year. There are opportunities to develop supporting businesses around the new facility and attract major media coverage in both cities. Our group is active in both sites, but Portland is much further along. To secure the financing, our investors have had to cross-collateralize the loan on the Seattle deal against the one in Portland. It's risky—if one site fails and the other can't pick up the slack, they both go under. But it's the best way to balance the risk. If I can negotiate the final terms, I'll be home tomorrow night."

I nod, sleepily pulling the comforter higher around my neck.

"Good luck," I say, trying to be supportive. I know how important this deal is to him, even if it means other things to me.

"Thank you, babe," he says, kissing my lips lightly. "I'll call you from the hotel tonight." He lifts his suitcase and I listen as his footsteps trail off down the stairs to the entryway, where he opens and closes the door behind him. I hear the sound of the key latching the dead bolt, which makes me feel safe, and loved, and cared for—all at the same time.

I stare at the ceiling. Cade's face appears in my mind, dirty and bearded. Those hollow eyes, razor-sharp cheekbones. I hear Grandma's voice, too. It reverberates in my ears. *Cade saved your life once. Now it's your turn to save his.*

I turn her words over and over again in my mind. And then I pick up the phone to call my editor.

"Jan, it's Kailey," I say.

"I just got off the phone with Melissa from the Hope Gospel Mission. She says donations are pouring in. The response to the first piece in your series has been incredible. Nearly a thousand readers have posted online, pro and con, inciting a heated debate about the fate of Pioneer Square. That's the kind of page traffic that makes advertisers

happy. We have to keep the momentum going, have the second piece
hit even harder—"

This is the professional moment I've been waiting for, but I'm
barely listening to the feedback.

"I need to take the day off today," I interrupt.

"Did you hear me, Kailey? We've got to get moving on that second
piece. Can you show me some of your raw data?"

"Something's come up." I take a deep breath. "Something I have to
deal with."

"All right," she says, immediately softening, her voice tinged with
concern. "You're not sick, are you?"

"No," I reply. "I just . . . need the day."

I park my car on the street in front of Le Marche and step out onto the
sidewalk. It's not quite ten, and I'm grateful that the sun appears to be
peeking out from behind a cloud. I survey the sidewalk and nearby
alley as I did yesterday—no Cade—then decide to stop at Starbucks for
an Americano before launching my little search party of one.

The line is long and it winds around the side of the espresso bar. In
front of me are two women who look like administrative assistants on
coffee runs for their respective bosses. The first woman tosses her shiny
brunette hair over her shoulder and makes a comment about the unbelievable number of calories in a slice of banana loaf. Her friend says
something in response and they laugh together.

Life is simpler in your twenties, especially when it comes to love.
You meet someone, you *choose* them and they choose you. Together
you can conquer the world. Move to Paris. Have a gaggle of children
or become vegetable farmers. All the stuff you wrote about when you
had a diary and a dream is now yours to live out in bright, bold colors.
Life is yours, together, and you take it by the horns and *live*. You pledge
your life to someone, fiercely, and the rest is history.

But when it doesn't work out, when the story has an unhappy
ending, the way my twentysomething love story did, it changes some-

thing in your heart. You go from a girl with a diary and a dream to a girl defined by her job, whose passion for social justice takes a backseat to business headlines. You're thirty, or thirty-five, and it's clear now that there are more rain clouds than rainbows and that you are the only one who truly has your own back. The dream has died. You lost the diary—no, you burned it.

And then you meet someone who is different than your ex in almost every way, and you wonder if you can do it. You wonder if you can love the way you did so long ago. You're not sure, but you try, and when you do, when you force yourself to go through the motions, you realize that your heart—asleep for so long—is groggily waking up, like a bear fresh out of hibernation. You're alternately hungry and grumpy, disoriented, a bit lost. It surprises you when you feel the spark again. And though it might not burn as hot as it did so many years ago, as it did with the man who loved you when you were wide-eyed and twenty-five, it burns steadily now. It keeps you warm. And one day you start seeing rainbows again. One shines out your window at work. Another when you emerge from the grocery store. A double one fills up the entire sky when you're having a glass of wine after a long day at the office. And that's when you realize that your heart, beleaguered, weighed down with baggage of all kinds, is ready to try again. And so you do.

I blink back tears as I reach the front of the line and order a double Americano and a banana loaf with its *fourteen billion* calories, which matter nothing to me in this moment. But I know that, somewhere in me, that twenty-five-year-old girl still lingers, and she tugs at my heart now in a way she hasn't done in so long. "Go find him," she whispers to me. "He's out there. He needs you."

I know deep down that no matter what's to come, good or bad, *she's right.*

I lean against the brick façade of Le Marche for a solid hour waiting, watching for any sign of Cade. I stop a homeless man and ask if he knows of a Mitchell. He doesn't. A woman with plastic bags wrapped around her feet and her life's possessions stuffed into a red Trader Joe's shopping cart doesn't either, but she tells me she's hard up for money to buy a meal. I give her ten dollars.

I wait, and I watch, and when the last drop of coffee is gone from my cup, I toss it into a nearby trash can and wander back down to Westlake Center, where Cade disappeared from my view yesterday.

I find my way to a park bench and watch a flock of pigeons fight over bread crumbs while a benevolent toddler squeals with delight. His mother looks on proudly. Somewhere around the corner, out of view, a saxophone sounds. At first I can't place the song, but then it comes to me: "A Kiss to Build a Dream On," that song by Louis Armstrong that my grandmother has always loved. I have, too.

The crowd parts enough for me to catch a glimpse of the opposite side of the square. Children watch as a man with a clown nose juggles tennis balls. A young couple reclines on a bench, embroiled in a heated makeout session. And then my eyes freeze on a speck of army green in the distance. I stand up to get a better look, and it's indeed a man in an army-green jacket. He's seated against the wall of Macy's, and his gaze is turned down, so I'm not quite able to identify his face, but my heart beats fast.

I cross the square to the street, and disregarding traffic, I barrel across. A taxi swerves and blares its horn at me, though I can scarcely hear it. My senses are dulled. All I can do is focus on the figure ahead of me. The man on the sidewalk in his crumpled army jacket, with his sad face, which I see now, plain as day. Cade.

Tears well up in my eyes as I make my way to him. The pull is magnetic, just as it once was. Two halves of a whole. That's how it used to feel, anyway. My legs are suddenly weak, and I steady myself as I take a few steps closer.

"Cade," I say in a faltering voice.

He doesn't look up, so I try again. "Cade," I say a bit louder. "I–I . . ."

His eyes meet mine, and every part of me freezes. I'm suspended in time, with waves of memories rushing back—one after the next. The day we met, our first kiss, all the promises, the tender, quiet midnight conversations, all the love.

"Hi," I say softly. "It's me." I take another step toward him, aware that I must go slow. I don't know his mental state. I don't know what he'll think or do.

He stares blankly at me.

"Cade," I say again. "Cade, do you know me? It's Kailey."

His eyes search mine.

I nod, fighting back tears. My hands are shaking. "May I sit down beside you? Just for a moment?"

He's silent, gaze fixed straight ahead to a spot on the street.

I crouch a few inches away from him. The cement sidewalk feels cold through my jeans, and I shift uncomfortably, finally tucking my knees to my chest. Feet pass in front of us. Swanky heels, freshly shined Italian loafers, ballet flats, and boots with elaborate laces. Someone tosses an apple core and it lands a few inches from me. Cade stares ahead.

I turn to him, nervous to speak again. "What happened to you?" I finally ask cautiously. "Please talk to me. How did you end up like this?"

He turns to me, and when our eyes meet I think I see a flash of recognition. And when I do, his current exterior melts away. The long matted hair melds into his old cropped haircut I used to run my fingers through. The unkempt beard disappears in a flash, revealing his beautiful tan skin. It's him. He's in there. But can I reach him?

"Cade," I say again. "Do you know me? Please, Cade, tell me that you know me."

His eyes search mine, and then he scoots back, suddenly frightened.

"Don't be afraid, Cade," I say, inching closer. "Please don't be afraid. It's me, Kailey. I want to help you."

A man in his twenties approaches. He's wearing a tailored suit and has an expensive-looking haircut. He sneers at Cade as he passes, and I wonder how many sneers, how many smirks, how much hatred Cade must field each day.

"Hey," I say, trying to get his attention again. "Cade, tell me if you know me."

He turns to me, but whatever flicker of recognition I saw in his eyes has vanished. "No," he says. His voice is hollow, lost, scared, wild. "No," he says again, shifting a bit to try to stand. His legs are weak and wobbly, and he uses the edge of the building to steady himself.

I stand, too, and reach out my hand to him. I touch his arm lightly. The once-strong muscles have atrophied and cling to the bone. "Cade," I plead through tears. "What happened to you? Please tell me. Please let me help you."

"No," he says again, taking a step backward. He reaches for a duffel bag at his feet and slings the strap over his shoulder, then turns his back to me and begins walking erratically down the sidewalk.

I follow. *I won't leave him. Not now.*

He walks down a few streets, then rounds another block until we're on Third, right by Wild Ginger, where we had our first date so many years ago. They're open for lunch now, and just ahead I see a group of people walking in the door. *Does he remember this place? Somewhere, deep down, is the memory still embedded in his heart the way it's surgically lodged in mine?*

"Please, Cade, stop," I say when he reaches the corner beside the restaurant. I'm hungry, and I know he must be, too. "Let me get you something to eat."

He turns around and waits. Instinctively I take his hand. It's rough and weathered. His nails are caked with dirt, but I don't mind. I lead him inside the restaurant, and he cautiously follows.

"Hello," I say to the hostess, who eyes Cade skeptically.

"Two for lunch," I say.

Her eyes dart around nervously. It's obvious that Cade's presence gives her pause.

I look out to the restaurant beyond her; half the dining room is empty. "Surely you can get us in," I say.

She looks at me, then Cade. "Well, I—I," she stammers.

Just then a woman approaches. Blond, with dark-rimmed glasses. I recognize Dawn, the manager, immediately. Over the years, she's become a reliable source on the downtown restaurant business, and I've quoted her in numerous articles.

"Kailey," she greets me warmly, stopping beside the hostess. "I read your piece on Pioneer Square. The restaurant values the potential business that new development may bring, but on a personal level I feel for the people who might be displaced. Your writing always makes me realize that there are two sides to every issue, especially the hard ones."

"Thank you," I say, forcing a smile. It's a tough moment to accept a compliment, given all that Cade has lost.

"Are you doing an interview?" she asks, assuming that Cade is a subject of my ongoing series.

"No reporting today. Just lunch," I say, turning to Cade. "Just . . . the two of us."

Dawn looks at Cade, then at me. For a moment I'm not sure how she will react.

"It would mean the world to me if you could find us a table," I tell her. "Maybe something in the bar, tucked away?"

Dawn is a consummate professional. She smiles, squares her shoulders, and turns to the hostess. "Jennifer," she says, "see Kailey and her guest to table nineteen."

"Thank you so much."

Jennifer selects two menus and begins to walk ahead. Cade and I follow. "Will you be comfortable here?" she asks, stopping at a table in the far corner of the bar. There are no other diners in the area.

"It's perfect," I say, smiling.

I sit down, and Cade continues to stand. "It's okay," I say, pointing to the chair beside him. "You can sit there."

He stares at the chair as if it's a foreign object from a strange land.

For a moment, I'm convinced he'll bolt, but then he drops his bag to the ground and sits at the table with me.

The waiter arrives next. If he's put off by Cade's presence, he doesn't show it. Dawn has probably briefed him; I'm relieved.

"Hello," I say to him. "What's your name?"

"Kyle," he says.

"Hello, Kyle. I'm Kailey, and this is"—I pause, feeling an unexplained surge of emotion—"Cade." It's important to me that this waiter knows his name. And I wish he could know so much more, that he once was a force in the music industry, that I once . . .

"Nice to meet you, Cade," Kyle says, pretending quite well the situation is like any other run-of-the-mill restaurant interaction.

Cade stares ahead.

"I think I'll just order for us both if that's okay," I say nervously.

Kyle nods agreeably. "Perfect."

"We'll have the chicken satay, the eggplant, and green beans. The prawns and pot stickers. An order of the sea bass and, oh, the pad Thai."

"I'll get that right in," Kyle says, spinning on his heels.

Cade keeps his hands in his lap, where his gaze is fixed.

I don't know what is going on in his head. I don't know what he must feel. But my heart is beating so fast, I worry that it might burst.

"Cade, you and I had our first date here," I say, letting out a nervous laugh. "You probably don't remember. It was a long time ago." I turn and point across the room. "We sat over there." I smile. I'm not sure if he's even listening. And I feel as if I'm talking to myself in the mirror. "I was nervous about my dress," I continue. "But you said I looked like Stevie Nicks. Remember?"

His gaze doesn't leave his lap.

"Well," I say. "That comment made me feel pretty cool." I sigh. "You always knew what to say." I keep my eyes on him, willing him to look at me. "You always made me feel special, wanted."

The waiter fills our water glasses, and I take a sip. Cade guzzles his, and Kyle instantly returns to fill it a second time.

"You saved my life," I continue, once we're alone again. "Do you remember?" I don't wait for him to respond. "I almost fell down a cliff."

Cade listens, but I'm not sure he understands.

When Kyle brings out our food, Cade surveys the table with big eyes.

"Go ahead," I say. "Dig in."

He cautiously reaches for a pot sticker, and I push the plate toward him. "Have as much as you want. All of it if you'd like."

He shoves the pot sticker into his mouth, and then another. With no regard to napkins or silverware, he reaches for a prawn and then a slice of sautéed eggplant. He crams a handful of green beans into his mouth next, then moves on to the pad Thai after I've spooned some of it onto my plate. I hand him a fork, and he takes it.

He's ravenous and focused, as if, without a moment's notice, the waiter will return and whisk all of this luscious food away and shoo him out the door in the process.

"I'm glad you're enjoying the food," I say as he polishes off the prawns.

"When you left," I say, "I didn't know why. I didn't know whether you needed a break from me, or if you needed to take time away from life, from the company. I waited, Cade. I waited so long." I wipe away a tear, and when I notice a bit of food in his beard, I inch my chair closer to him and dab my napkin to his face and beard. He doesn't flinch. I don't even know if he's listening.

I sigh. "But you never called. You never wrote me, not even once. You just . . . disappeared." I nod to myself. "And, just when I'm about to get married, I find you again. On the streets. And you don't know me. You don't even know me." A lump is forming in my throat, and I swallow hard. "But I know you. I could never forget you." I extend my hand across the table to him. "And I want to help you, if you'll let me."

He is unfazed, and his eyes remain cemented to his lap. Tearfully I pull my hand back.

The waiter returns to the table. "I'm glad to see that you two have enjoyed things."

"Yes, thank you," I say, offering my credit card. He returns a moment later, and I sign the receipt.

Following my lead, Cade rises to his feet and lifts his bag from the floor. As we weave through the restaurant on our way out, a few diners at nearby tables gawk and whisper, but Cade registers no response. I realize that at this moment, there could be a half dozen of Ryan's or my colleagues and friends looking on. But I don't care. All that matters to me is this moment. And all I can think is: *What next? When we get out to the street, then what? Do I let him slip away? What if I never find him again?*

It's a warm day for November, and the spicy food has made my cheeks red, so I peel off my sweater and tuck it into my bag. The brisk air feels refreshing on my bare shoulders.

I look Cade straight in the eye a final time. "Well," I say, my voice faltering again. "Thank you for letting me take you to lunch. I ... I mean, if you ... if you ever ..." My voice trails off. He doesn't know me. He doesn't want my help. I take a deep breath. "I wish you the best," I say. "I always will."

As I turn to leave, I feel a light hand on my shoulder, gently pulling me back.

Cade looks at me quizzically, then drops his bag to the sidewalk. As I face him, he touches my shoulder again, at the place where my tattoo resides. He delicately touches it, tracing the lines and swirls with his finger, then rubbing it lightly as if it might come off.

A moment later, he steps back and unfastens the last remaining button on his jacket and lets the right sleeve slide off, revealing a dirt-stained, torn T-shirt and a bony shoulder beneath. And then I see it, his tattoo, just like mine. Still just as vivid and beautiful as on the night we wandered into that tattoo shop in Belltown and, on a whim, like the wide-eyed hopeless romantics that we were, got matching tattoos. Just like that.

A decade later, we stand on this Seattle sidewalk, our tattoos the only evidence of that old life. But it is evidence, and my heart flips and flutters when I see a flicker of recollection in Cade's eyes. He's in there somewhere.

His eyes lock on mine. "Kailey," he mutters, his voice soft and timid but familiar. So familiar. "Kailey," he says again, as if he's learning how to form the word with his mouth.

"You remember," I cry. A single tear trickles down my cheek.

I close my eyes tightly, then open them again, looking up at the sky. Just above the buildings, painted across the sky in the faintest swath of colors, is a rainbow.

ten

"*L*et's go up to the deck," Cade says as the ferry slowly releases itself from the dock and forges out into Elliott Bay. I scrunch my nose. "Won't it be a little cold up there?"

"Nah," he says confidently, slipping off his black denim jacket and tucking it over my shoulders.

The crossing to Bainbridge is only thirty minutes, and fifteen minutes in I can see the island in the distance.

He offers me his hand, and together we walk up the narrow stairway that leads to the upper deck.

We've been dating about two and a half months now, and I still feel butterflies flutter inside when we touch.

On the top deck, he reaches for the camera dangling by a strap from his shoulder. "Wow, the light is beautiful out here. There's just enough cloud cover." He points to the railing ahead. "Stand over there. Let me take a picture of you."

"I don't know," I say shyly. "I've never liked having my picture taken."

"Humor me," he says, pointing ahead. "Just one photo."

"Okay," I finally say, walking ahead. I lean back, letting my arms drape across the railing on either side of me.

What I don't admit to Cade is that cameras have always made me feel anxious. Behind the lens, someone is looking at you, but you can't see them. It's one-sided and nerve-racking. And I feel vulnerable as Cade's camera flashes again and again.

"Try to relax," he says, lowering the camera and walking toward me.

"I'll do my best," I say, looking away. My cheeks feel stiff, my mouth awkward.

He lifts the camera back to his eye. "If only you could see what I see."

The wind is cold and it's whipping my hair across my face, this way and that. Cade takes one more photo, then walks to me, wrapping his arms, warm and strong, around my waist. And when our mouths find each other, he pulls me even closer. For a moment, a magical moment, we're so entwined in this embrace that I'm not sure where he begins and I end.

The ferry sounds its horn as we arrive on the island. We walk with a herd of other passengers off the ramp and through a long corridor that leads to the terminal. The little town of Winslow is just ahead, and we walk hand in hand along the sidewalk that leads to Main Street.

"Hey," Cade says, pointing ahead. "Let's rent a motorcycle and see the island in style."

On the next block, I see the rental company, with a lot of motor-cycles and scooters parked in front. "Really? Do you know how to ride?"

He grins. "Do I *know how to ride*?"

I flash him a playful smirk.

"I guess I'm going to have to prove it to you, then," he says, still smiling as we weave through the rows of bikes. Cade walks into the rental office and comes back with the key to a shiny black motorcycle trimmed in chrome. He hands me a helmet and then puts one on himself.

"Ready?" he says, straddling the bike.

"I guess," I say nervously.

He hands me his camera. "Mind stuffing this in your purse?"

"Sure," I say, fitting it inside my bag.

Cade pats the seat behind him, encouraging me to get on. "Don't be afraid, baby."

I swallow hard. "I've never ridden a motorcycle before. What if I fall off?"

"You won't," he says, handing me his jacket, which I immediately put on. "I promise. Just hold on to me."

"Okay," I say, climbing onto the bike and wrapping my arms around his waist as he guns the engine.

I close my eyes tightly as he peels out of the lot and into traffic. The engine sputters and pops as Cade careens right, then left, until we're on the main road that bisects the island. As he picks up speed, the wind has its way with every part of me. I hold on tighter to Cade. It's scary and exhilarating at the same time.

He turns right, and we find ourselves on a road that hugs the shoreline. We whiz by weathered homes and beach cabins, the scent of the sea ever present.

When we pass a little outlook beside a public beach, Cade slows the motorcycle and turns around. "Let's stop and check out the beach," he says, pulling into the parking lot beside the road.

We leave our helmets on the bike and follow a trail that leads to the beach, which is ours alone, aside from a seagull pecking at a clamshell ahead.

Cade walks to the water's edge, seemingly unfazed when a wave laps up against his shoe. The shore transfixes him, I can tell.

"Should we take a plunge?" he asks with a grin.

I smile a little self-consciously. "But we don't have towels or a change of clothes."

"All right," he says with a grin. "I'll let you off the hook this time."

I look away from the shore to the cliff behind us. "I bet we could hike up there and take some amazing photos from the overlook."

"It looks a little steep," he says.

I take his hand. "Come on, we can do it."

He smiles and follows my lead. "I have a daredevil girlfriend."

I grin as we begin climbing. The trail is steep and jagged, winding so close to the edge of the cliff that I feel a bit woozy when I glance below. "I guess this is more of an advanced hike than I anticipated," I say, a bit out of breath.

"Do you want to turn back?" he asks. "We can take some photos by the beach instead."

"No," I say. "Let's continue on."

Eight switchbacks become fourteen, and fourteen become twenty. "We've got to be close," I say. The sun is about to tuck itself in for the night behind the horizon. A band of orange and yellow streaks the sky.

"If we're lucky, we'll make it to the top by sunset."

"I hope," I say.

"Makes me think of that Robert Frost poem," Cade says.

I nod. "So dawn goes down to day . . ."

"Nothing gold can stay," he continues.

I smile as we round the last corner, which opens up to the top of the cliff. We both marvel at the views all around us—pristine tree-lined hills surrounded by sea. I feel both big and small.

"Stand right there," Cade instructs. "I want to take your photo. The light is incredible right now."

I inch closer to the ledge as he fiddles with his camera. I smooth my hair and instinctively reach for my necklace and give it a small tug, but when I do, the clasp breaks free and falls to the gravel at my feet.

"Oh no," I exclaim. "My necklace broke. That's never happened before." I fall to my knees and pat around the ground as Cade sets his camera down and walks closer.

"Don't worry," he says. "We'll find it."

Still facing Cade, I look over my shoulder at the edge of the cliff.

"What if it . . . fell?" I feel suddenly dizzy, my legs weak. And as I try to step closer to him, I lose my footing.

"Cade!" I scream as I slip backward. Time suddenly slows, as one terror-filled moment blends into the next. I feel myself falling over the ledge. I claw at the uneven hillside, which seems to melt beneath my grasp. And then strong hands meet my wrists. Cade's voice, solid and sure. "I've got you," he says. Rocks from the hillside are falling into the air. I feel dirt in my eyes. "Don't panic. Just stay still." His eyes are locked on mine. "I'm going to pull you back." My legs dangle over the rugged cliff. The beach is hundreds of feet beneath me. For a moment, I can see my end. The way the air would feel as I fall to the shore. The sound my body would make when it meets the rocky beach below. The blood trickling from my nose when Cade finally gets to me.

Cade slowly pulls me back to him. As he does, more gravel and rock fall from the cliff to the beach below. "Almost there," he says calmly. "I've got you."

I'm too scared to cry. Too scared to breathe. It might be a moment or a half hour by the time he's pulled me to safety; all I know is that I am alive. And Cade has saved me.

I crawl into his arms and weep.

"I'm so sorry," he says, kissing my face. "Baby, I'm so very sorry." He presses his sleeve to my nose. "Your nose is bleeding. Are you hurt?"

I shake my head as he helps me up. "I don't think so."

"Look," he says, pointing to the gravel at our feet, then kneeling down to pick something up. "Look what I found." My necklace dangles from his fingers, the locket still intact.

"Thank you," I say, tucking it into the pocket of my jeans.

Cade's eyes are fixed on mine. "I almost lost you."

"You saved my life," I mutter. "I . . . I don't know what to say." I swallow hard. "How can I thank you?"

"No thank-you necessary," he says.

I search his moist eyes, and wipe away tears from mine. "I will always be indebted to you."

"Better plan," he says. "How about you just save my life someday, then we'll be even?"

"I will," I say, smiling through tears. "I will."

We walk hand in hand off the ferry ramp, down the steps to the city. Cade's apartment is just a few blocks away.

"Want to go back to my place for a little while?"

All I want is to be near him, now and always. Especially tonight.

"Yes," I say.

We walk a block ahead, under the viaduct, then down the little side street to his apartment. I toss my sweater onto his sofa. My mind is so full of the events of the day that I'm grateful for a quiet moment while he fiddles with his record player.

I listen and hear our song, the one we listened to backstage, the one that was playing the first time he held my hand. When the chorus sounds, anything can happen, and then it does.

His arms are around me, his lips are on mine, and, as the lyrics command, I fade into him. I know exactly what I'm feeling, this thing I'm afraid of, this emotion that keeps bubbling up inside me like a pot on the stove that I'm trying desperately to keep from boiling over.

I open my mouth to speak, but he places his hand on my lips.

"I know what this is," he whispers, his voice faint above the music. "I've known it from that first night I saw you at the show, but now there's no doubt in my mind."

My gaze is entwined with his. Our eyes are locked and the key is gone. My heart feels full in my chest, heavy but in a good way.

"It's love," he says, letting the words slip freely from his mouth. And when they do, they fill the air and multiply like musical notes in a cartoon.

"Love," I say as the record crackles and skips.

"Love," he whispers back, weaving his fingers in mine.

And when I set my head on his pillow, and our bodies become one, for the first time in my life I feel as if everything in this crazy, complicated world makes complete and utter sense.

eleven

"Hi, baby."

"Hi," I say to Ryan later that night.

"Sorry to call so late," he says. "I just got back to the hotel."

I look up from my laptop and glance at the clock on the wall. It's half past ten.

"I had a productive discussion with the bank executives today," he continues. "Their concern in this tough market is our ability to secure high-profile tenants around the TV facility, but I walked into the meeting with contracts in hand. I think we may actually close this deal."

"Congratulations," I say, with a catch in my voice. This is terrible news for Hope Gospel Mission and all the people who depend on the shelter.

"I know you're caught in a hard place," Ryan says. "We don't have to talk about business anymore. Tell me about you. How was your day?"

"Oh fine," I say. "Just normal." I think of Cade, our lunch at Wild

Ginger, how he finally recognized me. When we parted, I didn't know what to do, so I told him to promise to meet me in front of Westlake Center at noon tomorrow. He nodded, but I'm not sure he understood. *What if he didn't understand? Then what?*

"Kailey, you there?"

I realize that Ryan has been talking and I've been lost in thought.

"Yeah, sorry," I say. "I'm just up ... working on a deadline." I eye the open browser on my laptop with a Google search for "homeless resources Seattle."

"Okay, well, I won't keep you, then," he says. "If the meeting goes well tomorrow morning, I'll take the early train back and we can have dinner together."

"Great," I say, feeling guilty for keeping this enormous secret from him, but I need more time.

"Oh," Ryan says before hanging up. "Were you by chance at Wild Ginger today?"

I sit up straighter as my heart rate quickens. "Uh, yeah, for lunch."

"Remember Jeff, from my office?"

"I think so," I say nervously.

"He saw you there."

I stay silent.

"But it was the weirdest thing. He thought you were sitting with some homeless guy."

My mind races. I can't tell Ryan about Cade. Not yet. "Oh, that," I say. "Yeah, it was an ... interview. For the series."

"Right," Ryan says with a yawn. "Yeah, I figured. All right, babe, I'm going to head to sleep. Early meeting in the morning."

"Good luck," I say.

"I miss you," he adds.

"I miss you, too," I say, feeling an ache in my heart.

And I do. I want him to wrap me up in his arms and say that it's all going to be okay when I tell him everything, every detail. I want it all to pour out of me like from a broken hydrant. I want to vomit the truth. But I can't. I have to go through this myself for now. It's scary and lonely and I don't know where the path will lead. All I know is that I have to keep walking down it alone.

"Morning," Jan says as I pass her office the next morning. I stop in her doorway and exhale deeply. Before we begin speaking, Lisa from the style department stops beside me. "Are you two coming?"

I give her a confused look.

"To Dana's baby shower," she says, pointing to the conference room. Dana, the style section editor, is thirty-seven weeks pregnant but one of those women who has miraculously managed to maintain her figure all the way through and could be an honest-to-goodness model for A Pea in the Pod's maternity catalog. "I got the cutest cupcakes," Lisa continues in almost a squeal. "They're pink and blue, with these adorable fondant baby blocks on top."

"Ah," I say, feeling my cheeks redden. "Thanks, I wish I could make it, but"—I pause, trying to will my mouth to spit out an appropriate response—"but I'm on deadline."

"Oh, okay," Lisa says, a little miffed. "Jan, how about you?"

She gives her a placating nod. "Yes, just give me a few minutes."

After Lisa walks off, Jan clears her throat. "Close the door," she says, "and sit."

I do as she says and sink into her guest chair, sighing, now safe from the newsroom listening in.

"What was that all about?" she says, pointing to the doorway.

I shift in my chair and sigh again. "Nothing," I say, composing myself. "I'm just . . . not that into baby showers."

Jan's gaze is unrelenting. "Give it to me straight," she continues. "Are you and Ryan breaking up?"

My eyes widen. "What? No!"

"Oh good," she says. "I, well, you haven't quite seemed yourself lately, and that's the only thing I could come up with. Kailey, in all your years working for the paper, you've never asked for a personal day." She takes her glasses off and cleans the lenses with the sleeve of her shirt. "I think you should use *more* personal days, but the request seemed wildly out of character." She gives me a long look.

"If it's not you breaking up with Ryan, what is it?"

I sigh. "It's worse."

"Worse?"

"I found Cade."

She shakes her head in disbelief. "As in, your ex? The one whose disappearance turned your life upside down?"

"Yep," I say. "That one."

"So that's why you didn't even bother to look at the stats on your piece."

I shake my head. "He's living on the streets of Seattle, maybe has been all this time."

"On the streets?"

"Jan, he's legitimately homeless. Skinny, dirty, rags for clothing, long beard, matted hair." I rub my forehead. "But the worst part about it is that it seems like he has lost his mind."

"Is he on drugs?"

"I don't know," I say. "I mean, I don't think so. It's more of a mental deficit. Maybe memory loss? Something happened to him, and I . . . want to help him."

"You should," she says, looking thoughtful. "I remember him well. He was something else. He was a force." She's silent for a long moment. "You loved him. Do you . . . still?"

I gasp. "What? No. I . . . how could I? In his state? Besides, I love Ryan. I'm marrying Ryan."

Jan clasps her hands together. "He was once a big deal in Seattle, wasn't he? I'm surprised he hasn't been recognized."

I shake my head. "He's almost completely unrecognizable. If I hadn't looked into his eyes that night, well, I wouldn't have made the connection at all." I'm quiet for a moment. "That's something I've learned, in my reporting, in the interviews I've done with the homeless. There's a certain anonymity about people on the streets. When I went to find him, no one even knew his name. They just called him Mitchell, because that's the name printed on the army jacket he wears."

I think back to the lunch at Wild Ginger, how it felt vital for the waiter to see Cade as a person, to know his *name*. "On the streets, people may see you, but they don't *see* you, you know?"

"Well put," Jan says. "And I must say, this new development in your life certainly ties into your series. You said you haven't decided on the final direction for the second piece. I don't suppose you'd consider adding a personal thread to bring dimension to the newsworthy elements? Like from record label executive to the streets—a real exposé on homelessness in our city. I don't want to be presumptuous, but this could be award-winning."

I shake my head. "I can't, Jan. Not this story. At least, not now."

"Well," she says. "However you write it, for publication or for yourself, I hope it has a happy ending for all."

"Me too," I say.

I'm on deadline. Determined not to include Cade in my piece, I start draft after draft, zeroing in on the profits that developers stand to make by eliminating the homeless presence from Pioneer Square. The tone of my prose feels analytical, ice-cold. Is this who I've become?

No, I tell myself, but actions speak loudest.

At precisely eleven forty-five, I get up from my chair, sling my purse over my shoulder, and head out. I told Cade to meet me in Westlake at noon. *Will he come?*

Rain clouds hover overhead. They may mean business, but I don't care. Let it rain. Let it *pour*. I march onward. All I can hear is the clack of my heels as I walk the six blocks to Westlake. One foot in front of the other.

When I reach Westlake, I can feel the first raindrop on my cheek. I make a beeline to the spot where Cade was yesterday, but when I arrive the sidewalk is empty, save for a man strumming a Dylan song that I can't immediately place. *Where is he?* I look around. I wait. Ten minutes pass. Twenty. *Maybe he's still coming.*

After forty disappointing minutes, I decide to head back to my office. Maybe that's it. Maybe I won't see him for another decade. Maybe . . . I turn around for one final glance, which is when I glimpse a distant figure moving slowly up the block toward me. *Cade? Cade!*

It's him, that's for sure. But why is he walking so slowly? Why is he *limping*? And then his face comes into focus, bloodied and bruised, swollen cheekbones. Adrenaline races through my veins as my legs instinctively begin moving.

"Cade!" I call, running to him. My heart is pounding when I reach his side. Fresh blood drips from his nose. His eyes are nearly swollen over, with dark crimson rings around each socket. A deep abrasion on his left cheek is four shades of purple and gaping open.

"Oh, Cade," I say, beginning to cry. "Who did this to you?" I take his hand in mine. "I'm going to get you some help. I'm not going to leave you this time. I promise."

When his eyes meet mine, I can see that he understands.

Traffic is light on this rainy day, and thankfully the cab ride to Harborview Medical Center is quick. When we reach the emergency room, I wave over a hospital employee, a bald man with kind eyes, to bring a wheelchair.

"Easy now," he tells Cade as he helps him into the wheelchair. I hand a ten-dollar bill to the cabdriver and follow behind as Cade is wheeled into the ER.

"They'll get you all checked in here," the man says, pushing the wheelchair to a stop at the front desk.

A young woman with a nose ring and a tattoo of a butterfly on her forearm eyes us as we approach.

"He needs help," I say. "Can we get him in to see a doctor right away?"

The woman gives Cade a long look and then sighs, as if my request is highly annoying. "Ma'am," she says, "you're going to have to take a seat and wait. We're incredibly backed up, as you can see." She points to the waiting room, which is filled with people in various states of distress.

"But look at him," I say. "He's badly hurt. He needs help."

"And we will do our best to help him, when it's his *turn,*" she says, clearly unaffected by my concern.

Just then a handsome-looking couple rushes in. The woman, with a white leather Coach bag slung from her shoulder, is in tears. She's beautiful in a formfitting black cashmere sweater dress and knee-high leather boots. Her husband, in designer jeans and a pair of black loafers, stands beside her, holding an ice pack to his head.

"He fell from a ladder," she cries. "He needs to be seen immediately."

The woman behind the desk nods and jumps into action. "If you could just fill out this paperwork," she says, offering a clipboard. "Just the top side is all. We'll get him in right away."

"Thank you," the woman says through tears.

After they've stepped away, I turn to the woman behind the desk. "I thought you said that you were full?"

"We are," she replies without emotion.

"But you're letting that man in."

She looks at me as if I somehow do not know the rules of a very elementary board game that everyone understands how to play. I want to pull the *Herald* card, but I'm here on a personal matter. I settle for "I think you're discriminating."

The woman rolls her eyes, then motions for me to come closer. I do.

"Listen," she whispers, looking beyond my shoulder at Cade. "I get your concern for this guy, I really do. But we have limited staff and resources here, and if we admitted every homeless dude with an owie, we'd have no room for the people who *really* need our help." She points over to the J.Crew catalog couple.

"I beg your pardon," I say, turning to look at Cade's bloodied face. "This is more than an *owie.* He's in serious pain, and the wound on his face is going to get infected if he's not treated."

The woman shrugs. "Look out there in the waiting room. Look at all of them, mostly junkies. We bring them in, treat them, give them what they need, then they go back to the streets, repeat their behavior, usually high, and we see them again the next week. It's a cycle."

"And have you ever seen *this* man?" I ask, anger beginning to rise in my chest. "He is *not a junkie.*"

She turns her gaze to Cade again and shrugs. "Maybe, maybe not. You can't always tell."

"He's a *human being,*" I whisper, worried that Cade might hear. "And he needs *help.*"

I pull out my cellphone and call Tracy. I'm grateful that she answers after the second ring.

"Trace, it's me," I say a little frantically. "I'm at Harborview. In the ER."

"Kailey, are you okay?"

"I am," I say, "but Cade is not."

"Oh no! What happened?"

"I don't know," I say. "But he's bloodied and bruised. Someone beat him up. He's going to need stitches on his face, almost certainly. And I think he may have a few broken bones. I need your help."

"Sure, anything."

"The ER is booked up," I say, lowering my voice. "And the woman at the check-in desk is not too keen on getting him in anytime soon."

"Yeah," Tracy says. "They see a lot of . . . uninsured people who kind of abuse the system. But still, it's no excuse."

"I need you to make some calls," I say. "See if you can pull some strings to get him in."

"Sure," Tracy says. "It just so happens that the head of my department is the best friend of one of the attendings over there. I'll ask him for a favor."

"Thank you," I say, exhaling. Cade stares ahead despondently.

"It's nothing," Tracy says. "Hey, how are you doing?"

I bite my lip and step a few feet away from Cade. "I'm . . . scared, Trace. I haven't told Ryan about all of this. It just feels so . . . monumental, like suddenly my whole world has been turned upside down."

"I know," she says. "But, Kailey, that's life."

"What do you mean?" I ask, wiping away a tear.

"Well," she says, "it's up and down. It's high and low, it's cyclical and scary and raw. That's being alive."

"I don't know if I can handle all of this," I say.

"You can handle it," she continues. "I know you can. For starters, this is a great first step. You're going to get Cade some help, medical attention, psychological attention. You're going to get him stable and sort out what happened to him. And then you're going to sort out everything you're feeling in that beautiful heart of yours, which, by the way, is the size of Arizona. No, Texas."

I laugh, but it comes out as a cry. "I love you, you know."

"I know," she says.

"Cocky."

"Or something." She's speaking in the background, but I can't make out the words. "All right, you sit tight. Let me make some calls. In the meantime, take care of your guy."

"My guy," I say after Tracy has hung up. The words roll off my tongue freely, but they sound awkward once they hit the air. I immediately think of Ryan and feel a pang in my heart that I cannot explain.

Someone with a heart the size of a major Southern state would not be deceiving her fiancé.

Eleven minutes, if that, have passed, when a nurse appears through a pair of swinging doors. "Cade McAllister?"

If he hears her, he gives no indication. "Yes," I say quickly. "That's us." I stand and push the wheelchair toward the reception desk.

"Assuming there is no insurance card?" the woman behind the counter asks.

"That's right," I say, unashamed.

She nods unaffectedly, as though she's seen the same scenario play out a thousand times. And I know, from my research, that Harborview will not turn anyone away. "I'm very sorry for the wait. We understand that Mr. McAllister needs immediate attention."

I nod. "Yes, he's badly hurt. Thank you."

She takes the handles of the wheelchair and pushes him down a hallway to the triage area, where she wheels him into a space with curtains for walls. A man moans loudly behind another curtain.

"Now," she says, extending her hands to Cade, "let's help you up." I watch as he takes her hand. He stumbles a little as he rises to his feet, but she's able to gently help him to the bed, where he sits. She reaches into a nearby drawer and pulls out a gown. "Would you like help putting this on, sir?"

He doesn't respond, so she takes charge. "Okay, let me get you undressed."

Cade is still as she unbuttons his coat. I feel a mixture of familiar affection and horror when I see his bare chest revealed, so thin. His arms, once so strong, are mere flesh and bones now, and I can easily make out each of his ribs.

If the nurse is concerned by the sight of Cade, it's impossible to tell. Her professional manner reveals nothing. His boots come off next, and though I've seen him unclothed so many times, I look away as she helps him unbutton his pants. "There," she says, tying the light blue gown in place. She turns to me. "Are you his sister? A friend?"

"A . . . friend," I say. I sit in the chair beside Cade's bed. He shifts positions and winces in pain.

"I'm so sorry," I whisper, squeezing his limp hand. "Help is coming soon, I promise."

A moment later, the doctor appears, and Cade flinches.

"No," he cries. "No, no!"

"Mr. McAllister," he says calmly, "I'm Dr. Green. I'm here to help you."

The look on Cade's face is one of terror, and it makes my heart hurt.

Dr. Green acknowledges me, but his eyes are on Cade. "No need to be frightened, Mr. McAllister. We're going to assess your injuries and fix you up."

Cade looks away but doesn't flinch when Dr. Green places his stethoscope on his chest. His blood pressure is taken next, and when the exam is over, the doctor makes a few notes in a folder, then turns to me. "We need to get some scans. He clearly has some broken ribs, but I'd like to rule out internal bleeding. He has some significant bruising in his abdomen."

I nod as the nurse comes in with a basin of warm water and a stack of washcloths. "I'm going to get those wounds cleaned up," she says.

As Dr. Green steps outside the privacy curtain, I follow him. "Doctor, may I have a word with you?"

"Sure," he says, turning around.

"This man didn't used to be like this," I say. "He didn't always live on the streets. He used to be the president of Element Records."

The doctor's eyes widen. "Element Records? That name brings me back to the nineties," he marvels. "I used to listen to so many artists on that label. What happened?"

"I don't know," I say. "Ten years ago, he left the company and Seattle, and I never heard from him again. I only recently found him on the streets." I shake my head. "It just doesn't add up. How could he have gone from the top of his field to . . . this?"

"There are many possible explanations," he says, "the likeliest culprit being addiction."

"No," I say. "I know him. He never touched any of that stuff. In fact, he was always disgusted by it. This is not addiction. This is . . . something else."

"Mental illness, perhaps," Dr. Green continues.

I shake my head. "Cade never struggled with depression or any related condition."

"Well, mental illness is a tricky beast," he says. "It can lie dormant for years before someone has an episode."

I sigh. "My best friend is a pulmonologist at Swedish. This case is outside her area of expertise, but she did mention the possibility of a brain injury of some kind. That would explain why he barely speaks and doesn't seem to know me, or even himself."

He adjusts his glasses and presses on: "You say he has memory issues?"

"At first he didn't know me," I say. "And I'm not sure if he does now. But"—I pull down my sweater to reveal my tattoo—"he remembered this, because he has a matching one."

"That's curious," he says, eyeing my tattoo. *"Toujours?"*

"'Always,'" I say, "in French."

He nods. "Well, I'd say a CAT scan is in order, maybe an MRI. We can get a sense of what's going on in there, perhaps detect some damage or past trauma."

"And if you find something," I say, "is there treatment available? Medication?"

"Brain injuries are tough," he says. "We'll get a neurologist to consult."

"Thank you," I say, "so much."

He smiles. "We'll do all we can."

The door to the room opens suddenly, and a little girl, about nine, maybe ten, barrels in. "Mommy," she chirps, staring at a bag of candy in her hands, "we found your favorite chocolates!" She's exuberant and sweet, and as she skips toward us, her ponytail flaps against her pink cardigan sweater. I glance at Cade, and then back at the little girl, and feel a pang deep inside.

"Oh," she says suddenly, looking up at us. "I'm sorry." She giggles. "I think I opened the wrong door." She points behind her. "My mommy just had surgery."

I smile. "It's okay, honey," I say as she finds her way back to the door. "Your mommy is lucky to have such a beautiful little girl."

She smiles and then disappears into the hallway. Cade doesn't notice me wiping away a stray tear.

An hour later, after Cade's wounds are cleaned and bandaged, the nurse wheels him down to the imaging department. I stay behind and scroll through my phone and see that I've missed two calls and a text from Ryan.

"Sorry," I type. "Busy day. You okay?"

"Hi," he responds. "Thinking of you. I'm on the early train back. See you at home at six?"

I look at the clock. It's already four, and there's no way I'll be home by six.

"Sorry, I have to work late," I type, feeling bad as I stare at the words.

"Okay," he replies. "Guess I'll see you later tonight?"

"Yeah," I write. "It could be late. Don't wait up."

"Okay," he responds.

My stomach knots as I toss my phone back into my purse and sink into the chair again. The air smells sterile yet sickly, like some awful combination of 409 and bedpans.

Several hours pass before Dr. Green returns. He's accompanied by a woman in her mid-fifties. She wears a white lab coat, and there's something about her face and gray chin-length hair that reminds me of Mrs. Ramsay, the high-school English teacher I always loved.

"This is Dr. Branson," he says. "She's the head of neurology here at Harborview."

I nod. "Nice to meet you. I'm Kailey Crain, an old . . . friend of Cade's."

"I understand that Mr. McAllister lives on the streets," she says. "I tried to speak to him, but he is unresponsive. In this case, given that we have no other record of his family, or power of attorney, I will consider you next of kin."

"Sure," I say. "Whatever I can do to help."

"Ms. Crain," she continues, opening up the laptop in her hands. She logs in and sorts through a series of scans. "Your friend most definitely has several broken ribs. While there's some swelling of his spleen, as you can see here"—she points to one of the images—"it's not of immediate concern, and I expect him to heal as a matter of course." She clicks to the next screen, and a new image shows up. She stares intently at what looks like the top view of Cade's brain. "Now, *this*," she continues, "is an image of your friend's brain. At first glance, everything appears normal." She zooms in on the image, and I'm fascinated. "But when we take a closer look, we can see that certain areas are brighter, indicating cerebral swelling. This could indicate trauma from his most recent injuries, but when I look at the overall composition of these images, I'm not convinced."

I shake my head. "What do you mean?"

"I mean that there could be evidence here that your friend sustained a traumatic brain injury some time ago. Dr. Green told me that he once owned a company, had a full life?"

I nod. "Yes, he did. He didn't used to be this way. I believe something happened."

"I do, too," Dr. Branson says.

My eyes narrow. "Like what?"

"A fall, a car accident, anything," she says. "We've seen the gamut. It appears that whatever trauma your friend sustained has left him in a state of confusion. I've only had a moment to examine him, but my initial assessment indicates TBI."

"TBI?"

"Traumatic brain injury," she says. "He also has significant cognitive decline, clear amnesia, and, according to your report"—she turns to Dr. Green—"spotty memory and understanding."

"Yes," I say. "I know he recognizes my tattoo, and I believe he remembers me, at least to some degree."

Dr. Branson nods. "It's possible that he may remember more, too. We call this Swiss cheese memory. It's the idea that there are a lot of holes in the entire picture. For many with TBI, as they recover, there will always be holes. Friends and family can do their best to fill in those gaps, though."

I sit up higher in my chair. "So are you saying there's hope that he might . . . recover?"

"Yes and no," she says. "Your friend has an uphill battle ahead. He'll need therapy, a lifestyle intervention. Even with the best treatment, it's unclear how he'll respond."

"How can I get him going with this treatment? What can I do?"

She nods. "There's a new program we're starting," she says, "one I think your friend would be an excellent candidate for. We've recently received funding for a center, much like a rehabilitation center or an assisted living facility but geared toward those with TBI. It's on the property, and we have twelve units. It's a slim chance, but there may be an opening for him."

"Wow, that would be amazing," I say. "When could he move in?"

She pulls a card from the pocket of her coat and hands it to me. "Call me tomorrow and we can begin the process of sorting through all the paperwork; that is, if there's space and he consents." She flips through a few pages of his chart. "One of my assistants will look through the past decade's medical records to see if a John Doe might have been treated here for a brain injury. When did you say your friend went missing?"

I close my eyes tightly, then reopen them. "It was the summer of 1998. I can still remember the last time I saw Cade. August first. He wasn't acting like himself. We had an argument. I left his place that day completely unmoored. I knew he was in a dark place, but I had no idea that I'd never see him again after that. It was as if he fell off the face of the earth."

"All right," she says. "It might be a needle in a haystack, but we'll review the undocumented patients over the years, see if we can make any connections. If we can find out what happened to him or have some sense of the nature of his injury, it could help his treatment plan."

I nod. "Thank you so much."

It's almost ten, and when the nurse finds me in the waiting room, I'm nearly dozing off. "We've moved him to the fifth floor," she says. "We'd like to keep him overnight to monitor him."

"Thank you," I say, taking a deep breath before standing and gathering my things.

"I could bring in a cot," she says, pausing, "if you'd like to stay."

I think of Ryan. "I . . . can't. But I'd like to come up and say good night to him before I go."

"Sure," she says. "Follow me, and I'll take you up."

The elevator lurches upward, and I can feel the nurse's eyes on me.

"He's special to you, isn't he?" she says.

At first I'm taken aback by her question. My eyelashes flutter. Cade used to notice when they did. He was the only one who could read me. "You're going 'walls up,'" he used to say.

"You're very observant," I finally say to the nurse. "Yes, he is."

The nurse leads me into Cade's room. It's dark, except for the faint light of the city shining in the window. The city he once loved so much.

"Mr. McAllister," the nurse whispers.

He doesn't respond, and by the pattern of his breathing I can tell that he's sleeping.

"Good," she whispers to me. "He needs the rest."

I nod, taking a few steps closer to him. His beleaguered body is covered by a light blanket. His face is puffy and bandaged. A nasal cannula delivers oxygen, and an IV line flows into his right arm.

"Good night, Cade," I whisper.

"Go home," the nurse says. "Get some rest. I'll look out for him tonight. Don't worry."

"Thank you," I say as tears sting my eyes. She notices them, I can tell.

"He's going to be okay," she says. "I have a feeling."

I take a deep breath to steady myself. "I hope."

I walk to the door, then turn back around and dig through my bag to find my iPod, where on a playlist there are hundreds of songs he used to love—*we* used to love. I gently attach a set of headphones to his ears, then turn the music on. His eyes flutter a little as the Gin Blossoms' "Follow You Down" begins to play.

. . .

It's after eleven before I'm home, and Eddie greets me at the door. "Hi, boy," I whisper, kneeling down to pet him. I see Ryan's suitcase and jacket, and I wonder if he's asleep. I wonder how much longer I can keep this secret from him.

Quietly I set my keys down on the side table. I glance at the stairs that lead to our bedroom, then turn to the couch instead, where I lie down and pull a wool throw over my tired body. As I close my eyes, I see Cade's face. He's standing on the balcony at the hotel we shared in Big Sur. The French doors are flung open. Waves crash onto the shore beneath the rugged cliffs, mirroring the intensity of my love.

twelve

"*L*ook," Cade says. "It's starting to snow."

I peer out the window of the cab to see flakes falling lightly outside. We're on the way to Mishu Sushi in Fremont, where I'll be meeting his business partner for the first time. Besides his aunt, James is the closest thing Cade has to family, so I'm honored to finally meet him, even if the occasion has been a long time in the making.

"I love snow," I say. "It makes me happy."

"Me too," he says. "But on these cold nights, I always worry about the homeless. There's this old man who's camping out in the alley behind my apartment. I brought him a cup of coffee the other day. His name is . . . Ivan, I think. It's got to be so cold tonight."

"It was easier being a kid," I say. "It could snow, and all that would matter was whether you'd miss school and get to make a snowman with your friends."

"Yeah," he says. "My aunt had the best sledding hill in the neighborhood. James and I used to be out all day until she'd call us in and make us hot chocolate."

"Those were the days," I say.

"They really were."

I smile. "Remember when you were little, and you'd go to the grocery store and come home with a kitten?"

Cade grins. "Yeah, there would always be some lady with a box of free kittens."

"Exactly," I say. "But that never happens anymore."

We both laugh.

"So what should I expect when meeting James tonight?" I ask, turning back to him.

"How to describe James," Cade says with a contemplative sigh. "Well, he's tall and charming, very smart. Come to think of it, kind of an all-around catch." He grins. "Don't go running off with him, now."

I laugh. "I'll try to control my impulses."

He squeezes my hand. "James and I are very different," he says. "But somehow we work as friends and business partners. Though it's not always easy."

I nod. "How so?"

"Take now, for instance. James wants to take the company in a new direction."

"Oh?"

"He thinks we should sign Flying Limbs. The lead singer thinks he's God's gift to music, even though he has a criminal record, and he's demanding an enormous signing bonus. I mean, they have a huge following, but"—he shakes his head—"I'm just not sure they're the type of people we want to work with."

"And James is?"

He nods. "Not only that, but he's taking matters into his own hands. The other day he took the band out for dinner without me. In the past, we've always taken talent out as a team." Cade shrugs.

"I'm sorry," I say. "So the leader's an ex-convict?"

"Yeah," he says. "I don't know the whole story, but he apparently assaulted a girl when he was a minor."

"Yikes," I say.

"I know." He shakes his head. "It's like James is going rogue. Last week he was talking about signing a string of one-hit radio wonders. You can only languish in the land of the Spice Girls so long before you want to gouge your eyes out."

"Spice Girls?"

Cade rolls his eyes. "They're a girl group that is blowing up in the U.K. Expect them to be on every major radio station in America by next summer, and prepare for some serious airwave pollution. Churning out commercial hits was never why I got into this business. To me it's all about the music. Good music."

I nod. "I get it. Can you two find common ground?"

"Eventually, but it's a constant battle," he says. "And sometimes it wears on me." He pulls out his wallet to pay the driver. A tall man matching James's description stands under a blue awning beside a woman with dark, curly hair. He extinguishes a cigarette on the sidewalk, which now has a light dusting of snow. "Oh," Cade says in a hushed voice. "I forgot to tell you that Alexis will be here."

"His assistant, right?" Cade has mentioned Alexis only a few times.

"Yes," Cade replies. "She's a whiz with the books. We hardly need to hire an accountant these days." He clears his throat. "Oh, and she and James are dating."

"Oh wow," I say.

Cade cracks his knuckles. "It's a little strange, I know. And I'm not sure Alexis is even that into him. But I'd rather stay out of it, if you know what I mean."

I nod.

As he steps out of the cab, the driver turns around. "Excuse me," he says. "I couldn't help but overhear your conversation. Are you Cade McAllister from Element Records?"

"In the flesh," he says.

"Wow," the driver says. "I'm Rod. I'm a big fan. I, uh, I've got a band. I play drums and a little guitar. We have a demo tape—uh, you might like to hear it."

"Rod, so good to meet you," Cade says warmly. "I'm just heading out to dinner now, but you're most welcome to send that demo tape along to the office and we'll have a listen. How does that sound?"

"Great," he says, grinning from ear to ear. "I'll do that."

"I'll bet that happens all the time," I whisper to him on the sidewalk.

"If I had a dollar for every time it did . . ." His words trail off as James and his assistant approach.

He's wearing a button-down shirt and blue jeans. His look is more preppy than hipster music executive, but it works for him. Alexis is petite, and under her unbuttoned black wool coat she wears a boxy black baby-doll dress, tights, and black Doc Martens with yellow laces. She's pretty, but not in a striking way, with her green eyes and dark hair. She reminds me of one of those girls in college who traded in their preppy Gap attire for hip Value Village vintage finds—and a nose ring. She smiles at us sweetly.

"Hey, man," James says to Cade, then grins at me. "So this is the lady." Cade was right, he oozes charm.

"Hi," I say, extending my hand. "I'm Kailey."

"It's really nice to meet you, Kailey," James says. "This is Alexis, my assistant."

"Nice to meet you, Alexis," I say.

"We've heard so many wonderful things about you," she says, smiling at me before fixing her eyes on Cade. James touches her back tenderly, the way one does in a relationship.

"It's great we finally got a dinner on the calendar," James adds. "Shall we go in and get our table? The sushi here is out of this world."

"They don't call Fremont the center of the universe for nothing," I say with a wink as we walk through the door.

Inside, James orders several plates of sushi for the table and an expensive bottle of sake, which arrives instantly and is poured into a small stone decanter and then into tiny stone cups.

"To new friends and good music," James says, holding up his cup.

"Cheers," I say, clinking cups. I catch Alexis's eye as I do, and she quickly looks back at James.

"Did Cade tell you we signed Ethan White today?"

I shake my head. "As in, Ethan White of that boy band on the radio?"

"Yes, the"—he makes air quotes with his fingers—"'boy band' that went platinum last year."

I remember laughing with Tracy at their music video for the song "All the Way." We decided that men really shouldn't wear all white. A T-shirt is one thing, but a T-shirt, pants, shoes, and hat? Well, it was *bad*.

"He's doing a solo album with us," James says. "And it's going to be huge."

Cade shifts in his seat and guzzles his sake, as if the very idea of this is about to make him break out in hives.

"A commercial success, maybe," he says. "But, James, you and I both know that this dude is musically bankrupt."

"Signing Ethan White is an enormous deal for Element," James counters, exhaling deeply.

Cade refills his sake glass. "I told you I still want to think this over," he says, a bit agitated. I've never seen this side of him, and it immediately puts me on edge.

James throws up his arms. "What's to think over? We have a Grammy Award–winning platinum artist who wants to make music with us."

"But it's not our kind of music, James, and you know that," Cade says, his voice a bit louder now.

James flashes a gentlemanly glance my way. "Guess you're getting the real view of a day in the life of Element Records."

Cade stands up. "I don't want to talk about this here, man," he says. "Let's step out for a bit."

James raises his eyebrows. "Whatever you want, dude." He turns to us with a smile. "Ladies, excuse us."

Alexis and I watch awkwardly as the two men walk outside to the sidewalk. She looks mildly grief-stricken, and I wonder if this is a scene she's witnessed often over the years. A moment later, through the window, we watch as they sort out their differences with animated gestures.

"They fight like brothers sometimes," Alexis says knowingly. She leans in as if she's about to let me in on a little secret. "But they love each other. They always work it out." She waves to a waiter and orders us another round of drinks. "Have another," she whispers with a laugh. "It's on the company's dime."

Ten minutes later they return, with their argument seemingly sorted out. We finish our sushi, chat about benign topics over another bottle of sake, then find our way to the door.

"Kailey, it was so good to meet you," Alexis says, squeezing my hand. She stumbles a little as she does, and I suspect that the sake has gone to her head, as it has gone to mine. My cheeks feel warm as I watch her turn to Cade and plant a kiss on his cheek. If this bothers James, he gives no indication.

"What time will you be in the office on Monday?" she asks Cade as James reaches for her hand.

He looks at me. "Hopefully not until well past eleven."

"Okay," she says, a little annoyed. "I have contracts for you to sign."

Cade nods and waves goodbye. We make our exit to the street and jump into a cab. I peer through the window as the car peels off. James and Alexis are a blur in the snowy night.

Cade seems exhausted and distracted when we get back to his place. He opens the fridge and stares inside absently. Outside the window, the snow falls heavier now. And despite the uncomfortable time at dinner, I love this night because I am with him. I plug in the strand of lights we have hung on the little Charlie Brown Christmas tree we picked up at the market in Queen Anne last weekend.

"You okay?" I ask, wrapping my arms around his waist. "You seem a little tense."

"Sorry," he says. "James has a way of getting under my skin. He always has."

"I can see why," I say. "I mean, he's nice and all, but there's . . . some intensity, for sure."

"Exactly," Cade says. "When we were first starting out, the excitement of our early success made it easy to ignore all of that. But now?" He shakes his head. "It's like he's turned into a complete egomaniac."

I nod. "Sorry."

Cade sighs. "What did you think of Alexis?"

My eyes meet his. "I thought she was nice, I guess."

Cade nods. "She's great—one of our first interns. I hired her right out of college. I asked her what her desert island music choices would be and she didn't hesitate. Nirvana. U2. The Beach Boys."

"Wow," I say. I'm surprised that he'd remember her interview question in such detail.

He pauses, then flashes me a knowing look. "You're doing it," he says with a grin.

"Doing what?"

"The walls-up eye flutter."

I shake my head. "The walls-up what?"

"You flutter your eyelashes when you're upset or unsettled by something."

"I do?"

"You do."

I smile nervously. "No one's ever told me that."

"It's endearing," he says.

I pull him closer to me. "Would you have hired me?"

"In a heartbeat."

I smile, but Cade's eyes are distant. "What are you thinking about?"

He sighs, sinking into the couch. "Just that the business feels different these days."

"That's nagging at you, isn't it?"

"Yes," he says. "And I'm not sure I can ever get it back to what it once was." He exhales deeply.

"I'm sorry," I say, pausing for a moment. I want to encourage him not to back down, to stand for all he believes. I want to tell him that in my mind and perhaps everyone else's, he is the reason for Element Records' success, the heart of the business. Instead I bite my lip and just rest my head on his shoulder for a long moment.

"You know what?" he says.

"What?"

"We've been in love for a few months now, but we never really talk about it. For me, it means that I feel at peace when I'm in your presence," he continues. "And . . . I miss you when you're not around."

I swallow hard.

"Sometimes it helps to channel my feelings through lyrics. You know that U2 song 'I Still Haven't Found What I'm Looking For'?"

I look into his eyes, and hum until I sing, "It was warm in the night."

"I was cold as a stone," he answers, completing the pair of lines at the end of the fourth verse.

He rises and pulls me onto my feet. There's no music playing, but our bodies sway together as if there is.

"I *was* cold," he says. "Cold and alone. I don't think we know what we're looking for until we find it," he continues. "And then I . . . found you."

I feel tears sting my eyes, but I blink them back. "And I found you."

"I was looking for you the whole time, Kailey," he says. "I just didn't know it." He takes my cheeks in both hands and swallows hard. "I love you more every day," he whispers.

I want to respond, but all I seem to be able to do is soak up his beautiful heartfelt words. I reach for his hand, but he's already turned and walked to the window.

"It's really coming down out there," he says, walking back to the couch, where he picks up the wool throw draped over the arm. "I'm just going to take this out to Ivan."

When he opens the door a stream of winter air hits my skin like light from a cold star, but it doesn't elicit even the tiniest shiver. I am warm from the inside out.

thirteen

I open my eyes to the sound of the coffee grinder in the kitchen.

"Sorry," Ryan says when he notices me sitting up.

I yawn and rub my eyes. "It's okay," I mutter groggily.

"Why didn't you come to bed last night?" he asks.

"I got in late," I say. The events of yesterday are coming into view now. The edges, blurred from a night's sleep, are taking on their sharp corners again. I shudder at the thought of Cade's wounds. "I didn't want to wake you."

He walks to the couch and sinks in beside me. "Next time," he says, pressing his nose against mine, "wake me, okay?"

I nod with a smile. "Okay."

The rain splatters the windows outside, and I'm struck with the desire to hole up here for the day, or maybe forever. Light a fire in the fireplace, pray for a blizzard so we can be snowed in and I can fall into

Ryan's arms, and try not to think of the emaciated man on the fifth floor of Harborview Medical Center.

"We should get a Christmas tree this year," I say.

"Really?" Ryan asks, flipping through a stack of mail. "Just seems like a bunch of mess and hassle, to be honest."

"Oh," I say, stung.

He looks up. "I mean, of course, if you want to get one, honey, we absolutely can."

"No," I say, "you're right. They're more hassle than they're worth."

I feel his strong arm around my waist. "I'm sorry," he says. "That was insensitive of me. I know how much you love this time of the year. Let's go get a tree. Maybe next week."

I smile and nod as he kisses my forehead lightly.

"Oh," he says, changing the subject as he gets up and goes back to the kitchen to check on the coffee, "I forgot to tell you that my parents called last night. They're flying in today."

"Tonight?"

He comes back and joins me on the couch, handing me a steaming cup of coffee with just the right amount of half-and-half.

"Yeah."

I frown. "I thought they weren't coming until this weekend."

"I know," he continues. "I did, too. But apparently Dad scheduled a meeting earlier, and Mom decided to come with him. I can have them stay at the Fairmont if you'd rather. It's—"

"No," I say. No matter how stressed I may feel, these are Ryan's parents. And while they sometimes rub me the wrong way, I haven't lived a lifetime without parents to finally get them and then banish them to a hotel. "They're family. They stay here."

He smiles. "They'll be here about nine. I thought we could have dinner with them tomorrow. I made a reservation at Earl's on Fifth. Seven o'clock okay?"

"Yeah, I, uh, I think so," I say, moving to top off my coffee. An enormous box of our "save the date" cards for our July wedding sits on the kitchen table. They need to be stuffed, addressed, and stamped. I pause to pick one up, remembering how I agonized over the exact shade of white for the envelopes, finally settling on "linen." How I long to return to the time when I was stressed about stationery.

"Are we ever going to mail those babies out?" Ryan says with a grin.

"Yes," I say quickly. "I . . . I meant to get a start on them last week. Things have just been so hectic."

"I can help, you know," he says. "My handwriting isn't *that* bad."

"Of course it's not," I say. "And I'd love your help. We'll get into wedding mode next week, okay?"

He nods, wrapping his arms around my waist, and grins. "You're not stalling?"

"Definitely not stalling," I say, smiling.

"You sure?"

I give him a quick smooch. "I'm sure."

My phone buzzes from an incoming email, and when I glance at my in-box quickly, I recall the interview I have with a panel of developers at nine-thirty. How have I forgotten this?

"Darn," I say to Ryan. "I have that big developer interview this morning." I shake my head. "It's the last thing I want to do right now, but I have to work the details of their plans into the Pioneer Square series."

"Need me to make a few calls? Ask them to be on their best behavior? Give you an exclusive look at their architectural renderings?"

"You're very cute," I say, "but that would hardly be professional. I'll be fine."

"All right," he says with a grin. "See you tonight." He grabs his coat. "Love you."

"Love you, too," I whisper after he's closed the door.

I arrive at a high-rise in Belltown an hour later and am ushered into a conference room with bottled water, mints, and zero personality. Five minutes pass, and five men stride in. Two are named Bob. A meek administrative assistant hovers. "Can I get you anything?" she asks in almost a whisper.

I shake my head. "No, no, I'm fine."

One of the Bobs begins to speak. "Ms. Crain, it's such a pleasure to meet you."

"You as well," I say curtly. The other men introduce themselves as Steve, Dan, and Phil. I am on one side of the long honey-oak conference table, alone. I reach for my purse and find my notebook and a pen. "Of course you know that I've been doing a series for the *Herald* on the future of Pioneer Square. I'm aware that each of you has been embattled with the city council about your interest in developing the neighborhood." I flip to a page where I took notes about Creighton Properties. "Bob," I say. "You're proposing to tear down the shelter on Main Street. Why?"

"Simple economics," he says. "If you build it, they will come."

"Explain what you mean," I say, taking notes.

"You may not remember this, but that shelter was built in 1996," he says. "And ever since, the homeless have been flooding to the neighborhood. You can't walk two feet without running into one of them."

I don't tell him that not only do I remember when the shelter was built, but Cade was living next door.

"But, Bob, you are aware that besides the shelter you're referring to, there are very few options for displaced people in this city."

"Displaced people?" He chuckles, and I notice the way his belly shakes. "Sweetheart, we're talking about mostly drug addicts here. These are people who mooch off of society and refuse to work. Bottom-feeders."

I clear my throat. "Bottom-feeders?"

"That's right," the other Bob says. "Now, listen. We do not have hearts of steel. If you've read through our proposal to the city, you'll see that we've included a nice relocation package that we believe is more than adequate."

"Relocation package?"

"Yes, yes," the first Bob adds.

"So you'd build a new shelter elsewhere?"

"Not exactly," one of the other men (Steve?) chimes in.

"Then what? If you tear down the shelter to build your high-rise condo, then where will the hundreds of people who rely on the shelter go?"

"How about Subway," Phil says. "Taco Bell. McDonald's."

I shake my head. "I'm not following you."

Phil smiles. "We're talking about work, Ms. Crain. We don't believe in handouts, we believe in work. And our plan includes a generous package geared toward attainment of this goal."

I set my notebook down. "I get what you're saying. And trust me, I believe in work just as much as you all do. But one thing I've come to learn through talking to people for this series is that homelessness is a complex problem." I think of Cade and the countless others like him who didn't choose a life on the streets.

Bob No. 1 shrugs. "I guess we'll have to agree to disagree," he says. "But we do hope you'll get our point across in your article."

"Oh, I will," I say, closing my notebook.

I call Jan on the way to Harborview. "Just got out of the developer interview."

"How did it go?"

I roll my eyes. "I'll fill you in later. But, for now, one word: ugh."

"You coming in today?" Jan asks.

"I'm going to be out again. Cade's in the hospital."

She gasps. "Oh no. Is everything okay?"

"Yes and no," I say. "He was badly beaten. A few broken ribs, but most of his injuries were superficial. The good news is that one of the doctors thinks he may qualify for a new program for patients with traumatic brain injuries, which they suspect he has. Anyway, I'm heading back to the hospital this morning."

"Take all the time you need," Jan says. "I mean that."

I exhale deeply. "You don't know how bad I feel about leaving you in a lurch like this." I sigh. "I feel like I'm leaving my entire life in a lurch."

"Well, don't worry about the work part of this lurch just now," she says. "I mean, don't go MIA entirely on me. But take a few days to sort things out. I'll cover you until then."

"Thanks," I say as I pull into the parking garage.

"Have you told Ryan?" she asks.

"No," I say. "I'm afraid to."

"You should tell him, Kailey," Jan says. "He deserves to know."

Cade is awake when I enter his room. The walls look dingier in the morning light. I suppose no amount of paint can cover the stain of illness.

"Hi," I say, walking to his bedside. In his lap are the iPod and headphones I left with him. I wonder if he enjoyed the music. He doesn't look up. "Have you eaten?"

He stares straight ahead as I reach for the phone on the table beside him.

"Hi," I say. "I'm with Cade McAllister in room 502. Has he eaten anything this morning?"

"Oh yes," the nurse says. "Mr. McAllister. We brought him breakfast an hour ago, but he refused."

I look at Cade, so thin, so lost. "What did you bring him?"

"Let me check," she says, sounding a little annoyed. I hear papers shuffling in the background. "Ah, yes, oatmeal. And prunes. With milk."

"He hates oatmeal," I say.

"Well, that's what our dietitian recommends for patients with broken ribs," she says. "Bowel movements should remain soft. You have to avoid—"

"I'd like you to bring him scrambled eggs and toast," I say. "With Tabasco. He loves Tabasco."

"I'll see what they can do," the woman says.

A half hour later, a young woman from the cafeteria arrives with a tray. She smiles at me as she sets it down on Cade's table.

"Thank you," I say as she leaves.

I take my sweater off and set it on the chair by the window, then walk over to Cade's bed again and lift the metal dome on top of the plate. Eggs and toast. I'm grateful to see a small bottle of Tabasco on the tray, and I sprinkle a few drops over the eggs and reach for a fork.

"Here," I say, holding up a bite to Cade.

He looks straight ahead, but I am not deterred. I lift the fork gently to his mouth, and, like magic his lips part. He takes the bite and looks to me for another, like a child. I give him one, followed by a bite of toast. With each morsel, he looks at me, eyes unwavering.

"We're going to get you healthy again," I say to him. "But you have to eat, okay? You're too skinny." I smile. "You were always thin, but you used to have a little gut. Remember that? I used to tease you about it."

He silently opens his mouth each time my fork reaches his lips. The memories keep coming, one after the next. The two of us sipping wine on the rooftop of my apartment. Me juggling a tray of appetizers at some party he hosted at his place for a new "it" band. Walking hand in hand through Pike Place Market.

"You always loved spicy food," I say. "I swear, even when you didn't like something I made, I knew that if I added enough red chili flakes or smothered it in Tabasco, you'd think it was divine." I smile as Cade takes the last bite of eggs. "It was my little secret."

I hold a water glass to his lips and he takes a sip, still keeping his eyes on me, as if he's willing his brain to know me, to remember me. A part of him does, I can tell. And I wonder what it must feel like to be trapped in a state of confusion. I can remember one morning when I woke up still hazy from a dream. I was at a real estate conference in Atlanta and had had a bit too much wine the night before. I remember opening my eyes and surveying my surroundings. For about ten seconds, I had no idea where or who I was. It was as if my mind had temporarily shut down or was at least sputtering to start its engine. In those seconds, I lay there in a suspended state of confusion. *Who am I? Where am I? What am I doing? How did I get here?* And then the engine kicked into gear. All the pistons started firing. My world came into focus again.

Would Cade's? I take the tray and set it by the window just as the door opens and Dr. Branson walks in. "Good morning," she says, walking straight to Cade. She adjusts his IV cord, reaches for a blood pressure cuff, and takes a moment to check his vitals.

She nods to herself and makes a notation in his chart, then turns to me. "My colleagues and I think that your friend would be an ideal candidate for the program I told you about yesterday, but there isn't space available, unfortunately."

"Oh no," I say, crestfallen.

"I did have an idea, though," she continues. "I spoke to my colleagues, and there's an apartment on the third floor that isn't quite ready yet, but we're looking into the possibility of having it completed, for Cade."

"Yes, yes," I say. "That would be wonderful."

"It would be a big step for him," she says, "independent living. But the building is monitored by medical staff. We feel it's the best way for TBI sufferers to assimilate back into society."

She hands me a packet of paperwork. "Admission is not for about two weeks, so he'll need temporary housing in the meantime."

My heart beats faster. "Temporary housing?"

"Yes," she says. "Surely you can help him with that in the interim."

I nod, thinking about Ryan, my in-laws, my life. "Yes, yes, of course."

"And while the program is subsidized, grants don't entirely cover it, and your friend is obviously uninsured, so there will be a portion of food and housing costs that will need to be paid." She hands me more paperwork. "About five thousand dollars."

I nod soberly. Ryan and I have the money. We recently combined our finances, and though we have plenty in savings, and this would be a mere blip on the map of our financial landscape, it still leaves me feeling uneasy. How could I pay for this without telling him about it first? Clearly it would be a violation of trust.

"I hate to rush you, but I'm afraid the deposit check needs to be submitted today to secure his spot."

I nod, reaching for my purse. "It's no problem," I say. "I'll take care of it."

I hand her the check, and she passes it to a medical assistant who has just arrived in the room. "Gail, take this down to my office and have John get Mr. McAllister's registration started."

We both look at Cade, whose eyes are now closed.

Dr. Branson lowers her voice to a whisper. "Do you mind having a word with me outside?"

I nod and follow her out to the hallway.

Once the door is closed behind us, she opens a folder and produces a stapled stack of papers. "My assistant did some looking around, and as I suspected, there was a John Doe matching your friend's description. He was admitted on August 4, 1998. The case file says he was brought in by an ambulance, completely unconscious, with trauma to the head and subsequent brain swelling. He had no ID on him. It appears that he was in a coma for two weeks and was released shortly after. There's a note in here from the physician who treated him. Let me read it." She pauses as her eyes scan the page, then raises one eyebrow. "Interesting."

"What?"

"Someone signed him out."

I shake my head. "I don't understand."

Dr. Branson nods. "It says here that the doctor tried to convince the person to enroll him in treatment for a suspected brain injury. But that obviously didn't happen. The next day, Cade left."

"Left?"

"It just says he was released."

"How?"

"Hospitals can't keep anyone against their will," she continues. "Whether Cade was taken or left of his own accord, we'll never know."

. . .

I spend the rest of the morning staring at the rise and fall of Cade's chest, wishing I could crawl inside his mind for just a moment, just long enough to see what he's feeling, what he remembers, what happened to him on that August night so many years ago. Because something happened.

Did James really pick up Cade from the hospital? If so, why didn't he tell me? I reach for my phone and step outside to the hallway, where I pull up his number. It's the prickly guy at the front desk again. Does he work seven days a week?

"Yes, I need to speak to James Keatley," I say. "Is he available? It's urgent."

"Who's calling?"

"Kailey Crain," I say.

"Oh," he says. "No, I'm sorry, he's unavailable."

"Unavailable?"

"That's right."

I sigh. "That seems to be the state of things over there. As soon as he comes up for air, please have him call me." I give him my number and he mutters some acknowledgment, then hangs up.

I put my phone back in my purse and look over at Cade, not sure what he's thinking or feeling, but my heart seizes when I see a tear fall from his right eye and trickle down his cheek.

"Cade, are you hurting?"

He stares ahead, chin trembling slightly. I want so badly to comfort him. To heal his brain. To snap my fingers and make it all right and good again. But all I can do is be here with him. I feel that familiar pull, and without thinking I walk to his bedside and lie beside him. My stomach presses against his back and my hand reaches around and gently rests on his chest. I can hear every beat of his heart. His eyes flutter and close, and so do mine.

. . .

"Excuse me." I hear a woman's voice in the distance. *Who? What?* I open my eyes. *Where am I?* A moment later, the room comes into focus, and so does the face hovering over me. A nurse. A hospital room. I sit up and look around. Cade is still sleeping.

"I'm sorry," I say. "I must have dozed off." I rub my eyes. "What time is it?"

"Just about seven P.M.," the nurse says.

"Oh no," I say, panicking. I texted Ryan earlier to say I'd be home by six. I stand and reach for my purse, catching my disheveled reflection in the window.

"I have to leave," I say. "I don't want to wake him. But I'll be back in the morning."

The nurse, the same one who was so gentle with me in the elevator, is now checking the various monitors attached by wires and cords to Cade. She nods. "Don't worry," she says. "We'll take good care of him."

"Thank you," I say, turning back to him, bearded and thin, his body in the shape of a crescent under the starchy hospital sheet. I hate to leave him, but I have to.

"Hi," Ryan says from the couch as I walk in the door.

"Hi," I say, setting my purse down on the bench in the entryway. "Remind me when your parents are arriving again?"

"Their flight's delayed," he says. "They may not be here until after eleven."

"Oh no," I say.

"I'll wait up for them, but don't feel like you have to. I know you've had a busy week."

I nod, grateful for the chance to disappear upstairs.

"Hey," he says, setting his laptop aside. "Someone from Harborview called an hour ago, left a message for you. Something about a brain injury center."

My palms feel suddenly sweaty. *Why would they call my home num-*

ber? Then I remember that it's the number on the top of our checks. "Huh," I say, trying to figure out what to say. Fast.

"I wrote the number down here," he says, setting a scrap of paper on the coffee table. "I mean, unless you have a brain injury you haven't told me about." He laughs. "I figured it was something for the *Herald*?"

"Yeah," I say. "I mean, no, I don't have a brain injury." I laugh nervously.

"Come over here," he says.

I nestle beside him on the couch and he weaves his fingers into mine.

"I just found out that I have to go back to Portland most of next week," he says. "We're at a crucial stage with the plans for the Pioneer Square project, and the details are too sensitive to handle by phone." He squeezes my hand. "It's a short workweek because of the Thanksgiving holiday. You could go with me, maybe. I know you prefer the beach, but we could walk along the river. You could write while I work. The change of scenery might do you some good."

Half of my heart wants to stay, and the other half wants to go. But I can't. Cade needs me. At least until he's settled in his new apartment.

"I'd love to," I say. "But I can't next week."

Ryan detaches his hand from mine and stands up abruptly. "I understand," he says in a voice that tells me that he does not in fact understand, as he walks toward the front door.

"Ryan, I'm sorry, I—"

"I get it," he says, reaching for the dog's leash. "I'm going to take Eddie on a walk. I'll be back in a bit." His eyes meet mine. I know he can detect my concern. "It's okay," he says as he zips up his coat.

But the thing is, I know that it's not okay. Nothing is okay.

The next morning, I wake before Ryan, dress quietly, and leave without disturbing Ryan's parents, even Eddie, who's too groggy to notice when I walk out the door.

I park at the hospital and make my way to the fifth floor. My heart beats fast as I grasp the door handle, but when I enter the room I practically bump into a man holding a vase of flowers, white carnations, and a Mylar balloon that says GET WELL SOON.

"Oh," I say, startled. "I'm so sorry. I must have the wrong room. I'm looking for 502."

"This is 502," he says. "My wife was moved here after surgery."

"Your wife?" I peer around his shoulder and see a middle-aged woman with short dark hair lying in the bed that once was Cade's. She's holding the remote and staring at the TV with a frustrated expression.

"Bill, how does this thing work? Can you get one of the nurses?"

"Sorry," I say, slipping out the door and heading directly to the nurses' station. *Maybe they moved him. Maybe he's on another floor.*

"Excuse me," I say. "I'm looking for Cade McAllister. He was in room 502 yesterday, but he's gone now."

"Oh," the young nurse says. "Yes." She turns to her colleague, an older nurse I don't remember from yesterday.

"About that," the older nurse says. "Your friend left."

I shake my head. "What do you mean, he *left*?"

She shrugs. "He slipped out at some point in the night," she says. "The nurse from the night shift said she went in to give him his pain medication at three A.M., but he was gone."

"How could you let him leave?" I exclaim. "He has a *brain injury*. He doesn't know what he's doing. He doesn't know who he is."

"Ma'am," the older nurse says, "we are a hospital, not a jail. We can't force people to stay. If they want to leave, they can leave."

I sigh. "Do you have any idea where he might have gone? Any at all?"

She shrugs. "Maybe back to the streets," she says, turning back to her paperwork. "They always end up back there."

She begins to say something else, but I don't listen. Instead I race to the elevator.

• • •

I spend all day searching for Cade. I wander through Westlake Center endlessly, scouring every alley, every sidewalk. I take on Pioneer Square next, stopping at shelters, soup kitchens, with no luck. By three I'm exhausted and disillusioned, so I decide to head back to my office, where I dejectedly slump in my chair. When Jan passes, she pokes her head in. "She shows her face."

"I'm sorry I've been so checked out," I say. I feel a rush of emotion and bury my face in my hands.

"And I'm sorry that you're going through this." She sits down. "Have you given any more thought to writing about it?"

I shake my head. "It's so personal, Jan."

"It is," she says, "which is what makes it such a compelling story."

"Oh, Jan. I don't know what to do." After keeping my guard up around Ryan, it feels good to be real.

"Thanksgiving is coming," she says. "Let's finish this series on Pioneer Square from Cade's perspective. Let's show the neighborhood through his eyes."

"I don't know," I say.

"Yes, you do," she counters.

I tell her about Cade's hospital stay, how he's disappeared.

"You'll find him," she says. "You didn't find him after more than a decade only to lose him again. Fate's not that much of a bitch."

I crack a smile.

"It will all work out the way it's supposed to in the end," she says, giving me a long look. "Now find him, and write something you both can be proud of."

Her words are as comforting as they are unsettling.

"Sorry I'm late," I say, giving Ryan a quick kiss as I squeeze into a chair at Earl's. Ryan's parents, Bennett and Melinda, look up at me, and my stomach instantly feels unsettled, the way it does before I have to speak in staff meetings. It's ten after seven, and while I left the office with plenty of time to spare, I sat in traffic on Mercer for longer than I expected. I look around the restaurant filled with well-dressed patrons. Weeks earlier, when I learned of Ryan's parents' imminent visit, I'd planned on wearing the new blue dress I recently bought at Nordstrom and maybe combing my hair and putting on mascara. But today—Cade—has gotten the better of me, and here I am in jeans and a wrinkled white button-down. I sigh, doing my best to smooth my rain-drenched hair.

"Hello, dear," Melinda says, blowing me an air kiss. She's dressed impeccably in a beige cashmere sweater set and black pencil skirt. Her perfectly coiffed blond hair makes me acutely aware of the state of mine.

Bennett smiles. "It's good to see you, Kailey."

"Sorry that I'm a bit disheveled," I say. "I came straight from work."

"Busy day?"

"Yes," I say.

Ryan smiles proudly. "Kailey's taking the lead on some key reporting for the *Herald*. She has important ideas on how to help Seattle's homeless in the midst of downtown development projects."

"My research is taking me to parts of the city I've never seen," I say. I want to explain, but I am unnerved.

"Well, isn't that wonderful," Melinda says. She obviously doesn't want to hear anything but pleasantries.

"How long will you be in town?" I ask, thinking of Cade, of everything.

"Just two nights, and then we're off to Atlanta," Bennett says. "Melinda's hosting a charity ball there with an old friend this weekend."

"To benefit cerebral palsy research," Melinda says.

It occurs to me what an accomplished fund-raiser like Melinda could do for the city's homeless. Perhaps she and I have more in common than I'm willing to admit.

"That's wonderful, Mom," Ryan says.

Melinda smiles at her son. "It's my calling."

"What's the latest on that Pioneer Squares joint venture? Did the financing come through?" Bennett asks Ryan. And suddenly father and son are immersed in a private conversation about how each of their various business interests is faring in the recession.

Melinda turns to me. "You look tired, dear. You're working too much."

I force a smile. "I'm trying to help people, too, through my words. Though at times it seems that no one is listening."

"Well," she says, narrowing her gaze. "Maybe you should consider volunteering your time after the wedding. Ryan makes enough money for the both of you, you know. You could touch lives more directly."

The waiter returns with a fresh wineglass and fills it from the bottle of expensive-looking French wine already open at the table.

"I really do like my job," I say after taking a sip.

"But, dear," she continues. "What about your home? What about a family? Surely you won't want an office job after a baby comes along."

My cheeks burn. "I can't really imagine not working. It's part of who I am."

Melinda squares her shoulders and folds her hands daintily in her lap. "I'm confident you'll find that there is great joy and fulfillment in being a wife and mother."

"Well," I say, smiling as sweetly as I can. I glance at Ryan to bail me out, but he is still deep in conversation with his father. "We'll see."

Bennett must have ordered more wine, because the waiter presents a new bottle. He has the look of a person who is new on the job as he fiddles with the corkscrew and struggles to free it from the neck of the bottle. He smiles nervously. "Well, darn," he says. "The cork appears to be broken."

I take a look, and it's not only broken, it's borderline decimated. My blood pressure rises in sympathy for his predicament. Ryan's parents are nice enough but prone to exaggerated disappointment when something doesn't go according to plan.

"That was a very expensive bottle," Bennett says, folding his arms. "I'd rather not drink bits of cork with it."

"Wait," I say, coming to the waiter's rescue. "I know how to fix this. Do you have a toothpick?"

Everyone gapes at me except the waiter, who may be my new best friend. He springs into action.

"Here," he says. I stand and carefully wedge the toothpick into the cork, then reach for the corkscrew. I insert it into the offending cork, then gently pull the corkscrew up. The combination works like magic, and the cork releases with a tiny pop.

"There," I say. The waiter exhales deeply. Ryan's smile is the biggest of all.

"Who taught you how to do that?" he asks, looking up at me proudly.

I swallow hard. "An old friend," I say.

Before I return to my seat, I refill Bennett's wineglass.

"Not a speck of cork," he says, pleased. "Marry this one, son." He winks at Ryan.

"I intend to, Dad," he says, grinning.

"Ryan, darling, where are you two going on your honeymoon?"

He wipes his mouth with his napkin, then tucks it back in his lap. "We've been so busy with work and settling into the new house that we haven't had a moment to talk about it." He smiles at me. "Kailey, is there somewhere in particular you'd like to go?"

"You know where we could go?" I say.

"Where?"

"Big Sur," I say.

Melinda looks pained. "Big Sur?"

"Yes," I say. "It's beautiful there."

Ryan looks surprised. "Funny, I don't think I ever knew that you went there. When was it?"

"A lifetime ago," I say with a summoned smile.

Melinda looks at Bennett, then shakes her head. "In our day, it was nothing but a hippie mecca."

"The beach is truly one of a kind," I say.

"Why not Paris?" Melinda continues. "Or Venice. Bennett and I absolutely adore Venice."

"Mom," Ryan says, picking up on my body language, "Kailey and I will plan a wonderful honeymoon. Don't you worry."

"Of course, dear," she says. "It's just that Big Sur is so . . . ordinary."

"It's where my parents met," I say. My voice isn't defensive but dreamy.

"Oh," Melinda says. "I didn't mean—"

"I understand," I say quickly. "I don't expect it to be special to you, but it is to me."

Dinner arrives, and our conversation, mostly small talk, ebbs and flows between bites of duck and parchment-wrapped halibut. When our plates are empty, Bennett pays the bill, and Ryan and his dad excuse themselves to the restroom while Melinda and I wait by the door of the restaurant.

"It's good to see Ryan so happy," Melinda says to me. She stares at me for a long moment, and I realize that her comment is less an observation than a warning to me. As in *My son is happy, don't mess it up. Don't hurt him.*

Bennett and Ryan return before I can respond. Ryan puts his arm around my waist as we walk outside. "I'm parked a block up," I say as Bennett hands the valet the claim ticket for Ryan's car. "I should have valeted." I glance across the street to the restaurant where I first saw Cade. My heart lurches in my chest.

"Let me walk you to your car," Ryan says, taking my hand. We start walking but turn around again when we hear Melinda raise her voice.

"Bennett," she calls, "this man is harassing me!"

Ryan's dad, who is talking to a young man at the valet desk, turns to his wife. When Melinda takes a step back, I feel the blood rush to my head. It's Cade. He's still wearing the hospital gown but with his army coat draped over it. He looks confused, more disheveled than ever.

"He means no harm," I say, rushing to Melinda's side.

"Well," she says with a gasp, "I suppose it's wishful thinking these days to expect you can have a meal at a nice restaurant and not end up being panhandled."

I shake my head. "I'm sure he wasn't panhandling," I say without thinking.

"He approached me for money," Melinda continues, aghast.

I shake my head. "This man doesn't speak."

"Are you accusing me of . . . lying?"

"No," I say, searching Cade's eyes.

"Well," Melinda says, pausing for a moment, "it wasn't what he *said,* but how he *looked* at me." She drapes the back of her hand against her forehead as if to drive home the point that she might in fact faint. "He frightened me."

"Are you okay?" I ask Cade, forgetting time and space and everything else.

His eyes lock onto mine and he reaches for my arm. I let him take it.

Melinda gasps. "Kailey, do you *know* this man?"

She and Bennett stand on the sidewalk in disbelief, waiting for my response. There might as well be a thousand spotlights on me. I'm on-stage, and the curtains have just opened.

"I, uh, I . . ." I falter as I search for the right words, any words. I feel Ryan's gaze burn my face. Confused. Worried. Two worlds are colliding right before my eyes. I could lie and say I interviewed him for a story. I blink hard, breaking my gaze from Cade's and freeing my arm from his grasp. If one can break her own heart, in that moment I break mine. "No," I finally say. "No, I don't know this man."

Cade's eyes mirror the pain I feel as Ryan takes my hand. "Here, man," he says, reaching into his pocket and placing some bills in Cade's hand. I stare at my feet. "Mom, Dad, why don't you take my car. I'll drive home with Kailey."

Ryan takes my keys. I'm glad, because I'm too shaken to drive. Every ounce of me wants to rush back, to rescue Cade from another night on the street. But how? Bring him home to our house and parade him in front of Melinda and Bennett? Tell Ryan everything? And then what?

With each stoplight, each mile, each moment that Ryan drives the car into the night, my insides churn. Tonight I feel as if I've just left my most valuable possession on the streets of Seattle, hoping that it will still be there, unfazed, unhurt, intact, by morning.

"Do you want to talk about it?" Ryan finally asks after a long silence.

I shake my head.

"When are you going to open up to me, Kailey? You know there's nothing you could tell me that would make me love you less. Nothing."

I nod and turn to the window, blinking back tears as the city whizzes by.

fourteen

FEBRUARY 18, 1997

"*H*appy birthday," Cade says, poking his head into my cubicle at the *Herald*. Startled, I look up from my computer screen to see him standing in my doorway holding an enormous bouquet of red roses. He wears a gray zip-up hoodie, jeans, and black Converse shoes. His hair is a bit tousled.

"You remembered," I say, standing up to kiss him.

"Of course I remembered," he replies with a grin. "And now I need you to go home and pack your suitcase, because we have a three-thirty flight to catch."

I shake my head. "What do you mean?"

His smile is infectious. "I'm taking you to Big Sur."

"Big Sur?"

"Yes, ma'am," he continues. "I figure everyone should see the place where their parents met. And don't worry, I talked to your editor. Your schedule is officially cleared for the next four days."

I bite my lip, hardly able to contain my excitement. *Big Sur!* "But do you have the time? Can you get away for that long?"

"For you, yes," he says with a smile. "James can handle things while I'm gone."

I recall an argument he had with James last week, something about the purchase of a recording studio, but I don't mention it. If he's okay with the trip, then I should be, too. And I am. I'm happy, and excited, and touched, all at the same time. It's been eight months since we started dating, and after Tracy and Mark went to New York last month, I've secretly been dying to travel with Cade, even just a simple adventure to the San Juan Islands, a few hours north.

"So you told her, then," Jan says, appearing in the doorway with a satisfied smile.

I nod. "Thank you," I say to Jan, reaching for my coat and bag. "I'm going to Big Sur!"

"I expect a column out of this," she says half-seriously.

I nod, unable to stop smiling.

"Happy birthday, Kailey."

Cade rents a convertible in San Francisco, and we put the top down and drive south to Highway 1, passing through Monterey and Carmel, cool wind in our hair, smiles on our faces, music blasting through the speakers. The road is narrow and winding, and I cling to my seat as the car hugs the edge of the cliffs that drop down hundreds of feet to the sea.

The terrain is breathtaking, the air intoxicating. I've never smelled anything like it, in fact—this aromatic blend of the bark of redwood trees and the spray of salty ocean air. No wonder my parents fell in love here. It's magic.

I glance over at Cade, who looks a slight shade of green. "You're carsick," I say, feeling a little queasy myself.

He nods and pulls over at an outlook ahead, where a group of tourists are posing for the camera.

"Wow," he says, taking a deep breath. "That drive is as beautiful as it is nauseating."

We laugh together, and then he reaches for his camera in the backseat and tells me to pause by the ledge. "Right there," he says, looking through the camera lens. I smile nervously, wondering what he sees. "Beautiful," he continues, clicking once, then twice, then again.

A man approaches us and smiles. "Would you like me to take a photo of the two of you together?"

"Thanks," Cade says, handing him his camera.

We've had a few Polaroids snapped at parties, but I realize that this will be our first photo together.

Cade kisses my cheek as the camera clicks, and I wonder if we'll look at this picture when we're old. I wonder if we'll show it to our children, and their children, if we'll come back to this place years from now and remember this moment.

We get back into the car and drive another few miles, then Cade turns onto a road that winds up a hillside. "This is Post Ranch Inn," he says. "I wanted you to stay in the most beautiful place in Big Sur."

I squeeze his hand as we pull into the circular drive. A man greets us and unloads our luggage. A few minutes later, we're whisked away on a golf cart to our room, a private, modern-looking cabin perched on the cliff. The furnishing is beautifully rustic, and I'm drawn to a painting on the wall of a coastal scene.

Cade lies on the bed, sinking into one of the pillows. "You know what I like to do in hotels?"

I flash him a curious smile. "What?"

He grins mischievously. "Back in the day, I traveled a lot for Element, was gone more than I was home. I spent so many nights in random hotels that eventually I came up with a way to entertain myself." He points to the painting on the wall that I'd been looking at. "Of course, that's really high-end, but hotel art is usually the worst."

I nod. "Like the kind of thing you'd find in a dentist's office."

"Exactly," he says. "So I started bringing index cards and pushpins with me on trips." He sits up and laughs to himself. "You know when you're at a restaurant or café and the art on display is for sale?"

"Yeah," I say.

"Well, I'd be in a hotel somewhere, and I'd pick the cheesiest framed print in the room, then write up a little index card for it. I'd title it something like *Drifting Through the Willows, in Retrospective* or whatever cheeseball name that I could come up with, and then I'd list a price underneath."

I laugh. "Why?"

"Well, just think about it. I check out, and the next person who has the room might be Myrtle and Bob from Orlando, Florida. Myrtle sees that there's a painting for sale.

"'Look, Bob, original art! It's only three hundred dollars. Bob, we have to buy it.' And Bob, wanting to please Myrtle, picks up the phone and calls the front desk.

"'Yes,' he says. 'This is Bob Smith in room 402. Yes, I'd like to buy the painting on the wall.'

"Long pause. 'I'm sorry, sir,' the hotel girl says, '*what* painting?'

"'*Drifting Through the Willows,*' he says, clearing his throat, '*in Retrospective.*' Long pause. 'The one for sale in our room.'

"'Sir, we don't *sell* the art in the rooms.'"

I fall onto the bed beside Cade, unable to stop laughing. "I'm going to pee my pants."

Cade stays in character.

"'Yes, you do sell art.' Myrtle is now fretting. 'I see the tag right here. My wife wants to hang it in our living room.'

"'Sir, I'm going to have to talk to a manager about this.'

"'Listen, my wife has become very attached to this painting, and we would like to buy it.'"

"I don't know where you come up with stuff like this," I say, laughing so hard that my eyes are tearing up.

He turns over onto his side, leaning into his elbow. His eyes sparkle, and I feel a surge of something I can't explain.

"Let's spend the rest of our lives together," he says, tucking a lock of my hair behind my ear.

I blink hard. "Are you saying what I think you're saying?"

His eyes don't leave mine. "It's what my heart wants. Does yours?"

"Yes," I say, feeling tears sting my eyes.

I put on a black dress with spaghetti straps and a pair of platform heels. I pull my hair back into a low bun, grab a sweater, then take Cade's hand as we walk up the path to the restaurant.

Along the way, a little girl in a floral dress runs ahead singing to herself. She must be four, maybe five. "Grace!" her father calls.

She giggles joyfully as her parents, walking hand in hand, catch up to her.

"Got you," her father says, lifting her into his arms. She giggles again.

"I've always loved the name Grace," Cade says.

"Me too," I say.

He watches the little girl skipping along, then turns back to me and nods as if he's made a definitive decision. "Grace."

When we reach the restaurant, the sun is flirting with the horizon, ready to set but not quite. The view is spectacular, and we choose to walk out to the deck so we can soak up the sky, painted elaborate shades of pink and orange, before being seated.

"Do you like it here?" he asks, tucking his arms around my waist, his body pressing against my back.

"I love it," I say, watching the waves crash onto the shore below.

"Let's walk down to the beach tonight," he says. "After dinner."

"Let's," I say.

"I can see why your parents were drawn together here."

I nod, thinking of their love story. I've heard it a thousand times from Grandma. Dad said she was the most beautiful woman he'd ever seen. And she thought he was the handsomest. They fit like two peas in a pod, Grandma said. They were . . . soulmates.

Unbidden memories wash in like waves, one after the next, crashing in with such force, I brace myself. I can smell the Coppertone sunscreen in the brown bottle. My hands are, once again, sticky with roasted marshmallows. The delphiniums in Grandma's garden stand at attention. I don't know where these thoughts are coming from. But then I realize that the reason these disparate snapshots from my childhood are bubbling up in my heart is the man standing behind me. I realize that with him, anywhere, I am home.

fifteen

NOVEMBER 24, 2008

R yan's parents talked of us joining them for Thanksgiving in North Carolina, but thankfully Ryan's work schedule won't allow for that this year. In some ways, it was nice to have them in the house with us. Their presence gave me an excuse not to confront the truth, and Ryan an excuse not to bring it up again. But it lingered, this truth that I am not ready to face.

"I'll be back from Portland on Friday. I'm sorry we'll be spending Thanksgiving apart," Ryan says on this Monday morning, suitcase in hand. He pauses, giving me space to say something, anything.

I clear my throat. "Ryan?"

He nods and takes a step closer.

My mind reels. *I have to tell him about Cade. I have to tell him everything.* "There's something I need to—"

I'm immediately silenced by the sound of Ryan's cell ringing in his pocket. "Sorry," he says, glancing at the screen. "It's my boss. I have to take this."

I nod and roll over, then pretend to be asleep when he kisses my cheek a few minutes later.

Tracy calls later that morning as I'm walking Eddie. "Did you *die?*"

"Sorry," I say. "Ryan's parents were visiting. And . . . I've been really lost."

"Because of his wacky mother?"

"No, I mean, yes, but not really that," I say with a sigh. "It's just . . . *everything.*" I kick a pebble on the sidewalk as Eddie sniffs around in the nearby grass. "I am caught in a horrible place. I haven't told Ryan about Cade. And then . . ." I tell her about the scene outside the restaurant the other night, how I denied knowing Cade. How I walked away and left him there.

"Oh, honey," she says. "Don't be so hard on yourself. What else were you supposed to do? Have a confrontation with Ryan's parents right there? Embarrass Ryan? You did what you had to do. And I know how much it hurt."

"I don't care about me," I say. "I just worry that I ruined whatever seed of trust I was building with Cade. Trace, I'm worried that I've lost him."

"I checked your horoscope this morning," Tracy says. "There's no way you've lost him. In fact, something tells me you're about to find him."

I spend the morning at the office, answering emails, giving the latest article in the series another read-through. And then, with Jan's words ringing in my ears, I open up a blank Word document and type at the top of the page, "The Faces of Homelessness."

The words flow from there, and I don't censor them.

In the late nineties, Seattle knew Cade McAllister as a successful music executive. Today he is homeless.

As I write more, I can see Cade in my mind's eye, the Cade of long ago, with his beloved bottle of Tabasco and the world at his fingertips. The image haunts me. So does the image of him looking at me on the sidewalk the other night, so scared and lost. And the image of me walking away from him.

"Knock knock."

I turn from my computer to see Jan in the doorway.

"Glad to see you writing," she says.

I sigh. "I don't know what else to do, Jan."

She nods. "Yes, you do." She's resolute and sure. "And, I'm giving you an assignment for today—well, for the week. An important one." She dabs a napkin to my cheek, whisking away fresh tears. "Go find Cade. Bring him home. Nurse him back to health. Help him find his way, and in the process you'll find yours."

"But I—"

"No buts," she says. "This is an assignment. And I want you to write about it."

I crack a smile.

"And don't think I'm giving you preferential treatment," she says in her best boss voice. "If you don't turn in good copy, I'll put you back on the city council beat."

I grin.

"Now go find him."

I park my car on the street in front of Le Marche and set out to find Cade. I look everywhere, just as I did last week. Westlake Center. All along Fourth, and Fifth, then back down to Second. Shelters. Parks. I even lift a blanket off a man's face on a park bench, but the figure beneath is not Cade.

Hours pass like minutes, and before I know it, it's after six and people in suits are filing out of office buildings and into restaurants and bars.

When the sun sets, I tearfully decide to return to my car. I sigh and insert my key into the ignition, flipping on the radio. As I merge into traffic, the hair on my arms stands on end. Mazzy Star. "Fade into You." I turn up the volume and my eyes fill with fresh tears. When I pass the entrance to I-5, I keep going, as if my car is on autopilot. And instead of driving home, I drive to the place my heart wants to go: that ivy-covered brick building in Pioneer Square.

I pull the car over and get out without bothering to turn off my headlights. They shine into the dark street like a spotlight on my past. Cade's old door is straight ahead. At once I am twenty-five again. We are walking hand in hand, coming home from a show. He's whispering something funny in my ear, and I throw back my head and laugh. And then we arrive at his door, and he presses me up against that brick wall and kisses me with the fire of every star in the sky.

I blink back tears, remembering every detail of what happened, and what didn't happen. The life we might have had. The future that was robbed from us.

I kiss my hand, then press it to the door as I take a step back. How do you say goodbye to a dream you still wish were true?

I hear the shuffle of footsteps in the nearby alley and decide to head back to my car. As I slowly drive away, I take a final glance back, and a shadow in the rearview mirror catches my eye. I brake and roll down the passenger window to try to get a better look, then put the car in reverse.

It's him. He stands on the corner, looking right, then left.

I slam on my brakes and turn the engine off. "Cade!" I cry, jumping out of the car.

He looks up. He sees me.

"Cade," I say again. "It's me."

He looks away, but I reach for his hand, and when I do, his eyes meet mine.

"I'm here," I say. "And I'm not going to leave you again. I promise." I pull him toward me into an embrace, and we stand like that for what seems like an eternity. And maybe it is. I'm not sure.

"Come with me," I say, taking his hand and leading him across the street. I open the door to my car. "I'm taking you home."

sixteen

JULY 17, 1997

"My grandma's going to love you," I say.

Cade grins. "And what about your grandpa? I'm more worried about him."

"He's old-fashioned," I say proudly. "So as long as he feels like you respect him, you'll be golden. He was in the army."

"And he loves his granddaughter."

I smile. "He does. He's been a true father to me."

"He's protective, as he should be," Cade says, kissing my cheek. "And I'm completely honored that you want me to meet them."

"It's a big deal that they're coming," I say. "Grandma's afraid of flying." I look at my watch. "They'll be here in an hour!"

He squeezes my hand. "Hey, sorry again about last night."

Work stress got the better of him. He snapped at me for no reason. It hurt, but I tried to let it roll off my back, knowing that hadn't been his intention. It wasn't our first fight, and it wouldn't be our last. I'd be foolish to believe that there won't be more lovers' quarrels in our future. Hundreds of them, maybe. And probably more. But there will be makeups, too. And the makeups are electric.

We take Cade's car to the airport to pick them up, and when I see them standing on the curb beside the Delta Air Lines sign, I wave and Cade pulls over. I leap out of the car and wrap one arm around each of them, blinking back tears.

"Kailey," Grandma says. "You look beautiful."

"There's my girl," Grandpa chimes in. It's been only a year since I've seen him, but he looks much older than I recall, and it pains me to see him struggle with his luggage.

Cade idles the engine and steps out. "Welcome to Seattle," he says, extending his hand to my grandfather, who eyes him skeptically.

Grandma hugs him, like she'd hug any of my friends. "We're so happy to meet you," she says warmly.

Cade takes her bag, but Grandpa doesn't relinquish his. Instead he stubbornly lifts it into the trunk. I give him the front seat, and Grandma and I take the back. She tucks her arm in mine, and I feel like I am nine again, pigtailed, with cherry ChapStick on my lips.

"Are you hungry?" Cade asks as we merge into traffic.

"Gerry ate on the plane," Grandma says. "But I could use a bite."

"Do you like Mexican?" Cade asks.

"We sure do," Grandma replies, giving me an approving smile.

"Great," Cade says. "I know just the place."

Grandpa sits in silence while Grandma is abuzz with conversation. Does Cade have any family in Seattle? Has he always been interested in music?

At a little spot we both love on Lake Union called Agua Verde, we settle into a table by the window. Kayakers glide by on the lake as we dip our chips into green salsa.

"I've always loved this place. The food is authentic Mexico, but the setting is pure Seattle," Cade says, ordering a round of margaritas for the table. Grandpa's face seems to brighten.

"You say the word *always* like a Midwesterner," Grandma says.

Cade smiles. "Do I? No one's ever told me that."

Grandma nods. "Kailey's mother, Lucinda, was born in Alton, Illinois. She only spent her first six years there, but she never lost that touch of the Midwest in her words. Somehow Kailey didn't pick up the dialect. You always know by the way someone says the word *always*."

I smile, saying the word aloud. Cade repeats it, too. "You know, you do say that word differently. It's almost like you're saying 'all-was.'"

"Am I?"

"Yeah," I say. "Say it again."

"All-was," he says.

Grandma smiles as the margaritas arrive. "You still wear your necklace," she says, pointing to my locket. "I assume Cade knows the story."

I feel Cade's hand on my leg under the table. He's reassuring me that while he knows the story behind the necklace, he'll never worry my grandparents by telling them about the day when I almost lost the locket—the day all three of them almost lost me.

"Yes, it was one of the first I told him," I say, my cheeks feeling warm.

I open my necklace and let the tiny shard of green fall to my palm. "Grandpa said it was his lucky charm."

"Wow," Cade says. "That's—"

"I'll never forget that beach," Grandpa says, clearing his throat. "It was unlike anything I'd ever seen. Rocky cliffs along the shore, with this sand that was"—he pauses to recall the image—"the color of amber. That beach was special. When I found the shell, I tucked it in my pocket. Its luck is why I dodged a land mine on the way back to camp. I kept that part of the story from Kailey when she was young."

"That's amazing," Cade says, swallowing hard. "My father served in Vietnam. Marines. But he died. I . . ."

I squeeze Cade's hand. "Cade lost both of his parents, too."

"I'm sorry, son," Grandpa says. And just like that, I can see that he likes him. There's newfound acceptance in his eyes. I tuck the shell into my locket and lean back in my chair, watching the people I care most about in the world chat about big things and small over plates of Mexican food.

The week sails by, and though Cade is busy at the office, he spends as much time with us as possible, taking Grandpa and Grandma on a tour of Pike Place Market, to dinner at Wild Ginger and the Space Needle, and on a walk along the waterfront.

"They're wonderful," he says after we drop them off at the airport.

"And they adored you," I say, weaving my fingers into his.

We stop at a little Italian place near his apartment for dinner, where we're seated at a table with a red-and-white-checked tablecloth and a drippy white candle flickering from a Chianti bottle.

"Cheesy but charming," I say. "Just my style."

Cade nods and pours us each a glass of red wine from the carafe in front of us. The candlelight accentuates the dark circles under his eyes. He's mentioned that things at the office have been rocky, but when I asked him about it yesterday, he brushed off my question. "Just the usual," he said.

"You okay?" I ask.

"Just tired," he says.

"What's going on at Element?" I ask, reaching my hand across the table. "I know you hate to think you're boring me with work stuff, but I promise, I want to know."

He grimaces. "And spoil this beautiful night?"

"Nothing you say could spoil this night, Cade," I assure him.

"Well," he says, taking a big sip from his wineglass. "I blew it. I convinced James to sink fifty thousand into a new band, and they've tanked."

"What do you mean, they tanked?"

He rubs his forehead, then takes another long sip of wine. "Their album, which we were over budget on to begin with, bombed. And now they want out of their contract but refuse to give us back the signing bonus."

"That doesn't sound legal," I say.

"It's not," he replies. "But even so, these are losses the company has to eat."

I nod. "Don't be so hard on yourself," I say. "You've had dozens of successes with the label. You're allowed to strike out now and then."

Cade shrugs. "James doesn't see it that way. He's a perfectionist."

"And is *he* perfect?" I shake my head. "I don't think so."

"He promoted Alexis to head of business operations," he continues.

"Alexis? She's nice enough, but is she really qualified for the job?"

Cade shakes his head. "She may have a degree in accounting, but she knows nothing about music."

"Cade, it's your company, too," I say. "Don't let him railroad you."

I can tell the conversation is wearing on him, and after the waiter takes our orders, I change the subject.

After dinner we step out to the street. It's a warm night, and instead of cabbing back to Cade's apartment, we decide to walk.

"Hey," he says, suddenly perking up. "I know a band playing at the Crocodile tonight. Want to go?"

"Sure," I say, loving his spontaneity.

Hand in hand, we wind up several blocks. Cade's name is on the guest list, and we slip past the line of people waiting at the door.

He buys us each a double vodka soda, and we find our way to the stage. "These guys aren't on a label yet," he says.

"Who are they?" I ask.

"Death Cab for Cutie," he says. "A little indie band from Bellingham. I saw them play a small venue a few months ago, and I haven't been able to get their music out of my head. That's when you know." He takes a sip of his drink. "I'm trying to get James to agree to sign them. But it's a losing battle."

"Not if you don't want it to be," I say. "If you believe in them, sign them."

The band takes to the stage and the lights dim all around. The crowd applauds. "It used to work that way," Cade continues. "I think I'm losing my edge. And I think James knows it."

"No way," I say.

The band begins to play, and I'm struck by their sound, especially the singer's voice. "Wow, they're good," I continue. "Really good."

We stay until their last song, then follow the crowd out the door. I feel light and airy from my cocktail, so when Cade suggests that we stop at a bar on the next block for one more, I don't say no.

Two drinks later, each of us is laughing. Whatever troubles Cade carried with him hours prior have disappeared into the night. "You're magic," he says from the barstool next to me. "You make everything happy."

I giggle, running my hand along the right side of his head. "Magic, huh?"

He nods, eyes relaxing closed at my touch. "Put a spell on me."

I wave my straw, pretending it's a magic wand. "Hocus-pocus," I say.

We get up from the bar, laughing, and stumble out to the sidewalk. I feel numb, in the very best way. And I can't remember drinking this much . . . ever. Cade takes my hand. "Where to next, my lady?" he asks, passing a tattoo shop on our left. He stops. "Wait, neither of us has any tattoos. Let's get one."

"Tonight?" I say with a hiccup. "Really?"

"Why not?" he says.

"Well, I can think of a few reasons . . . like maybe the overwhelming feeling of regret we might have in the morning."

Cade runs his hand through his hair, and like a dark cloud overshadowing the sun, I watch as the carefree grin on his face melds into something more serious.

"The problem with you, Kailey, is that you don't take any risks. You're afraid of stepping too far out of your comfort zone."

I gasp. "That's not fair."

He shrugs. "It might not be fair, but it's true."

I let out a nervous laugh. "Well then, if you think I'm too cautious, I think you're too impulsive." My cheeks burn. *How can he be so insensitive? So . . .*

"Listen, babe," he says, taking my hand. "I shouldn't have said that. I just . . ."

"You just want me to jump when you say jump?"

"No," he says solemnly.

"Cade, I'm not one of your band friends. I'm not—"

"I know," he says, taking my hands in his. "I was out of line. I don't know why I said that."

"Well, you did."

"Listen," he continues. "Forget what I said. You aren't too cautious. You're smart, beautiful, and wise."

"And," I add, "apparently deeply flawed because I'm not running into the tattoo parlor right now ready to get a dolphin inked onto my ass."

I can't help but laugh. He does, too.

"Now, that's a tattoo I'd like to see," he says with another chuckle.

"You know what?" I say, glancing back at the tattoo joint. "Why the heck not?"

Cade's eyes widen. "The dolphin?"

"No," I say. "But something." I nod. "Why not? You're right. I am too cautious."

"And you're right," he replies. "I'm too impulsive."

I exhale deeply. "Let's do it."

"Really?"

"Yes," I say with a certainty I didn't know I had in me. "What should we get?" I ask, eyeing the images of dragons, roman numerals, and tribal art in the window. "No sea mammals."

Cade scratches his chin. "Matching butterflies?"

We both laugh.

"How about a word?" he suggests.

"Like what?"

He steps closer to me and lets his eyes fall on my face tenderly. "How about *always*?"

"Always," I say, then smile. "Or 'all-was.'"

I follow him inside, where a large bald man, like Mr. Clean but with tattoos, sits on a chair in the back.

"Evening," he says. "How can I help you?"

"We'd like to get two tattoos." As Cade says the words, my heart leaps. *Are we really doing this?*

"All right," he says.

Cade scratches his head. "Do you know how to say *always* in French?"

"Toujours," he says. "I spent a quarter abroad in France."

"Toujours," Cade says, turning to me. "For you. For us. For Normandy."

We flip through a book of fonts and finally settle on a script, which the tattoo artist tells us is something very special from the 1940s. Evidently it appeared on a Frank Sinatra album cover back in the day.

"I'll go first," Cade says, sitting in a chair. The tattoo artist makes a quick mock-up of the design for us, and we settle on the size. Cade decides he'd like it on his shoulder, and I watch him wince as the needle hits his skin. I look away when I see blood, and when it's finally my turn to sit in the chair, I waver. "Maybe I shouldn't," I say.

"Do it for me," Cade says. "Do it for us." His eyes are intense, and I know, right in this moment, that there isn't anything I wouldn't do for this man.

I close my eyes tightly. "Okay," I say, pointing to my right shoulder. "Right here. Let's do this."

The pain is real, and when I feel the first prick of the needle, I flinch.

"Try to be as still as you can," the tattoo artist says. His voice is deep and soothing, and I listen as he tells a story of a couple who'd been in earlier to tattoo wedding bands onto their ring fingers. I can't help but think of Cade and my forever.

When my tattoo is complete, I have a look in the mirror, but my skin is swollen and puffy. It's hard to get a complete sense of what it will look like. And to be honest, in this moment I really don't care.

Cade pays the tattoo guy, then takes my hand. As we walk home to his apartment, my shoulder throbs, but I hardly notice. I feel connected to him in ways I've never been before. More than the tattoo, more than the words we've uttered to each other in moments of love, Cade and I are entwined. And I know we always will be.

seventeen

"This is where I live," I say to Cade as we walk in the door of the house I share with Ryan. It feels surreal to see him standing in the entryway. He stands by the door, paralyzed, as I take off my sweater and set my purse down.

"It's okay," I say softly, reaching for his duffel bag. He holds on to it tightly at first but then relents, and I set it by the door. "You can come in."

Eddie runs past me and directly to Cade, who reaches out his hand to him. *Does he remember?*

He takes a step forward and silently surveys my living room. I flip on the lights and see that his wounds, though less swollen, look just as bad as they did in the hospital.

"You're probably hungry," I say nervously. I walk to the kitchen and peer into the refrigerator. For the first time in years, I have no idea what to cook. None at all. "What do you feel like?" I ask, not expecting a response. "I could make a burrito, maybe spinach quesadillas?" I nod, pulling out a bag of spinach, some cheese, and tortillas. "There," I say, assembling the ingredients, then reaching for my trusty cast-iron skillet, which I've been cooking with since the days of living with Tracy in our little downtown studio. It was my grandma's—she doesn't do much cooking anymore. I like to think about all the meals it has provided over the years.

Cade watches as I make the quesadillas. When they're ready, I cut them into triangles and put them on a plate for him.

"It's not Wild Ginger," I say, setting the plate on the table, "but plain ol' quesadillas hit the spot sometimes." I point to adjoining chairs at the table. "Please, sit. Make yourself comfortable."

He slowly sinks into the chair beside me; Eddie plants himself on the rug at his feet.

"Here," I say, pushing the plate toward him. He doesn't reach for a quesadilla, so I lift one to his lips, just as I did in the hospital. It works, and he takes a cautious bite.

When his plate is clean, I clear the table and nervously try to make a plan for the evening. "You can stay in the upstairs guest bedroom," I say. "You'll probably want to have a bath. I'll get you a towel and some fresh clothes." He picks up the conch shell on the coffee table and turns it over and over, surveying every crevice. "If you'll come with me, I'll get you settled."

As I climb the stairs, he follows, and I'm aware of every step I take, every breath that seeps from my lungs. I take a towel from the linen closet, then flip on the bathroom light. "I'll get your bath started," I say. "Soap is right there, and shampoo."

He just stands and stares.

"Okay," I say with a big exhale. "I'll leave you now. Let me know if you need anything."

I walk to my bedroom and sit on the edge of the bed, listening to the sound of the water running in the other room. Minutes pass, and I start to worry. Should I go check on him? I stand up, then sit down again. Then stand, slipping out of my clothes and into a tank top and leggings, my typical sleeping attire.

"Excuse me," I say, peering into the bathroom through the barely cracked door. I push the door open wider to see Cade standing, fully clothed, in the same spot I left him ten minutes ago. "Everything okay?"

He doesn't respond, so I slowly venture in and turn the faucet off. The tub is nearly overflowing.

"You need some help," I say, nodding. "Let me help you."

I take a deep breath, then step closer to him. My fingers unfasten the button on his coat and I let it fall to the ground. I remove the hospital gown next, revealing his thin bare chest and the familiar tattoo on his shoulder. I wonder if he notices mine now.

I swallow hard when I touch the button on his pants and tug it free. His chest rises and falls with every breath, accentuating the concave of his stomach. I feel a familiar flutter inside as I pull the zipper down. I look away as his pants fall to the ground, then slowly let my eyes drift back to the body I once knew so well. I had memorized every bit of his topography, like a well-studied map. Every freckle. Every inch of muscle and flesh.

I take his hand and lead him to the bath, testing it first with my free hand. "It's just the right temperature," I say. "Go ahead."

He stares at the bathtub as if it's Olympic-size and he's just been asked to breaststroke across and back. "It's okay," I say, encouraging him to get in. "It'll be relaxing."

And then he steps in slowly, at first with trepidation. But once he lowers himself beneath the water, I can tell he finally feels at ease. I kneel beside him and use the spray attachment to soak his hair before I reach for the shampoo. I scrub and lather, then rinse his hair clean, offering him the bar of soap next. He doesn't take it, so I rub it along his arms and chest. He watches me as I reach for a washcloth, then dip it into the water and onto his skin. The water is dark. While the hospital gave him a sponge bath, he has hardly been bathed properly, and when I help Cade up and wrap a towel around him, days, maybe even years, of grime from life on the streets washes down the drain.

I lead him to the bedroom and peer into the closet, where I select a pair of Ryan's jeans and a blue college T-shirt, well worn at the edges. From the dresser, I grab a pair of white boxer briefs and add them to the stack. "Here," I say. "You can wear this."

I help him slip the T-shirt over his head, and his arms find their way through the sleeves. If he's at all shy when the towel slips to the floor, he gives no indication. I carefully guide his legs through my fiancé's boxer briefs, then help him into his jeans, buttoning them up the way I might for a small child.

"There," I say when he's dressed. He places his hands on the jeans, about two sizes too big, as if he's never felt anything quite like the wonderful texture of freshly washed denim. Dressed and scrubbed, he looks more like the Cade I remember, aside from the long hair and beard. I look into his eyes, tilt my head to the right, and somehow expect him to snap out of it. To smile and say, "I'm back. And by the way, where can I get a haircut and shave?"

But that Cade is still locked away in the abyss, deep in the maze of his mind, perhaps where he keeps memories of me, of us. I sigh. "You must be exhausted, let me ..."

As I speak, he sinks into my bed, laying his head on the pillow. I watch him shift uncomfortably to avoid putting pressure on his ribs. I hear Eddie's footsteps on the stairs, barreling up and into my bedroom. He leaps onto the bed and nuzzles into the place between Cade's stomach and right arm, tucking his chin over Cade's left arm.

I smile to myself, then find my way to the guest bedroom. I glance at my phone; Ryan has sent me a few texts. Portland is beautiful. How am I? Instead of replying, I set my phone on the bedside table and lie awake for a long time, staring at the ceiling, thinking. When I finally close my eyes, I dream of Cade and the sea.

When I open my eyes, light streams through the bedroom window. Birds chirp in the tree outside, and I sit up and yawn, wondering if Cade has rested as well as I have. The old wood floors creak underneath my bare feet as I walk to my bedroom, where the blanket and sheets are turned back, the bed empty. I look around the room, then walk to the bathroom, peering inside the open door. Also empty.

"Cade?" I say from the stairway. "Are you here?"

Eddie trots down the stairs behind me as I have a look around the first floor, quiet except for a slow drip from the kitchen faucet, which Ryan had scheduled a repairman to fix tomorrow. *Did he leave?* I feel panic rise in my chest, and I run to the back door to have a look at the empty yard behind the house. "Cade?" I call out again into the quiet house.

Then I notice a scant sliver of light coming through the front door. I open it, stepping out onto the front porch, which is where I find Cade, sitting on the steps, staring ahead.

"Oh," I say, exhaling deeply. "There you are."

I sit down beside him. For a moment I wonder what the neighbors might think of me, sitting on the front porch with a strange bearded man. But then Cade turns to me, smiles, and says two words that render any concerns meaningless. "Good morning."

I squeeze his arm, beaming. "Good morning!" And the birds chirp. And the sun shines. And I am happy.

I pour coffee from the French press and watch him take the first sip from his mug, closing his eyes as he takes another, as if he's trying to remember coffee, me, life.

"I thought I'd make us an omelet," I say, opening the fridge. I pull out a carton of eggs, butter, some spinach, shredded cheese, and a few green onions that look as if they've seen better days.

I pour myself a second cup of coffee, then chop the spinach and trim off the wilted ends of the onions. Butter sizzles in the pan as I whisk the eggs together in a white ceramic bowl. Ryan loves my omelets, and I make them for him often. As I pour the eggs into the pan, watching the edges firm and the middle bubble slightly, I feel overcome with guilt. When Ryan comes home, Cade will hopefully soon be settled in the brain injury program at Harborview, and I'll tell Ryan everything. *He'll understand,* I reassure myself. Ryan always understands.

I divide the giant omelet into two, then dish up a serving for each of us. Cade's hand shakes a little as he holds the fork, and a few bites fall to the plate before they reach his mouth, but he eats, and when he finishes his plate I offer him the rest of mine, which he happily takes.

I think of all the things I have to do: plan the wedding, get Cade set for the brain injury program, begin the monumental task of finding out what happened to him, including figuring out what James knows or doesn't know. And write about it all. But I don't want to do any of it. I just want to be right here, in this moment.

After breakfast, I quietly clean up the kitchen while Cade sits on the couch with Eddie. By eleven he's dozed off, and I suspect that he's years behind on his rest.

I slip out to the porch to call Tracy, letting him sleep as long as he needs to. "Hi," I say quietly.

I hear the hospital in the background. "Why are you whispering?" she asks.

"Cade is here. He's sleeping."

"Cade's at your *house?*"

"Yeah," I say. "I brought him back here last night. I didn't know what else to do."

"Is Ryan cool with this?"

"He's not here," I say. "He's on a business trip to Portland this week."

"Oh, Kailey," Tracy says. "And so, what, he's just sleeping in your guest bedroom?"

"Well now, yeah, but last night he actually slept in my bed. I mean, not with me. He just sort of fell asleep there." I swallow hard. "I gave him a bath, got him cleaned up. He's wearing Ryan's clothes."

"Wow," Tracy says, taking it all in.

"I know," I say nervously.

"He's going to start that program at Harborview soon, right?"

"Yeah," I say, pausing for a moment. "But I was thinking, maybe it would be better just to have him stay here. I'm the only one who really knows him. He could live here, in the guest bedroom, until he's well enough to be on his own."

"But, Kailey, you're not a medical expert. Cade needs rigorous therapy and rehabilitation. I mean, don't get me wrong, I'm sure you would take excellent care of him; it's just that he needs more than that." She's quiet for a moment. "You and I both know that Ryan's never going to be comfortable with the idea of you caring for Cade for an extended period of time."

I shake my head. "Ryan would understand."

"Really?" Tracy counters. "Here's a man you once loved with all your heart, and he resurfaces, and you take it upon yourself to be his personal nurse and caregiver."

"He'd do it for someone in his past, too," I say.

"I'm not so sure he would, or that anyone would. I think that for you, this is different. I know you. You lost this man once and your heart can't handle losing him again. I get that. But, Kailey, playing house with Cade isn't going to save him. If you care about him, you'll make sure he starts the program at Harborview. You'll let him go so that he can get better."

I sigh. "You're right."

"You know I am." She's interrupted by a work matter, then returns to the phone. "I've gotta go," she continues. "But, Kailey, I think there is one huge way that you can help Cade."

"What do you mean?"

"Find out what happened to him," she says. "Ever since you told me about the John Doe report matching his description from 1998, I've just had the creepiest feeling."

"Me too," I say.

"Cade had a full life and a thriving business when he left, or when we thought he left," she says. "I think someone may have wanted a cut of that, maybe someone who had something to do with his state today."

I nod. "Yeah," I say, lowering my voice again when I see Cade through the window stirring on the couch. "I think so, too. Something's not right."

"Help him make it right," Tracy says before hanging up.

The rest of Tuesday passes, and by Wednesday morning, I'm struck with how time can barrel along when you're not doing much of anything. In my case, sitting on the porch with Cade, sharing quiet meals at the table, telling him stories that I'm not sure he remembers or even understands. But for every split second he looks at me as if the light has blinked on, it warms me in a way I cannot describe. This happens mostly when I play him music, old records we used to love. In those moments, I see his spirit lift. I see the old spark in his eyes.

When Ryan calls that evening, I step onto the back porch to answer the phone.

"Hi," he says.

"Hi," I reply.

"I miss your voice. I miss you so much."

"I miss you, too," I say, tugging at a stray piece of yarn on the sleeve of my sweater.

"How's your week been?"

"Ah, good," I say.

"I tried calling you at the office, but you haven't been answering."

"Sorry," I say. "It's been nuts."

"I know it has, honey," he says. "Listen, can I just say . . ." He pauses, "You've just been so distant. I know you have something on your mind, something you're not telling me or aren't ready to tell me, but whatever it is, please, I hope it's not going to come between us. Kailey, I can't bear to lose you."

My eyes well up with tears, for Ryan, for me, for my past and my future.

"You're not losing me," I promise him. Inside the house, I hear the sound of glass shattering. "But, Ryan, I'm sorry. I have to go. I'll call you later, okay?"

Cade stands in the living room staring at his feet nervously. The Chihuly piece, a ridiculously expensive gnarled blend of multicolored blown glass that Ryan's parents gave us for an engagement present, lies in pieces on the floor.

"It's okay," I say, rushing to his side.

He kneels and picks up a shard of glass and then another, pushing them together in an impossible attempt to fix it. A moment later, I notice blood trickling down his hand and I gasp.

"You're hurt," I say. "Just leave it. I'll clean it up later."

I jump to my feet and return with a damp cloth and a bandage. "Here," I say, taking his hand in mine to tend to his wound. He doesn't let go when I'm finished. Instead he squeezes my hand in his.

"Thank you," he says in the voice I knew so well. A voice that made me laugh and cry. A voice that told a thousand stories and uttered even more "I love you"s.

eighteen

I glance at the clock on the wall in my apartment: six thirty-five. Cade's an hour late.

"You look agitated," Tracy says, looking up from the couch, where she's watching a rerun of *Friends*.

I open my mouth to speak, but Tracy continues. "Did you read your horoscope today?"

I shake my head.

She nods. "Mercury's in retrograde. It's throwing everything off, but particularly for Aquariuses." She frowns. "I hate to say this, and I know how much you and Cade love each other, but things are looking a little rocky in the relationship department."

"Well," I say with a sigh, "you know I normally don't buy that stuff, but"—I glance at the clock again—"I have to be honest: I'm starting to."

"What's going on?" she asks.

"Cade's late again," I say. "He was supposed to be here at five-thirty." I stare at the dinner I've made—sea bass and steamed asparagus, which is now cold—and sigh.

"Did he call?"

"No," I say, slumping on the couch beside her. Jennifer Aniston's hair looks perfect on the screen as she sips coffee from an oversize mug. I run my hands through my hair and consider a new haircut, maybe changing the color. Maybe changing everything.

Tracy nods knowingly.

"Something's wrong," I say.

"How so?"

I shake my head. "It's Cade. He's . . . changed."

"Changed?"

I sigh. "Cade is the most brilliant person in any room, the funniest, the most engaging. I knew it when I met him, and ever since that day I've been swept up in his whole being. When his sun shines on you, you just . . . feel it. But when it shines elsewhere, it's cold."

Tracy turns off the TV. "It's only a phase, a bump in the road," she says. "Every relationship has them. You two are meant to be together. I know it. You know it, too."

I nod.

"And besides," she continues, "your horoscope says that you can work through this rough patch and come out stronger."

I force a smile, then turn to the door. It's Cade, looking sheepish in the doorway. "Hi," he says, running his hand through his hair. "I'm so sorry I'm late." He walks toward me and places a quick peck on my lips. I smell alcohol on his breath and turn away from him.

"I'll just head out for a bit and . . . let you two talk," Tracy says, standing up and reaching for her sweater before going out the door.

"Baby," Cade says, taking my hand. "My meeting ran late, and then Steve from Everland—you know that band we just signed—stopped into the office, so I took him out for a drink, and I—"

"Cade," I say, "it's fine."

"But it's not," he says tenderly. "I can tell."

I sigh, looking out over the city. The maple tree with its brilliant orange leaves practically looks on fire on the street below. My heart actually feels on fire. I turn to face the man I love. "You seem off lately," I say. "You've been late to everything we've planned to do, and it just seems, well, that maybe you're losing interest in me . . . losing interest in us."

"Oh, Kailey," he says, his eyes narrowing, concern washing over his face. "That's so far from the truth."

"Then how can you explain it?"

"I'm just overwhelmed, I guess."

"With work?"

He furrows his brow. "Yes. And other things."

"Like what?"

He looks away. "Nothing to worry about."

"Cade, tell me," I say.

"Listen," he says, raising his voice a decibel. "Trust me when I tell you not to worry." He stands up and walks to the window. "I don't want to involve you in something that . . ." He pauses, then turns back to me. "Oh, baby, I'm so sorry. My tone, it sounds terrible. Forgive me."

I nod, feeling tears well up.

Cade kneels beside me. "I promise," he says, "just give me a little more time and things will be better."

He reaches for my hand, and I let him take it.

"Whatever you're going through," I say, "I'm here. Just please don't shut me out."

"How could I ever do that?" he asks.

But I fear he already has.

nineteen

NOVEMBER 26, 2008

Cade sits quietly with Eddie on the couch. Earlier, I called Dr.
Branson and learned that he can move into his new apartment in the brain injury program as soon as the day after
tomorrow. And while it's good news, I hate the idea of seeing him go,
and the unsettling feeling of knowing that without my protection he
could just get up and leave and disappear again for a day, a year, or
maybe even forever.

I sit beside him and notice how he continually brushes his long
hair from his eyes. I remember the electric clipper upstairs in the bathroom cabinet. Ryan occasionally uses it to trim his sideburns. I run
upstairs to find it, along with a pair of haircutting scissors.

"Let's give you a haircut," I say to Cade, smiling.

He gives me a confused look.

"I can do it," I say, pulling out a chair from the table. "In the
kitchen."

He doesn't move from the couch, so I walk to him and take his hand. "I'll be gentle, I promise."

Cautiously he follows me to the kitchen and sits in the chair placed on the tile floor. I drape a towel around his shoulders and plug in the clippers, remembering the way Cade's hair used to be. Short up the sides and a little longer on top. He flinches a little when I run a comb through it. "It's okay," I whisper, first cutting off some of the length before shaving up the sides. His brown hair falls to the floor in clumps. He sits still, hands in his lap, as I snip and trim and comb his hair into submission. I move to his beard next. "Let's just get this trimmed up a bit."

He doesn't protest as I run the clippers over his face, freeing inches of coarse facial hair. I brush off the hairs from the back of his neck and set the towel aside, then step back and have a look. He stands and runs his hands through his hair, then touches his face. The transformation brings me to tears, and when he catches his reflection in the mirror on the wall he looks deeply moved, as if he's seen a ghost. A ghost from his past.

"You look … great," I say, equally if not more moved. "Just as I remember you."

He continues to stare at his reflection as I sweep up the hair on the floor and tuck the haircutting supplies back in the case. There's a stack of dishes in the sink, but I don't feel like dealing with them right now. Instead I walk to the record player, the one that made Ryan affectionately roll his eyes. A carryover from my days with Cade, who swore that everything sounded better on vinyl. I rarely use it anymore, but I can't bear to part with it. Even if my old records, precariously balanced on a bookshelf, do nothing but collect dust, their mere presence gives me comfort.

I select my favorite Mazzy Star album, *So Tonight That I Might See,* and pull it out of its sleeve, setting the needle to the first track. The opening notes of "Fade into You" take me back twelve years to the night I met Cade. I don't expect him to remember. Maybe he does.

Maybe he doesn't. But I do. And as I rock slowly, I remember the way he took my hand that night and led me backstage so we could watch together. I remember the way he looked at me. The way time passed so quickly in his presence. I close my eyes tightly, then reopen them when I feel his hand on my waist. At first I think it must be a dream, that I imagine his touch. But then he places his other hand on my waist and turns me around to face him. And when my eyes meet his, I can see his tears. His hands are still on my waist, and my arms, operating on instinct or muscle memory, move upward. I slide my hands up his chest, then to his thin shoulders, until my arms are draped around his neck. He pulls me even closer as we sway to the music, one track after the next, locked in this embrace, holding each other.

I know I should pull back. He's too ill to know what he's doing. Too lost. But this moment feels too real to deny. He holds me just like he used to. I want to say a thousand things to him. *You remember, don't you, Cade? Do you know how hard it was for me when you disappeared? Do you know how I mourned you? I didn't ever stop mourning you. I didn't ever stop loving you. Do you know that, Cade? And now you're here, and you're holding me in my living room. And I don't know what the hell to do. I'm scared—terrified, really. For you, for me, for the life I've built while you were gone, which feels like it's about to come crashing down.*

These thoughts swirl around me like dandelion seeds in the wind, free and wild. And I'm suspended, too. I'm somewhere between two worlds, one foot in each, one heart pulled in two directions.

I lift my head from Cade's chest and look at him for a moment. "The other day," I say, "you said you remembered. Cade, I have to know. Do you really? Do you really know me? Do you remember the life we had together, the life we planned together?"

Tears stream down my cheeks now, and he tenderly wipes them away and nods.

Just then I hear a key in the door. Startled, I turn around to find Ryan standing, suitcase in hand, in the entryway, mouth agape.

"Ryan?" I step back, falling out of Cade's embrace.

"Kailey, what's going on?"

"Uh, well, I, you see—" I look at Cade, then back at Ryan.

He sets his bag down. "I definitely *see*." He remains on the tile in the entryway, as if there's some invisible and impermeable line between us that he cannot cross.

"Ryan, this is Cade," I say.

"Cade," he says, nodding. "Of course."

"Ryan, it's not like that," I say. "He's been on the streets. He suffered a significant brain injury."

Ryan gives Cade a long look. "This is the guy from in front of the restaurant. The one who practically accosted my mom?" Ryan nods. "That explains things."

"Ryan," I plead. "He needs our help."

"Sure he does," he says, rubbing his forehead. "And I see you're doing a great job *helping* him."

"I got him into a program at Harborview for people with traumatic brain injuries." I turn to Cade, who's now staring at his feet, and I hate this. I hate this confrontation for Ryan, but especially for Cade. "He's going to be admitted Friday. He just needed a place to stay in the interim."

Ryan shakes his head. "And you kept all of this from me?"

"I was going to tell you," I say. "I just needed to find the right time. I feared you'd react . . . like this."

Ryan sighs. "Like this? Kailey, how do you expect me to act? We're getting married, and you can't bring yourself to mail the save-the-date cards. I feel like I don't even know you anymore." He brandishes his keys.

"Don't go," I say, taking a step toward him. I feel like I'm caught between two crumbling worlds and I am powerless to save either one.

Ryan pauses for a long moment, gazing at me with those handsome eyes. Waiting.

"I'm going," he finally says in a quiet, defeated voice. "I'll stay at my friend Matt's until we figure all of this out."

"Ryan, please," I plead. "I have nothing to hide."

He looks at me, then Cade, and his face says everything. "Nothing to hide?" He shakes his head. "Oh, my dear Kailey, you've been hiding from the very thing you can't ever escape: the truth. It's time you face it, even if it breaks my heart to watch you do it." He reaches for his suitcase. "Good night."

Cade stands behind me as I stare at the closed door, wondering if I should run after him, plead with him to stay, to understand. Surely he can understand. But my legs won't move, and my voice, well, it's been swallowed up. I am paralyzed, and I fall to my knees and weep. I feel as if I'm drowning in my own sorrows, unable to stay afloat. Then Cade places his hand, like a life raft, on my shoulder.

Ryan doesn't answer his phone that night; the next morning I call his friend Matt, who will be the best man in our wedding.

"Matt, it's Kailey," I say. "Is Ryan with you?"

"He was," he says. "He said that if he can't be with you, he wanted to be alone."

"So I'm guessing he told you about . . ."

"He did," Matt says.

"I was going to tell him myself, but he came home early from his trip, and the way it went down . . ." I sigh. "Oh, Matt, the timing couldn't have been worse."

"Kailey," he says, "you're really going to leave him for a . . . home-less guy?"

"First of all," I say, "I'm not leaving him. And Cade isn't just some homeless guy. He's my ex-boyfriend. I spent two years with him."

"So you can see why Ryan's devastated," Matt says.

"I know," I say. "It's a mess, and I want to make it right. But I do have to help Cade. He has no one." I lower my voice so as not to wake Cade, who's still asleep upstairs. "He's only been staying with me be-cause he has nowhere else to go. Tomorrow I'm taking him to Harbor-view. He's being admitted into a program for people with brain injuries. He'll live there, supervised by experts who can help him get his life back in order. He's going to have to relearn almost everything."

"I understand," Matt says. "And I'm not judging you, Kailey. It's just that . . ."

"Ryan's your best friend," I say. "I know. Please know that I never wanted to hurt him."

"Thanks," he says before hanging up.

On Friday I select a fresh change of clothes from Ryan's closet and help Cade dress. He's silent in the car as I drive to Harborview, and I am, too.

"Good morning," Dr. Branson says when we reach the second floor. We spoke a few times earlier in the week about Cade when she called to check on him. "This is my assistant, Tess. We'll take you over now, if you're ready."

I nod for both of us, and we walk down a long hallway to a different set of elevators.

"I'm assuming you will be his emergency contact?" Tess asks, glancing at the clipboard in her hands.

"Emergency? What emergencies?"

"Just a precaution," she says, "in case something happens, like a patient wanders off. As I briefed you on the phone, TBI patients are prone to volatile behavior."

"Oh, sure," I say, swallowing hard as we reach the ground floor and walk outside to a pathway that leads to what looks like a brick office building. "Yes, of course, you can put my name down."

Dr. Branson points to the building ahead. "Here we are," she says, smiling. "The Edward Miller Center for Brain Injury Treatment and Recovery." She turns to Cade. "This will be your home for the year to come. You'll have your own apartment. In fact"—she points to the corner window on the top floor—"I believe that one right there is yours."

He looks up, then at me. I can't tell if he's scared or confused or both.

"The facility is staffed twenty-four/seven, and each day you'll have a series of talk and physical therapy, brain scans, and rigorous rehabilitation to help you relearn everything you lost after your injury." She places her hand on Cade's arm. "We intend to help you get your life back."

The elevator lurches up, and we step out on the third floor. Tess walks ahead to a door marked 304, and inserts a key. We follow her inside the studio apartment. It's small, and the air smells of Windex and floor wax—certainly a far cry from Cade's Pioneer Square apartment, but it's clean and sunny, and the high ceilings mitigate the boxy layout.

I watch Cade walk the perimeter of his new home, first stopping at the twin bed with simple white hospital-grade linens, then turning to the brown love seat and coffee table. The tiny kitchen consists of a sink, some cabinets, and a mini fridge.

"For the safety of all, we insist that our residents refrain from using ovens or stoves during their tenure in the program. All meals are provided in the first-floor cafeteria. Breakfast is served at eight, lunch at noon, and dinner at five sharp."

"I hope he will thrive here," Dr. Branson says to me.

"Me too," I say.

"Now," she continues, "it's time for you to say your goodbyes. He has a full day today. Orientation, meeting his occupational and physical therapists. A team of neurologists will be here at two for an evaluation. The idea is to establish a baseline so we can monitor his progress over time."

I nod and take a step back.

"It's always hard to leave them," Dr. Branson says. "But I promise he's in excellent hands here."

"Thank you," I say, glancing at Cade once more before turning to the door. He's at the window, looking at Seattle's Capitol Hill neighborhood, an expanse of record stores. The Space Needle pokes up over the cityscape. "I'll come by tomorrow and check on you."

He stares ahead; I'm not sure if he hears me. Tracy is right. As much as I yearn to keep him hidden away from the world so as not to lose him again, I need to set him free. And this is the safest place to do that. But as I take the elevator to the ground floor and find my way back to my car in the parking garage, I can't help but feel as if I've left a piece of myself in apartment 304.

I drive through Pioneer Square. The second article in the series has stirred up even more passionate debate than the first, but that doesn't change the fact that there are still too many people on the streets with nowhere to go. The third article, profiling the developers and their proposed "displacement packages," was all facts and figures. Yet I haven't yet managed to complete the piece on Cade. The article is unfinished because Cade's story is unfinished. But slowly I am writing it. It's always on my mind, as is he.

I'm so lost in thought, I hardly remember sitting in traffic, or merging onto I-5, or taking the Forty-fifth Street exit home. But when I park on the street, my heart warms at the sight of Ryan's car.

"Hi," I say from the entryway, where he stood last night with a face that looked as if his world was crashing down.

"Hi," he replies, glancing up from his laptop at the kitchen table.

"I didn't expect to find you here," I say.

He stares at me for a long moment, then stands to walk to me. "Kailey, I've had a chance to think," he says. "I'm hurt, but I may have overreacted the other night." He takes a deep breath. "How can I fault you for the things I love most about you? You are generous and kind. You care deeply about people. And you are loyal."

My eyes well up with tears as he takes my hands.

"The past is hard to face, but it's just that: the past. And you have pledged your future to me. If you still feel the same way, I'd like to continue that journey to the future, because I love you. Plain and simple. I love you more than I've loved anyone. And I'm willing to see you through this. I'm willing to give you the time and space you need." He looks at me intensely, eyes ablaze. I know he's hurting. I know he's frightened. "What I'm trying to tell you is that I want to marry you no matter what. I want to love you and take care of you and spend my life with you. And I don't think your past, or mine, should complicate that."

I nod, falling into his embrace and letting my tears spill out. "Oh, Ryan," I say.

He holds me for a long moment, then pulls my face upward so that my eyes meet his. "I think we should take a trip together," he says.

"What do you mean?"

"Five days in Mexico," he says. "I was just checking flights and hotels. I can book us at the Pedregal, that resort I showed you in *Travel and Leisure* recently, remember? Every room has its own infinity plunge pool. We can sleep late, and drink margaritas by the pool, and while the days away napping and talking and getting massages." He smiles. "We could leave in a week or two. How does that sound?"

"Wonderful," I say. "But can we really get away? We both have so much going on at work, and . . ." I think of Cade just starting out in his new apartment. Can I leave him? Will he be okay?

Ryan silences my worries with a long, passionate kiss. "We'll make this our holiday celebration, and we have so much to be grateful for," he says. And when he pulls me closer to him with the strong arms that have comforted me and loved me for so many years, I melt into his embrace.

"Okay," I whisper. I close my eyes as his lips move from my face to my neck to my shoulder.

twenty

DECEMBER 31, 1997

"Y ou look like a total babe," Tracy says from the doorway
of the bathroom, where I'm applying glittery gray eye
shadow to my lids.

"Aww, thanks," I reply, turning around. "Do you
think this dress is too . . . ?"

"No, Cade is going to *love* you in it," she says.

Black, fitted, and covered in sparkly sequins, it was on a sale rack at
Nordstrom last week and I bought it on a whim. But I feel like an im-
postor somehow.

"Really?" I ask, tugging at the waist. What I don't tell her is that
I'm doubting everything from my dress to Cade's love. He's been so
distant lately, so . . . not himself.

"Trust me," Tracy says. "You are going to be the hottest girl at the
party."

"Well, next to you," I say with a grin.

She looks down at her red sleeveless dress and shrugs. "We'll see if Mark even notices."

I knew they were having trouble of late, but I was happy to hear he would be joining us for Cade's annual Element Records party.

"He will notice," I say. "You look beyond gorgeous tonight."

She takes a long look at herself in the mirror over my shoulder, tapping her fingers to the imaginary bags under her eyes. "It's hard to date in medical school," she says. "It's all one exhausting and emotional blur." She sighs, then laughs. "Maybe I should have ended up with Wes."

"The Mormon?"

"Yeah," she says nostalgically. "He was in love with me."

"But you weren't in love with him," I say with a smirk.

"But he was so handsome, and so . . . nice."

"Mormons are very nice."

She nods. "But he had braces."

"The poor guy," I say. "Didn't he leave on his mission only to come home and be dumped by you?"

"A solid two years in Jackson, Alabama, yes," she says, deep in thought. "But he was a terrible kisser."

"The braces," we both say at the same time, bursting into laughter.

"Ready?" I say, brushing my hair a final time, then pulling it back into a tidy low ponytail.

Tracy looks at her watch. "Yeah, Mark gets off in an hour. He'll meet us there."

We'd walk, except we're in heels, and it's one of those miserably frigid days when it's cold enough to snow but the atmosphere doesn't quite have what it takes, so Tracy hails a cab outside the apartment. When we arrive at Cade's, it's five after eight, and about a dozen people have already arrived.

"Hello, gorgeous," he says, making a beeline to the door when he sees me walk in. "You look unbelievable."

"Thanks," I say, grinning.

His apartment has been transformed into party central. The furniture has been pushed aside to make room for dancing, with a strobe light and glitter ball adding to the effect. A bartender stands at attention in Cade's kitchen, and one of the interns from Element (I think his name is Tom or Tony) is manning the stereo.

"I have a surprise for you," he says, motioning me to the kitchen.

I follow him around the corner, where a couple of women with bleached-blond hair are kneeling down beside a black Lab puppy.

"Happy early birthday," he says, smiling.

My eyes widen. "Cade!"

"You always said you wanted a black Lab, and, well, I wanted to get you one."

I kneel down, tears in my eyes.

"I thought we could raise him . . . together."

The puppy nuzzles my face as I lean toward him. "Hello, little fellow."

Cade kneels down beside me as the blond women look on, smiling. "What should we call him?"

"Eddie," I say, lifting him into my arms.

"Eddie it is, then," he says with a smile.

After a few minutes, more people arrive, and I suggest that we keep Eddie in the guest bedroom. The commotion of the party might be too much for him.

"What would you like to drink?" Cade asks after settling the puppy with a bowl of water and a few blankets.

We meet Tracy at the bar. She asks for a martini, and I decide on the same. Cade stows our coats and purses in his closet, and we make small talk with a few Element employees as more people arrive, old friends of Cade's, musicians from bands I've never heard of and a few I have, like Dave Grohl from the Foo Fighters, who introduces himself to Tracy and me and throws down a shot of Jägermeister. And then James and Alexis walk in. James looks distracted and tired, as if this is a check-the-box event that he'd like to hurry up and get over with. If Alexis feels the same way, however, she doesn't show it. She smiles at me.

"Hi," I say, waving. James's frown softens when he sees me, and he and Alexis walk over to us from the bar.

"Happy New Year," James says, holding up his martini glass for me to clink.

"James and Alexis, this is my roommate, Tracy," I say.

"Nice to meet you," James says.

Cade is across the room switching the record, and when our eyes meet, he gives me a knowing smile.

Tracy presses her hand to her chest. "I love this album."

"Me too," Alexis says. "Neil Young is so timeless."

I clear my throat. "You mean Harry Nilsson, right?"

Alexis's cheeks turn pink. "Oh, yes, right," she says.

"I mean, I suppose they sound a little alike," I say, helping her save face.

"Neil Young and Harry Nilsson?" Cade chuckles. "Hardly."

I give him a stern look. "Well, they do have that seventies sound."

James smiles as Alexis's eyes dart around the room. I can't tell if she's mortally wounded or just a teeny bit embarrassed. Her expression gives nothing away.

"How long have you two been dating?" Tracy asks, doing her best to break the ice.

Alexis opens her mouth, but James talks over her. "About a year," he says.

"And what do you do?" Alexis asks, changing the subject. Her eyes follow Cade to the bar.

"I'm in my residency at the University of Washington Medical Center," she says.

I grin. "Dr. Greenfield will see you now."

James laughs, but Alexis's face remains unchanged. "That's fantastic," he says. "I can't even begin to imagine how intense medical school must be."

Tracy nods. "It's intense. In fact, it's a pure miracle that I even got the night off to be here."

"I'm glad you were able to come," James says, pointing to her glass. "You're empty. Let's get you a refill." Tracy smiles, looks at me, then walks to the bar with James. Alexis trails behind distractedly.

Cade returns and kisses my cheek. "How's my girl?" His words slur together a little. He has another drink in his hand, and I've seen him down at least six. But I need to let Cade enjoy the night; it's New Year's Eve.

I glance at the bar and watch James laughing with Tracy, who looks a bit uncomfortable. He touches his hand to her back once, then her arm.

"James, what a player. It's beyond me," Cade says, just as Alexis appears beside us.

"Sorry," Cade says quickly. "I—"

"It's okay," Alexis says, unfazed. If she's hurt by her boyfriend's behavior, she doesn't show it in the slightest.

"Great party," she says, glancing directly at Cade. She looks pretty in her black dress and maroon Doc Martens.

"Can I get you a drink?" Cade asks.

She smiles. "A stiff one."

He grins, then turns to me. "Kailey?"

"I'm okay," I say.

"Well," he continues, "I need another." Alexis follows him to the bar, and I feel a twinge of jealousy when I see Cade touch her shoulder. Silly, I know. Cade would never cheat on me, much less with Alexis, and yet I can't deny my feelings of insecurity lately. Our connection, so strong for so long, feels weakened somehow, like a heartbeat growing fainter, and I can't figure out why.

I haven't wanted to face it, or even talk to Tracy about it, but I'm worried about Cade. He's seemed more anxious than usual, and his drinking has gone from occasional to frequent.

I walk to the bar and nestle my hand around his waist. Alexis turns her gaze from Cade to her drink and takes a long sip. "I'll have another of the same," Cade says to the bartender. "Actually, make it a double."

James gives Cade a disapproving look. "What is this, man, number four? Or is it five?"

"What's it to you?" Cade replies. "I didn't know you were counting."

"It's a lot of booze," James says. "Just saying, man."

"Just saying what?"

James puffs up his chest. "Just saying that maybe if you stopped drinking so much, you could actually come into the office once in a while and, I don't know, maybe get some work done."

"How dare you," Cade says, taking a step closer. "I work my ass off, and you know that."

James shrugs. "When you're not drunk."

Cade lunges at his friend. "No," I say, placing my hand on his chest. All eyes in the room are on the two of them. "Cade, no. Don't do this."

He looks at me, then takes a step back. Before I can stop him, he bursts through the crowd of people, grabs his leather jacket, and leaves.

"What was that all about?" Tracy asks, finding me a moment later, leaving James and Alexis in the corner of the room.

"Cade and James have a lot of bad blood between them right now," I explain.

"Why?"

I shrug. "They have entirely different ideas about how to run the company; it's really come to a head lately."

Tracy and I mingle, and talk, and drink. I look at the door every few minutes, hoping Cade will return. And when he doesn't, I start to get nervous.

I check on Eddie in the bedroom, find his leash so that I can take him out. "I'm going to go look for Cade outside," I say to Tracy. I find my coat and walk out to the sidewalk. The air is bitter cold as I make my way down the alley and up the block. Cade is around the corner, sitting on a bench talking to a homeless man.

"Oh, there you are," I say to him, letting Eddie sniff around a frozen patch of earth and relieve himself.

"Hi," he says. "Sorry. I had to get out of there."

"Is it James?"

Cade shrugs. "Ivan," he says to the homeless man, now wearing Cade's leather jacket. As he speaks, his breath sends out puffs of steam, and I reflexively bounce in place to stay warm. "This is my girlfriend, Kailey."

"Pleased to meet you," the old man says, flashing a toothless smile.

"You too," I say with a smile, blowing warm air into my hands, then turning to Cade again. "Shouldn't we get back? It's getting late."

Cade throws back the remaining drink in his glass as Ivan takes a swig from a bottle in a brown paper bag. "I can't stand it anymore," Cade says. "All those people in there. The company we built. It's turning into something I despise."

"But Element is your dream," I say.

"I love the company I started." He points down the block toward his apartment. "But that? Did you see the people in there? Rich guys with their coked-out girlfriends." He shakes his head. "That's not the kind of Element Records I know and love."

"Then change it," I say.

"I'm afraid that's a battle I can no longer win," he replies.

"Well, that's a Cade I don't know, then. You're someone who doesn't take no for an answer. You're someone who fights for what he believes in. You don't give up. That's not you. So don't give up now."

The corners of his mouth form a brief smile as I reach for his hand. "Now, come on," I say. "Let's go back inside. Let's put this all behind us and go make a New Year's toast."

He stumbles to his feet. "I guess this is good night, Ivan," he says.

Ivan grunts in return and then chuckles.

"Aren't you going to take your coat back?" I whisper.

"Nah," Cade says. "He needs it more than I do."

My words must have had an effect on Cade, because when we return to the party, he snaps back, immediately beginning a conversation with some musicians by the door. I squeeze his hand, then move through the partygoers to find Tracy. I love how Cade can work a room. I love how everyone wants to talk to him but that he'll always circle back to me. I watch each guest in turn light up as he greets them, offering a kind word for their latest song, thanking them for celebrating with him. When my eyes meet his, I love the fluttery feeling deep inside.

Tracy glances nervously at her watch. By eleven-thirty, she's looking at me tearfully. "He's not coming. I know it."

"He probably just got caught at the hospital," I say. "Or maybe . . ."

Tracy shakes her head, then takes a long sip of her drink. "If he really wanted to be here, he'd be here."

Before I can respond, I hear a scuffle at the door, followed by someone shouting.

Tracy and I turn around to see a circle of men, young, dressed as if they just stepped offstage at a punk rock show. At its center, Cade is slowly picking himself up from the floor. Without hesitation, I run to him.

"What happened?" I cry.

He touches his hand to his lip. "Nothing important. They're gone."

"Cade, who are they?"

"Band guys," he says. "It doesn't matter. They're not welcome here again."

"You're bleeding, Cade."

Tracy runs to the kitchen and returns with a paper towel and ice. "Hold this on it."

I help him to his feet. "Cade, I'm worried about you," I whisper.

"It's no big deal," he says. "Let's not let this ruin our New Year's Eve."

"Okay," I say reluctantly. The door opens, and Mark appears. Tracy runs to him.

"Hi," I say to Mark a moment later. He looks tired, or distant, or sheepish, or all three.

"Crazy night at the hospital," he says. "Sorry I'm late." He turns to Cade. "Hey, man, good to see you."

Cade nods distractedly, then catches someone's eye across the room and waves. Tracy returns from the bar with a drink and offers it to Mark. "Nah," he says. "I don't think I'm going to drink tonight. In fact,

I really should get back to the hospital. I just, uh, wanted to come wish you a Happy New Year."

Tracy sets his drink down on a side table. She looks deflated, as does Alexis, standing beside James a few feet away.

Cade reaches for two champagne glasses and hands me one. He looks exhausted, mentally and physically. There's a hollowness to his gaze that I don't recognize. He's had way too much to drink, and when he stumbles as he nestles in closer to me, I feel a lump in my throat. He's standing beside me, and yet somehow it feels like he's not even here.

Ten, nine, eight. I look at Cade. *Seven, six, five.* My heart aches. *Four, three, two.* And just like that, one year ends and another begins.

twenty-one

O utside my kitchen window, the light filters through the cherry tree, casting a jagged shadow on the sidewalk, menacing and dark. I'm struck by the duality of life—the way the world can be both beautiful and cruel.

Today. The anniversary of . . . I blink back tears, remembering. When I let myself face the memories buried so deep in the annals of my brain, it's all there. The color of the paint in that little hospital room with its shabby white curtain separating the two beds, threadbare at the edges. These memories, the ones I've long since hoped to banish, still linger stubbornly. Maybe they always will. I take a deep breath and make a double shot of espresso from the fancy new machine Ryan's parents sent.

I reach for my keys and drive to Harborview to see Cade.

From the doorway, I watch him eating breakfast with two other residents in the cafeteria. He looks stronger, more alert somehow, when a staff member comes to his table to check on him. I take a few steps inside, pausing a moment to quietly listen to their interaction.

"Do you have any hot sauce, by chance?" he asks.

The cafeteria employee smiles. "Is Tabasco okay?"

Cade pauses and smiles. "I used to love Tabasco."

I smile to myself. *Cade and spicy food.*

"Look at him," Dr. Branson says, leaning over my shoulder.

I beam as I watch him proudly, amazed at how far he's come. There is strength in his eyes, strength that hasn't been there in a very long time.

"He has a long way to go yet, but he's making excellent progress," Dr. Branson says, echoing my thoughts. "We've put him on a new medication. It's an off-label use of the drug, but there was a study out last year showing that it could be a very effective novel treatment for TBI patients. It's too early to know if this will be the key for him, but his brain scans show measurable improvement."

"I'm so happy to hear that," I say. "I'm leaving for Mexico tomorrow. Can I see him for a bit?"

She looks at her watch, then nods. "Yes, as a matter of fact he has the morning free."

"Also," I say, "I wonder if I might take him to see an old friend."

"Who is this friend?" she asks.

"His childhood best friend and former business partner," I say.

"I don't know," Dr. Branson says. "That's a tough call. If this person has any association with traumatic incidents in his past, well, then I wouldn't advise it."

"But that's just the thing," I say. "I don't know what happened to Cade, and meeting with James might help us find out."

"Then I'll leave the decision to you," Dr. Branson says. "Part of recovery is reentering the world. We can't shield our patients from the hard things in life." She pauses. "Just use your discretion here."

I thank her and wait for Cade to finish his breakfast. When he walks out to the hallway, I catch his eye. "Hi," I say.

"Hi," he replies.

I hold up a paper shopping bag. "I brought you a few things."

"Thanks," he says.

I look ahead to the elevator down the hall. "Do you want to go up to your apartment and we'll drop this bag off?"

He nods, and together we make our way upstairs in the elevator to the third floor. The sun streams through the big windows inside his little room, and I sit down on the love seat while Cade sits on the edge of the bed.

"How are you enjoying the program?" I ask. When the words formed in my head, they sounded normal. But they come out sounding awkward and patronizing.

He nods his response.

"I've been so worried about you," I say. "And I'm hoping this was a good choice for you. You like it here, right?"

"Yes," he says.

"I'm so glad," I say, beaming. "I hoped you would."

I set the bag down on his counter. "Before long, you're going to start remembering. You're going to get your life back, Cade. I know it." I remove clothes from the bag—two pairs of jeans, a sweater, and three T-shirts—and place them in a neat stack on the coffee table. "Speaking of that," I continue. "I thought we might go see James today. Your old friend."

Cade appears unfazed by the name. "James," he says, as if trying out the word for size.

"You two grew up together," I explain. "He was your business partner."

Cade nods.

"Dr. Branson indicated that you were hospitalized back in 1998, and according to the medical records, someone apparently refused further treatment for your injuries."

Cade sits quietly.

"I know this all must be a lot to take in, but I thought if we saw him, we might jog your memory a bit."

"Okay," Cade says.

• • •

We drive until we hit Fourth, and find parking on the street. "James's office is on the seventh floor."

Cade looks up at the building cautiously, and I squeeze his hand. "It'll be okay," I say.

We make our way up in the elevator, and it stops with a jerk. I'm relieved to note the absence of the surly bow-tied assistant from the reception desk. We're clear to proceed.

"He's just down this way," I say to Cade. James's office is in view. He's on the phone, seated at his desk, his back facing the glass door.

"Knock knock," I say, opening the door and poking my head in.

James turns around, and when he sees Cade, his eyes widen. "I'm going to have to call you back," he says, quickly ending the call. "Kailey and . . . Cade, wow. I . . ."

"Here he is," I say, smiling.

James walks to Cade and extends his hand, then laughs awkwardly and opens his arms to embrace his old friend. Cade's arms remain stiffly at his sides.

"It's been so long," he says. "How are you?"

Cade just stares ahead.

"You look good, man," he says. "After Kailey told me about your . . . predicament, well, I guess I expected things to be . . . different."

"Cade is in a rehabilitation program," I say, "at Harborview."

James's eyes flash. "Well, that's great. I'm glad to hear you're getting some help. If I can do anything for you, man, just let me know."

He speaks faster than usual, and I'm surprised by his offer to help Cade, given my last visit, when he seemed put out by the very idea of his old friend being in Seattle.

If Cade is listening, he doesn't let on. Instead, he walks to the wall of James's office, where he pores over the array of framed photos and mementos. Beautiful family portraits. Certificates of achievement. James shaking hands with George W. Bush. I notice Cade's eyes stop when he sees the photo of Alexis and James on their yacht. I remember seeing it the last time I was here, and I can easily imagine all the fun they've had sipping champagne when Cade was huddled beside some rusty dumpster on Fourth Avenue.

"James, I do want to ask you about something," I say.

"Sure," he replies.

I lower my voice. "Cade's doctor checked the back records, and it seems that someone matching his description was admitted to Harborview in August 1998 with significant trauma. He was in a coma for some time but ended up leaving the hospital." I take a deep breath.

James shrugs.

I eye him skeptically. "James, is there something you haven't told me?" Cade is still staring at the wall of photos. "Please," I continue, in almost a whisper, "you once loved him like a brother. I'm just trying to help him get his life back in order. Can you help me?"

James walks around his desk to a side drawer and pulls out a checkbook. "Sure," he says. "How much do you need? Maybe a down payment for a car so he can drive to a job? Grocery money? What's your amount?"

I shake my head. "I didn't come here for your money," I say. "I came here genuinely hoping that you could help sort out what happened to him."

James shakes his head. "I'll tell you what happened to him. Your boyfriend cracked up. He had a nervous breakdown and left Element Records in shambles when he did. He didn't even protest when we offered him the buyout package. He wanted out, just as I told you. I was the one who had to pick up the pieces and salvage whatever could be salvaged, which, let me tell you, wasn't much. And you waltz in here and act as if I owe him something? Well, I'm sorry, Kailey, but I just don't buy it."

"Shhh," I say, pulling his arm until he's out in the hallway. "He's not deaf. He *hears*."

"Well then, let him hear," James says.

I close the door behind us.

"Cade McAllister," James continues, saying the name as if it's up in lights. His voice is tinged with equal parts nostalgia and anger. "He could charm the pants off anyone. And he did. He charmed you, didn't he? He always got his way. The company logo. The hiring and the firing. Hell, he even had a pinball machine shipped to our office. It cost six grand. Did he ask me, his *business partner,* for permission? No. He just did it. Do you know what it was like to work with someone like that? It was all I could do to keep the company afloat. And then Cade lost his shit when I confronted him about our financial situation. The record label was going under, but he was in denial about it. He was always in denial."

I shake my head.

"I know you never wanted to believe all of that, but it's the truth," he says.

"Cade really had a nervous breakdown?"

James nods. "I'm sorry to say, he did. It was one of the worst days of my life. Our entire staff saw it. It was the beginning of the end."

"So if you didn't sign him out of the hospital that day, who did?"

James looks exhausted, and for the first time I notice dark circles around his eyes and deep crevices between his eyebrows. "Who knows," he says.

"All right," I say. "We'll go now."

He holds up his checkbook again. "Let me at least write you a check."

"Keep it," I say. "As you say, you've already given enough."

I drive Cade back to his apartment and sit with him on the love seat for a few minutes before his two o'clock session begins.

"I'm sorry about today," I say. "James is : . . well, there is a lot from your past friendship with him that is a bit complicated." I turn to him, but his gaze is fixed out the window. "I suppose that's to be expected when two people run a company together." I pause for a moment. "I was worried about how that interaction would affect you, but I'm trying to find answers for you."

He turns to me and begins to speak. "So he was my friend?"

I'm still getting used to him speaking more than one or two words to me; hearing his voice form a sentence, well, it slays me.

I squeeze his arm. "Yes," I say, smiling. "It's hard to believe, but the two of you were once very close, like brothers."

"I'm trying to remember. But it's so hard."

"Yes." I nod. "I can only imagine what it must be like to lose your memory. It must be so frightening. But look at you. You're here, and you're making progress, and I'm so proud of you."

He smiles. "Proud." He says the word aloud as if trying to understand it.

"Proud," I say.

"Kailey," he says.

My eyes fill with tears.

"I'm remembering."

"I'm so happy. And I will be here with you every step of the way until you're back. And you're going to get back. I know it." I pause for a moment, remembering my trip to Mexico and wishing I didn't have to go. But I promised Ryan. "Cade, I have to go on a trip tomorrow. I'll only be gone five days, and during that time I won't be able to visit you. I . . ."

"Mexico," he says.

I smile. "Mexico."

"I always wanted to take you to Cancún."

My heart leaps as our eyes meet, and somewhere past the veil of brain injury, through the layers of confusion and disorientation, the old Cade is piercing through. For a moment I can see him, that old spark in his eye. For a moment he is himself again.

Just then we hear a knock at the door.

"Come in," I call out. A moment later a man in a suit stands in the doorway. I notice his red bow tie immediately.

"Hello, I'm Dr. Friedman, part of the neurology team," he says, pointing to a badge on a lanyard around his neck. "I'm going to be working with you today, Mr. McAllister."

Cade's eyes widen as he leaps to his feet, looking strangely agitated. With each step Dr. Friedman takes toward Cade, he takes a step back, until his back is wedged against the window.

"Is everything all right, Mr. McAllister?" the doctor asks. He looks at me, then back at Cade.

"No!" Cade screams. "No! Don't. Don't. Don't!"

Cade is suddenly panicked and scared. When Dr. Friedman cautiously takes another step forward, it frightens Cade even more and he sinks to the floor in the fetal position, tucking his knees to his chest and covering his head with his arms.

I rush to his side. "Cade, it's okay," I say. "Dr. Friedman would never hurt you."

"No, no, no!" Cade cries over and over again.

I look up at Dr. Friedman, who is doing his best to remain calm. "He's having an episode," he explains in a steady, slow voice. "It's not unusual for our patients to have lapses in memory, or confusion, or to project a traumatic memory from the past onto a present situation."

"Cade," I whisper, hoping my voice will draw him back to the present and out of whatever horrific place his mind has slipped into. "It's me, Kailey. Dr. Friedman is here, too." He looks up cautiously. "We'll make sure no one hurts you. You don't have to be afraid."

Dr. Friedman gives him an encouraging smile.

"It's okay," I whisper. "I promise."

Cade nods and gets to his feet.

"Great," Dr. Friedman says. "Now, if you're ready, I'll take you down to your appointment."

Cade takes a deep breath, then looks at me a final time.

"You'll be fine," I say, trying to disguise the tremor in my voice. "I'll be back before you know it."

I park the car in the driveway, but instead of going inside the house, I wander down the block, taking in the smells of dinners long since cooked and enjoyed. Stir-fry, maybe, to the right, or perhaps some sort of Asian chicken. Birds flutter in a bush somewhere nearby as I round the corner, passing the house with the little picket fence and the cherry tree with a trunk so big, it looks like it belongs in a forest, not a city neighborhood.

I stop in my tracks when I notice a red ribbon on the pavement, which probably slipped from a little girl's ponytail earlier in the day. I reach down to pick it up, and as I do, my heart is flooded by the memory of Tracy spotting a red ribbon tied to a cherry tree downtown. It was so many years ago, but I can hear her words echoing in my ears, and in my heart: *Tie a red ribbon around a tree branch for your one true love.*

I take a deep breath, then tie the abandoned ribbon on a low-hanging branch. So much has changed since that day, and yet so much has remained the same.

twenty-two

I'm finishing up a column at my office when my phone rings. "Have you taken the test yet?"

I wince. "No," I say. "Not yet."

"Kailey, take it," she says. "It's probably fine. You've been stressed at work. I'm sure that explains it. But you'll feel much better once you know for sure."

I stare at my purse as if it holds a ticking time bomb inside. I confided in Tracy when my period was five days late. Now, on day seven, it still hasn't come. I stopped at the drugstore on my way to work and purchased a pregnancy test. "Okay," I say with a sigh.

"Call me after, okay?"

"Okay," I say, hanging up the phone.

I reach for my purse and wind through the rows of cubicles to the women's restroom down the hall. I haven't told Cade that I'm late. Not yet. Besides, how could I be pregnant? I remembered to take my pills this month, except for one day. And everyone knows that missing one day is no big deal. Or is it?

I stare at the stick, then look away. Three minutes. The results won't be valid until three minutes from now. I take a deep breath as a bit of color, pink, begins to appear on the little window of the stick. One line, then two.

What does this mean?

I scramble to find the instruction pamphlet inside the box. *Does two lines mean pregnant or not pregnant?* My heart beats faster. And then I have my answer.

I am . . . pregnant.

I gasp, clutching the side of the bathroom stall. Pregnant.

I wander back to my desk numbly. I don't call Tracy. I don't call anyone. I just stare at my blank computer screen until the phone rings, and rings, and rings, and rings.

Al, the copy editor in the office next to mine, calls over the divider, "You going to get that?"

"Oh," I say, as if coming out of a trance. "Yes, sorry."

"Hello?" I say robotically.

"Kailey, it's James."

I sit up in my chair.

"Yes, hi, James."

"Do you have a minute to talk?"

"What is it?"

"The company's board met today, and we're all in agreement that Cade should no longer be a part of Element Records."

I shake my head. "What board? Cade never mentioned a board."

"That's just it," James says. "We've always had a board. But Cade never cared about those details, important details that make or break a company."

"Regardless," I say, "what in the world do you mean about voting Cade out of Element?"

"Kailey, surely you're aware of his drinking problem," he says.

"Yes, he has a few too many sometimes," I say, "but I don't know that I'd call it a *problem*. He still works harder than anyone, James. And he's constantly at shows, constantly doing work for Element."

He clears his throat. "I didn't want to have to tell you this, but—"

"Tell me what?"

"The thing is, Cade has developed a pill addiction."

"Pills? What are you talking about? Cade is completely antidrug. I've never seen him take anything."

"Then he does a damn good job of keeping it from you."

"I don't believe this," I continue. "How do you know?"

"One of the interns found a stash of Vicodin and Percocet in his drawer. She was looking for a stapler and instead discovered a year's worth of narcotics."

"This makes no sense," I say, but at the same time I worry that it does. Cade hasn't been himself lately. I asked him why his hands were shaking the other day. He said it was just low blood sugar, but could it have been because of drug use?

"I know," James replies. "But what also doesn't make sense is allowing this pattern of behavior to continue."

"Did you talk to him about it?"

"I did," he says. "Of course he denied everything."

"Well, maybe someone set him up?"

"Impossible," James continues. "I know this is hard to take, but I wanted you to know so you could be there for him after we dissolve the partnership."

"James, please," I plead. "You can't do this."

"I have to," he says. "The company leadership voted, and we've decided to buy him out. It won't be much, but then again Element isn't worth much right now."

"There's no way he's going to agree to that," I say.

"We're going to strongly encourage him otherwise," James replies. "Maybe you could encourage him, too?"

"Encourage him to give up the company he founded for pennies on the dollar?"

"Cade's time at Element has come to an end," James says. "He can either take our buyout package or he can drain his savings and hash this out in court, where any reasonable judge will see that his actions have hurt the business. Kailey, the label has grown into something that Cade doesn't even want anymore. He should go on to do things he loves." He sighs. "And he should get some help."

I place my hand on my belly lightly and keep the phone to my ear until I hear the operator's recorded voice: "If you'd like to make a call, please hang up and try again."

I don't bother to call before driving over to Cade's apartment. What has happened to him? To us? Surely, we can make a plan. If he needs help, I'll stand by his side. My mind churns with ideas about rehab and talking James out of this ridiculous buyout scenario. And the baby . . . We are having a baby. We'll talk about that, too. We'll talk about everything.

I feel a surge of nausea as I park my car and round the block to Cade's place. It's well after noon, and when he shows up at the door his eyes are bleary and there's a crease from a pillow on his cheek, making it obvious that he's just rolled out of bed.

"What time is it?" he asks, rubbing his eyes groggily.

"Almost *one,*" I say. I hate that my words sound accusatory, like I'm a bitter wife, but I'm jarred by my conversation with James.

"It was a late night," he says, yawning.

"So you went out last night?"

"Yeah, just with a few band guys."

"You never called," I say, hurt.

"Sorry, baby," Cade replies, raising a hand to his forehead. "I have a killer headache. You don't have any Advil, do you?"

"No," I say, folding my arms across my chest. "But I hear you might have something heavier in one of your desk drawers at the office."

His face freezes. "So you talked to James."

"I did."

I follow him inside, where he rummages through a cabinet in his kitchen, producing an orange pill bottle. He opens it and pops two tablets into his mouth. "You know I have back pain, Kailey."

I let out a long sigh. "Cade, I don't know what to believe anymore. You stay out late. You drink yourself into a stupor, and then you sleep away the days. You haven't been yourself for months."

He reaches for my waist, but I pull away, pausing when my voice starts to falter. "I don't even know how you feel about . . . me."

He reaches for me again. "Kailey, honey, you know that I love you. I love you more than life itself. Please don't let anything James says make you think otherwise." He cringes at the light streaming through the blinds in his living room. "Damn this headache."

I look away, heart beating fast, thinking about our past, our future, the tiny life growing inside me.

"Look," he says. "I know I need to make some changes, and I will. For you. For us." He rubs the tattoo on his shoulder. "I'll do whatever it takes."

I look away.

"Let's go to Mexico," he says. "Cancún. We could leave next week."

I shake my head. "Mexico? Next week? Cade, I have work. Are you completely out of touch with real life?"

He looks hurt, and I instantly wish I could retract my words. "I mean, I—"

"It's okay," he says. "It's just this city." He pauses and rubs his forehead. "I just need to get away." He looks over his shoulder as if someone might be watching him, which is when I notice a fresh bruise under his left eye.

"What's that?" I ask, touching his face lightly.

"It's nothing," he says, looking away.

"Clearly it's something."

He nods. "I got into it with an old friend."

"Who? Do I know him?"

"It doesn't matter," he says, shaking his head.

"Cade, it does," I say as he pulls me to him. "I'm worried about you."

"Things will get better," he says. "I promise."

I shake my head. "James is going to force you out of the company."

"He's going to do *what*?"

"He said the board agreed, and they're going to offer to buy you out."

Cade's face looks ashen as he sinks into the couch. Eddie leaps onto the cushion beside him. Like a child of divorce, he has spent as much time at my apartment as Cade's.

"They can't make you do anything," I say softly, sitting beside him, then scratching Eddie behind the ears.

Cade just stares ahead. "He's right. I'm a drain to them all," he says. "It would be better if I just left."

"No," I say. "You know that's not true. Cade, you have to—"

We both look up when we hear a knock at the door. Cade doesn't budge, so I answer the door for him. Outside is a woman, barely twenty-one, if that. She smacks her gum, adjusts the pink bra strap on her right shoulder, and looks at me in surprise. "Oh, sorry. I must have the wrong place." She takes a step back, looks at the address on the side of the brick building, then checks the scrap of paper in her hand. "Yep, this is it." She pauses, then laughs to herself. "Wait, you're not his *wife*, are you? Because that would be . . . awkward."

Cade appears behind me.

"Hi," the woman says, taking a step forward.

Cade looks both confused and embarrassed. "I'm sorry," he says. "I don't remember you."

"We met last night," she says. "At the bar. I'm Alicia. You said I could come over and look at your record collection. I love records." She has bleached-blond hair and a bubbly voice, the kind of girl who probably went to church youth group all through high school, then in community college got a nose ring after dating a boy in a band. The easily corruptible type.

"I'm sorry," Cade says again. "I really can't place you. I, I . . ."

"Okay," she says, spitting her gum out onto the sidewalk. "I see that you're . . . busy. Well, you have my number." She points to his pants and smiles. "In your pocket."

He looks down at his pocket, then back at me.

"Call me sometime."

Her words echo, escalating the hurt I feel into a blind rage. I pull Cade back inside.

"In Big Sur, you promised to spend the rest of your life with me. I didn't know that included strangers in pastel lingerie." I reach my hand in the right pocket of his jeans and find the scrap of paper with her number on it. *Call me, Alicia xoxo,* it reads beneath the digits she scrawled.

"Wow," I say, setting it on the coffee table.

For once, Cade is speechless. He's never seen me like this.

I want to go on, to rail at him for his unforgivable behavior. But as quickly as the anger comes, it is replaced with sadness. My eyes fill with tears. "I get it," I say. "I'm not enough for you."

"Oh, Kailey," he pleads. "You are more than enough for me. You are everything to me."

"Then what was *that*?" I cry. "Who was *she*?"

"She was nobody," he says. "Look, I had a few business deals go south and maybe I've been drinking too much."

"Maybe? Cade, you're drunk by noon every day."

He sighs. "Okay, I had too much to drink last night. But nothing happened. You have to trust me. Girls come on to me all the time. It's the music biz. You know that. Have I ever acted on it?"

I throw up my arms. "How should I know?"

"But you do *know*," he says, reaching for my hand. "You know my heart."

I shake my head. "No, I *used* to know your heart," I say, reaching for Eddie's leash and attaching it to his collar. "Now I hardly recognize it."

I turn to the door with an awful feeling of finality. It surges through my veins like adrenaline-fueled poison.

"Kailey, wait!" Cade cries. "Please, don't go. Not like this."

I look at him once more. His blue eyes, so sad, pierce mine. I love him with every ounce of my being, and I always will. But I have to go now. Cade is lost, and I can no longer light his way. I can no longer be his map. He has to find his own inner compass.

Tears stream down my cheeks as I reach the end of the block. Before I round the corner, I turn back once more, hoping to find Cade in the street running to me, calling my name, but he's not there. He's nowhere. I touch my belly lightly, and Eddie and I walk on.

twenty-three

R yan takes my hand as we step off the plane in Cabo. I've never been to Mexico, though I'm struck with a sudden memory of Cade that final day at his Pioneer Square apartment. He asked me to go to Mexico with him. To Cancún. If I had, would it have changed history? I take a deep breath and walk ahead. The air is warm and arid, and I'm glad I opted for my white linen sundress as opposed to the jeans I almost slipped on. When I turn my phone on, it buzzes with a few voicemail notifications, but I ignore them, determined to stay in the moment and focused on Ryan.

We catch a cab to the hotel, where we're greeted by a concierge who holds two salt-rimmed margaritas. He takes us to our room, a third-floor suite with an ocean view.

"This is truly gorgeous," I say to Ryan as we walk in, in awe.

"I thought you'd like it," he says.

"It's perfect," I say, having a look around the room. And it is. Sleek and modern but warm at the same time. The bed, with its turned mahogany posts, looks luxurious topped with a white starched duvet and pillows with pink and turquoise-blue embroidery. The adjoining bath-room, separated by a curtain, features an elaborate bathtub for two and a steam shower. Perfect, and yet I can't help but feel an ache in the pit of my stomach when I think about the way people live on the streets, the way Cade lived for so long. A divided world, one part beauty and the other darkness, with a line drawn right down the middle.

On the bar is a complimentary bottle of high-end tequila, limes, and a dish of salted cashews. Ryan pours us each a shot and walks out to the balcony, which features, as promised, our own private infinity plunge pool. He slips on his swim trunks, I quickly change into my blue bikini, and together we slip into the warm water.

"To us," Ryan says, smiling.

"To us," I repeat, throwing back the shot. It burns my throat but feels warm and comforting at the same time.

I gaze over the balcony and watch the waves crashing onto the shore. They're fierce and mighty, pummeling the sand again and again without relenting. I'm in awe of their power, in awe of forces beyond our control. The way the sun sets and the moon rises. The way the tide ebbs and flows. And I think about how we're drawn to people, too. How I was drawn to Cade so many years ago. Our attraction was mag-netic, undeniable.

I was drawn to Ryan, too, of course, from the very beginning—but in a different way. Ours is a quieter attraction, a gentler pull. Does that make it better, more lasting? I love him intensely, but our waves have always been softer. It's safe to swim in our sea. With Cade? The tidal wave conditions would close down the beach. I nod to myself.

Ryan nestles closer to me and wraps his arm around my waist. I take comfort in his presence the way I always do, and I nuzzle my head into the crevice of his neck, breathing in his love for me, soaking it up, resting in it.

"I'm glad we're here," he says, popping a cashew into his mouth. "Sometimes you have to get away to appreciate home."

I turn to him. "You don't think I love the life we're building together?"

"It's not that, exactly," he says. "We dream together about this future of ours. It's like a house we've been designing for so long. You picked the windows; I picked the front door. We've argued about the trim and the tile in the bathroom, but somewhere in the process we found a compromise. And now we're ready to break ground. The permits are all in. Cement trucks and bulldozers stand by." He pauses and looks deeply into my eyes. "But I don't think you're quite ready to pour the foundation."

He's right, and he knows it. And for the first time, I realize that I may lose this beautiful, wonderful man if I'm not careful.

"The beach looks rough. Want to head down to the main pool?" Ryan asks. "The rock waterfall looked amazing in the magazine spread. I can't wait to see it in person."

"Sure," I say. "You go ahead. I'll meet you down there. I just want to change and unpack a few things."

"Whatever you want, baby," he replies with a grin.

Mexico is beautifully lonely. I think about that as I lie on a chaise by the pool, watching Ryan swim laps as the bartender mixes us two more margaritas. Yet even the perfection of this place can't soothe the ache in my heart.

Next to me are two empty chaise lounges. "Mind if we take these?" a voice asks.

I look up to see a couple about my age approach. She's wearing a white bikini with a black mesh cover-up wrapped artfully around her waist. The man beside her is tan and tall, in navy-blue swim trunks and a pair of Ray-Ban Wayfarers.

"No, no," I say. "Go right ahead."

"Thanks," the woman says. "I'm Allie."

"Hi, I'm Kailey."

She smiles and takes a sip of the fruity blended cocktail in her hand. "Are you on your honeymoon, too?"

Ryan sits down on the chaise beside me and smiles at the couple.

"No," I say. "We're just on a . . . vacation."

Ryan leans into the conversation. "We're getting married soon," he says. "So I guess you could call this a practice honeymoon."

Allie laughs. "I wish Dalton had thought of that," she says, looking at the man beside her. "We got married last weekend."

I feel Ryan's gaze on me. "Congratulations."

"Will you two come back here for your . . . actual honeymoon?"

"I don't know," I say. "We haven't really decided that yet."

"Really?" Allie looks shocked. "We booked this place a year and a half ago," she says, gazing affectionately at her husband. "Anyway, it's nice to have the wedding behind us. I just love referring to Dalton as my husband. There's nothing like it." She turns to me, eager to share a confidence. "But I did love planning my wedding. I had twelve brides-maids."

"Wow," I say. "That sounds . . . big."

"Six hundred people, yes," she says.

I feel a little woozy suddenly, and I rub my clammy palms together. Did the bartender make my margarita a double?

"I had roses and freesias in my bouquet," Allie chirps. "And the cake! Five tiers of white chocolate with fondant. Dalton and I saved a section to have on our first anniversary."

My heart is beating fast. I feel strange, like I'm in a confined space with locked windows and doors.

"It was all so beautiful," Allie continues. "I loved my dress. Would you like to see a photo?"

No. I don't want to see a photo of her wedding dress. No, I don't want to talk about her wedding, or mine, or any shade of happily ever after.

I stand up suddenly. "I'm sorry. I, I . . . I think I've had too much sun, or too many drinks, or both. I don't feel well. I'm going to go lie down in the room for a while."

My head is spinning. Beads of sweat dot my brow.

"I'll go with you," Ryan says, concerned, grabbing my bag.

"Feel better," Allie says, her voice tinged with equal parts confusion and concern.

In the room, two maids are making the bed. Ryan politely asks them to leave, and I sink onto the bed.

"Here," Ryan says, sitting beside me. "Drink some water. The sun is hot. You're dehydrated."

I take the glass and gulp it down. If only water could cure what ails me.

At dinner that night, Ryan orders a bottle of wine from one of our favorite vineyards in Napa. "Caymus," I say, trying to cheer up.

"How perfect that they have it, right?"

I smile, remembering how he surprised me with a trip to Napa five months after we began dating. We both became instantly smitten with that little winery. The windy road was lined with wildflowers, and I asked Ryan to stop so I could pick a red poppy. I long for those days now.

As the waiter pours us each a glass, I notice the couple from the pool. They're seated at a table on the other side of the dining room, leaning so close to each other that it looks as if their noses are touching.

"My brother's going to fly in for the engagement party," Ryan says, swirling his wineglass, then taking a long sip.

"That's great," I say, realizing that until this moment I've forgotten about our party. Ryan reserved the event space at Serafina, a restaurant in Seattle's Eastlake neighborhood that we both love. But it was a favorite of mine long before Ryan. And the truth is, every inch of the city holds a memory for me. Memories of another time.

"I saw on the Evite RSVP list that Gregory and Katie will be coming, too," he continues. "I didn't think they'd drive up all the way from Portland."

I think of all the people who will be there. Gregory and Katie. Mike and Lisa. Evie and Jonathan. Jan. Tracy. Ryan's boss. That cute couple on the corner of our street who are expecting their first baby before the end of the year. All of them coming to celebrate our love. I feel the buzz of my phone in my purse and I pause to dig for it. I gave Dr. Branson my number and told her to call or text if Cade had any problems.

"Kailey," Ryan says softly.

I look up from my phone. Just a text from Tracy.

"Is it too much to ask to just have you all to myself tonight?" he says. "I don't want to share you with anyone. Not your phone. Not your past. And definitely not that ex-boyfriend who may or may not still be tugging at your heart."

I force a smile and reach across the table for his hand. "Of course," I say, blinking back tears. "Ryan, you have me."

"Do I?" he asks. His voice is tender, vulnerable.

"Yes," I say, squeezing his hand. "Yes."

It's after nine when I open my eyes the next morning. I'm wrapped in Ryan's arms, and I don't want to break from his embrace. I love the warmth of his skin, and the way he's holding me. I feel safe and sound, cocooned from the world. But my phone is ringing across the room. Ryan stirs as I extricate myself to answer it.

I don't recognize the number. "Hello?"

"Kailey, this is Dr. Branson. I'm sorry to bother you. I know you're out of the country. But it's Cade."

"What happened?"

Ryan sits up in bed.

Dr. Branson clears her throat. "He left, and we've been unable to find him."

"What do you mean, he *left?*"

"We do have staff here at all hours," she explains, "but our front desk attendant must have stepped out to use the bathroom when he walked out. The security camera shows him exiting this morning around four A.M."

"This is terrible," I say.

"It is," she continues. "But I don't think we should panic. It's possible he'll return later. I've notified hospital security to keep an eye out for him nearby."

I look out the open doors that lead to the balcony. Waves ripple onto the sugar-sand beach below. Everything about the scene is peaceful and placid, but inside all I feel is terror. Cade is on the streets again. And I am thousands of miles away.

"I'll catch an early flight back," I say. "I can find him. I know where he goes."

"I hate for you to have to do that," she says. "But I—"

"He'd do it for me," I say.

Ryan doesn't say anything when I set my phone down. "Cade's missing," I say. "You probably heard."

He nods and leans back against the pillows propped up behind him. I can't tell if he's upset or annoyed or both.

"I'm so sorry," I say. "But I have to go. I can't be here knowing that he's on the streets again. He's lost, Ryan. He needs my help. And I know that it may be hard for you to understand, but I have to help him."

Ryan sighs. "Of course I don't want you to go," he says. "But you have to do what you have to do. Our relationship has always been about that sort of trust, and freedom to do what we need to do."

"Thanks," I say as I frantically pack, then call the airline to change my flight. If I can get a cab immediately, I'll be able to catch the eleven A.M. flight home to Seattle.

I slip on a pair of jeans and put my hair into a ponytail. Before I wheel my suitcase to the door, I walk back to the bed, where Ryan is still lying shirtless beneath a sheet.

"I hate to go," I say. "But I have to."

He looks at me for a long time, then pulls me to him. "I wish you didn't have to," he says. "But do what you need to do, baby."

My eyes well up with tears as I kiss him goodbye. "Thank you. You don't know how much that means to me, Ryan."

twenty-four

OCTOBER 10, 1998

The pain is excruciating.

"Keep breathing," Tracy says as she drives her Volvo up James Street to Swedish Hospital. "We're almost there."

I nod and take a deep breath, then exhale before crying out in pain again. Towels are wadded up beneath me on the seat. I've never seen so much blood.

"Hold on," she says. "Just a few more minutes."

I'm dizzy and weak. I know what's happening to me. I'm aware the baby Cade and I conceived may be leaving my body, just as Cade left me. Left the planet, really. I turn to Tracy and cry out. "It hurts so much." And I think then that physical pain is nothing compared to the anguish my heart feels. Bearing this alone. Can I do it?

"I'm here," she says, swerving into the hospital parking lot. "You're going to be okay, I promise."

"I hate him," I scream through the pain ripping through my abdomen. "I hate him for not being here."

"Breathe, honey," Tracy says as she drives up to the hospital.

Tears stream down my cheeks as she rolls down the window and shouts at a hospital employee in blue scrubs near the elevator. "We need a wheelchair!"

Moments later I'm rushed in a dizzy blur to the fifth floor. Medical staff hover around me.

"My God, she's bleeding out!"

"Get the doctor!"

"Where's the father?"

"Hurry, get the IV in!"

"Her blood pressure is falling!"

It's like a nightmare where you want to scream, but you can't. I am alone with my pain, both physical and emotional. I moan and weep; Tracy speaks for me. She squeezes my hand and wipes the sweat from my brow. I feel pain shooting like daggers from my back to my stomach.

I feel everything when I so desperately want to feel nothing.

"Tracy?" I cry.

"I'm right here."

"I lost the baby, didn't I?"

She squeezes my arm. "I'm so sorry, Kailey."

I roll to my side and moan as a doctor with a soft voice and dark-rimmed glasses approaches holding a syringe. "This will take care of the pain," he says.

The needle pricks my skin, and moments later I'm enveloped in a blanket of calm. Nurses and doctors buzz around my outstretched legs, carving out the remnants of a life that will never be.

When it's over, I stare out the window despondently. The cherry trees that line James Street are starting to lose their leaves. Two years ago,

Cade and I walked hand in hand along that street when they were in full bloom. He stopped to shake a branch and let the pink blossoms flutter down. "Snow, for my beloved."

"Excuse me, Kailey," the doctor says, approaching me cautiously. "I thought you might like to know"—he swallows hard—"that it was a girl."

My heart surges. My daughter. Cade's daughter. We are a family now, joined together forever by this little life we created. But he's gone. They're both gone. And the world is dark.

Tracy reaches for my hand. "Oh, Kailey. I'm so sorry. I'm so very sorry." She places her hand on my arm. I close my eyes and weep.

twenty-five

I am restless on the plane home to Seattle. I shift into a million positions, lose interest in the in-flight movie, try to sleep but can't, and am basically miserable. Flying has always fascinated me: the concept of being thirty thousand feet high, suspended between here and there. In no place, really. While it used to give me comfort, this middle place—this idea of being neither here nor there but in between—it doesn't now. The pilot can't fly this thing fast enough, and as I watch the clouds out the window I'm plagued with worry. *Cade, I'm coming. I'm coming.*

I speed-walk through baggage claim to customs, then outside to flag down a cab. I call Harborview, but when they transfer me to Cade's building there's no answer, so I instruct the driver to take me to Cade's apartment. I ask him to wait while I rush to the reception desk. He's still gone.

We drive downtown next, past Le Marche, past his old Pioneer Square apartment, up and down Fourth and Fifth six times.

"Miss, you want me to take you somewhere else?" the driver says, turning to me at a stoplight.

It's the most expensive cab ride of my life, but I don't care. I tell him to circle downtown once more. We do, but Cade is . . . nowhere.

"I guess you can take me home now," I say, dejectedly giving him my address.

Ten minutes later, we're parked on the street in front of my house. I pay the fare, and the driver lifts my suitcase out of the trunk. I stand on the sidewalk as he drives away, then turn to the house. My eyes widen when I notice a figure sitting on the second step of my porch in the shadow of the wisteria vine.

I drop my bag when I see him, hands at his sides, knees propped up slightly on the steps. "Cade!"

His face brightens when he sees me. "Hi," he says.

"Cade, what happened? Why are you here?"

He rubs his forehead. "I don't know. I, I . . . I missed you."

I feel a burst inside, sort of like the first taste of a lemon. It's intense and all-consuming. "You did?"

"You were gone for so long," he says.

"Just three days," I assure him, reaching for his hands. "I came home as soon as Dr. Branson called and said you were missing."

"I'm sorry," he says. "I just . . ."

"I won't leave again, not for a while. Not until you get more set-tled. You're making such good progress. The new medication seems to be working."

We walk inside the house, and when he reaches for my suitcase, at first I shake my head. But he insists, so I let him carry it.

Cade nods. "I'm remembering. More and more."

"Like what? Tell me something."

He smiles. "Like . . . you. And boats."

"Boats?"

He nods. "We took a ferry ride, didn't we? To an island."

"We did," I say. I pull my cellphone out of my pocket and scroll through my photos, old and new, that I scanned and saved, to find the one Cade took of me on the ferry so many years ago. "Do you remember this?"

He blinks hard, reaching out for my phone. He takes it and stares at the image longingly. "I do."

He smiles. "It's like a blurry dream."

"You saved my life that day," I continue. "Do you remember?"

He nods.

"Funny that when I asked you what you remember, you said boats."

A cloud falls over his face then. I sit down on the couch and he sits beside me.

"What is it?"

"There's something else I remember," he continues.

"What?"

His face is strained, as if he's recalling a horror he'd just as well let slip back into the cobwebbed corners of his mind. And I'd like him to, but I have a feeling this memory is significant somehow.

"Cade," I say, placing my hand on his arm. "Tell me."

He stares straight ahead. "It was dark. There was water." His hand trembles in mine. "I felt something hit my head."

"Something? What?"

"I don't know," he says. "It was cold. Waves crashing all around. I could taste blood in my mouth."

"Cade, are you sure? Dr. Branson said your memories would return, but that sometimes they'd be jumbled."

"I don't know," he says. "Maybe."

"Is there anything else? Anything more specific?"

He's quiet for a long moment, and I don't try to fill the air with chatter. I want to give him space to remember.

"Princess," he says.

"What?"

"That word was on the side of the boat."

"Are you sure?"

He nods. "I think so. It was painted in navy-blue letters."

I pull up my phone and open a browser window. "Maybe it's a type of yacht." I Google "princess yachts" and sure enough, there's a company of the same name.

"Okay," I say. "I'm going to look into this."

"What do you think it all means?" Cade asks.

"I'm not sure," I reply. "But I promise you, I'm going to find out."

I drive Cade back to Harborview. Together we take the elevator up to his third-floor apartment.

He makes me a cup of coffee with the coffeemaker I bought him after receiving the green light from Dr. Branson, and I smile when he hands me the mug. "You used to love coffee," I say.

"Did I?"

I grin. "You bought one of those enormous La Marzocco espresso machines, like the ones they have at cafés."

"I did?" He laughs.

"You did."

"It was red."

I nod.

He sits down on the love seat, and I join him. There isn't much space, so our thighs touch, as do our arms. "What was I like?" Cade asks, looking suddenly thoughtful.

"You were larger than life," I say. "You loved music and vodka martinis with cheese-filled olives."

He raises his eyebrows.

"You loved travel and people, and owned a thousand records. You told the funniest stories. In the two years I dated you, you never ran out of stories, and you never stopped making me laugh."

"Two years," he says, a little in awe, a little regretful.

"Yes," I say. "And I loved every day, even those hard days at the end."

"Why were they hard?" he asks. It's as if Cade's mind is on fire, exploding with questions, his brain's circuits firing so rapidly that his speech is having trouble keeping up.

I tell him about the drama with Element Records. I tell him about how he began drinking heavily. I share James's accusations.

He turns to me, eyes so big and earnest that I want to pull him to me and hold him tight. "I wish I could still make you laugh." He nods. "Like I used to."

"Oh, Cade," I say, feeling an intense rush of emotions wash over me. "I'm just so happy I found you again. I've missed you. Every day since you've been gone. And I looked for you around every corner of this city. I was always looking for you, even when that voice deep down told me it was time to stop. I had to mourn you like you were dead. I had to say goodbye. And I've never been the same since."

He touches my cheek to wipe a tear away. "What did you do all those years?"

I swallow hard. "I got a job in New York working for a magazine. It was grueling. I had a boss from hell, and I pretty much hated every minute of it." I laugh. "My apartment was infested with mice."

He smiles, listening intently, patiently.

"I moved back four years ago when my editor offered to bring me back to the *Herald*. I met Ryan after that."

Cade looks at his feet.

"Sorry, I . . ." My voice trails off. I don't know what I'm beginning to say, or even what I want to say.

"Do you love him?" Cade says suddenly.

"Yes," I say. It's the complicated truth.

He nods. "I was so lucky."

"What do you mean?"

"To have had you in my life," he replies earnestly, regretfully.

"But you still have me in your life. And you always will. That will never change."

"I wish . . ."

I wish, too. So much.

His eyes meet mine, and their pull is magnetic, so I close mine tightly. I can't. It isn't right. He's not himself, and I'm . . .

I feel his fingertips on my lips and a wave of emotion washes over me.

"Open your eyes," he says suddenly with the same swagger and confidence that once possessed him. "I need you to see me."

I obey, and when he pulls me to him, I don't protest. I melt into his embrace. My arms wrap around him, then my legs as he pulls me onto his lap. Our bodies press against each other, and then he kisses me. When our lips meet, the past, the future . . . none of it matters now. Only us. Only this moment.

I pull back when I hear a knock at Cade's door. I quickly jump to my feet and nervously run my fingers through my hair where his hands were moments before.

Cade opens the door. It's Dr. Branson.

"Cade," she says. "It's so good to see you back. I hope you won't leave us again anytime soon."

He nods, then looks at me.

"Hi," I say. "I was just . . . helping Cade get settled again."

"Of course," she says, stepping back into the hallway. "I won't keep you, but I would like to run some tests later."

After she's gone, we stand in silence. I feel guilty and scared. As much as I want to turn back to him, to pick up where we left off, to shower him with all the love I still feel, I know it's not right. I'm going to marry Ryan.

"I'm sorry," I say, breaking the icy silence. It cracks all around us like a winter lake on a sunny day. "We shouldn't have done that."

He looks confused, but then nods.

I take a step toward the door.

"You could . . . stay," he says.

There is longing in his voice, and I want so desperately to go to him, to fill the void in my heart with his love, the love he once gave me so freely. But I can't.

"I have to go," I say. "I . . ."

He sits down, staring out the window.

"Please," I say. "It's not that I don't want to. But I just . . . can't."

He continues to sit in silence as I place my hand on the door.

"I'll be back to check on you tomorrow afternoon. I promise."

Ryan calls from Mexico on my drive home.

"Hi," I say, my voice weary and distant, as if I've lived three lives in the span of just this afternoon. My heart feels heavy with guilt.

"So, did you find your missing hobo?"

I'm momentarily annoyed by Ryan's tone, but I know I don't have the right to be. "Yes," I say. "I found him and got him back to Harborview."

"Good," he says. "I thought about flying home today, but the hotel is nonrefundable at this point, so I might as well stay and enjoy the sun."

Rain splatters my windshield. Everywhere outside it's gray. The light. The clouds. The pavement. The world is bleak on bleak.

"It's okay," I say. "Just stay."

"I love you," Ryan says. "I don't always understand you, but I love you."

"I love you, too," I reply, haunted by the words that just flew out of my lips. They echo in my head after I've hung up the phone.

I grasp the steering wheel tighter and begin to cry.

twenty-six

"The feedback on your series keeps breaking records," Jan says that morning at the office. "Good fodder for the editorial page."

I sigh, thinking of Ryan's Pioneer Square projects inching closer to completion. "Maybe we should just leave it at that. After all, I've covered both sides. Both the homeless advocates and the developers have had their say."

Jan shakes her head. "And yet there's still a missing piece." Her eyes pierce mine. I know she's right.

"When are you going to let me read it?"

I know exactly what she's referring to—the article about Cade. I've made progress with it, for sure, but it's far from complete.

"Soon," I say, letting my eyes fall upon the framed engagement photo of Ryan and me that sits on my desk.

"Your engagement party is this weekend, right?"

I nod.

"I'm going to try to make it," she says. "At least for a bit."

I smile.

"Kailey, you don't have to go through the motions if you don't want to."

"I'm going to marry Ryan, Jan," I say. "I'm going to marry him, and you are going to come to our tenth and our twentieth, and our fiftieth wedding anniversaries."

I turn for the door before I can see the look on her face.

I meet Tracy for lunch before stopping to see Cade. She tells me about a new guy she's dating named Trent.

"I like everything about him," she says, "except his name."

I can't help but laugh. "What's wrong with *Trent*?"

"Everything," she replies. "Trents are never any good. They're either really boring accountant types with bangs that are cut evenly across their forehead, or they're heavy-metal, thrasher-rock dudes."

I smile. "So it sounds like you found the world's best Trent."

"Exactly," Tracy exclaims. "He's got to be in the Trent Hall of Fame. He's cute, smart, and, oh, he has a boat, and we're very compatible from an astrological perspective."

"I'm happy for you," I say, smiling big. "Are you bringing him to the engagement party on Saturday?"

"Yeah," Tracy says. "You'll get to meet him. And can you actually believe I was able to get that night off work? I mean, I may or may not have had to kill for it."

I grin. "I expect no less from my best friend."

I fill her in on Cade—well, everything but what happened at his apartment yesterday.

"So it sounds like Ryan is easing into all of this," she says. "He's such a good guy; he's always so understanding."

"He is," I say wistfully.

I tell her about Cade's recollection of being on a boat.

"Is he sure?"

"I don't know," I say. "His doctor said that his memory could ebb and flow. That not all of the details would connect or even match."

"Right," Tracy says. "I had an amnesia patient once. Her memory was fluid in the same way Cade's doctor describes. She kept insisting that what was clearly a childhood incident happened on her forty-third birthday."

"Did she ever recover?" I ask, a little afraid to hear the answer.

"She had a remarkably patient husband. He went over the time line with her until she closed the gap," Tracy says.

"In this case," I say, "we might not have time for that approach. I wasn't there that night, but even if Cade doesn't remember what happened, there must be someone who does. I'm going to try to piece it all together if I can."

I find Cade in the common area of the apartment building when I arrive. He's playing a game of chess with another resident and looks up and smiles when he sees me.

"Hi," I say.

"Hi," he replies.

I sit beside him as he finishes the game with a winning move.

"Nice," I say, smiling as the other resident, an older man, stands up and leaves.

"It's funny how stuff like this can just come back to you," he says.

"You're making amazing progress," I say.

He smiles.

"I was thinking," I say. "It's almost Christmas, and you need a tree in your apartment."

His face brightens.

"Would you like to go pick one out with me?"

"I would," he says.

After signing Cade out, together we walk to my car and drive to a tree lot on Capitol Hill with a blow-up Frosty the Snowman.

"How about this one?" I say to Cade, pointing to a little tree at the back of the lot.

He studies it carefully, then nods. All around us are families and couples. A little girl with blond pigtails and pink rubber rain boots races up and down the rows of Christmas trees.

"Grace!" her father calls playfully. "I can see you!"

Cade looks at me when he hears her name. He remembers, just as I do. The skin on my arms erupts in goosebumps.

I pay for the tree and a worker offers to rope it to the top of my car, but Cade holds up his hand. "I've got it," he says.

I watch as he lifts the tree up and secures it on the top of the car. He isn't as strong as he used to be, but he's just as determined. I watch, beaming with pride, as his arms thread the rope to the roof rack. "This baby better not fall," he says with a laugh, then turns to me. "What do you think?"

But I'm not thinking about the tree. I don't care if it falls into a ditch on the side of the road. All I care about is this man before me and how, in this moment, his injury, like a suit of armor, appears to be falling off him before my very eyes.

"Should I put some more rope by the trunk?" he asks. The Christmas lights strung above us make his eyes twinkle, and I will away the tears that are flirting with the edges of my lids.

"No," I say. "It's perfect. You've done a perfect job."

We drive to the local drugstore and find our way to the holiday aisle, where I stack our cart with my favorite multicolored lights, boxes of red and silver ornaments, and a tree stand. On a whim, I throw in a pack of silver tinsel.

"Merry Christmas," the clerk says, handing me my change at the register. I stuff it into the Salvation Army bell ringer's red bucket on our way out.

Back at Cade's building, we carry the tree and decorations to the elevator, then up to his apartment. He sets the tree in the stand, and I fiddle with the radio I brought over for him a few weeks ago. It isn't anything near the level of sound system Cade once owned, but it plays music, and that's good enough.

At the sound of Bing Crosby's voice singing "White Christmas," I stop the dial. Cade has set the little tree up by the window, and together we unwind the lights and string them around the branches. Cade is quietly focused as we hang the ornaments, then finish with the tinsel.

When it's complete, we turn the lights off and sit on the love seat, admiring our little tree. I lean my head on Cade's shoulder. It feels natural, like it's a resting place made just for me, always for me.

My mind churns. *Ryan. The wedding. Cade's healing.* There is so much to do, so much to figure out. A world of decisions to make. But for now, this is enough. The Christmas tree, like life, isn't perfect. It leans to the left a little, and it's missing a star. There are no presents underneath, no tree skirt. But even so, it's just right.

twenty-seven

"Ryan," I say from the bathroom while I'm getting ready for our engagement party. I can barely focus on my dress, which needs to be ironed, or my hair, which I suppose I should curl. "Do you know any forensic accountants?"

"Sure, why?" he replies, poking his head in the doorway while tying his tie.

"It's just some stuff that came up with Cade."

His expression changes momentarily. "Oh," he says.

"The thing is," I continue, "I think there's a very good chance that his business partner took everything from him."

"Wow," he says. "Well, it could be worth looking into, but, Kailey, those guys aren't cheap."

I know it's not fair to expect Ryan to pay any more out of pocket for Cade's well-being. He's already aware of the Harborview costs but hasn't questioned them, and for that I am grateful. "You might find someone to work on commission, based on what they could find and recover."

"Good idea," I say, selecting the pair of diamond stud earrings that Ryan gave me for Valentine's Day last year.

He pulls his phone from his pocket and scrolls through his contacts. "Here," he says. "Davis, Emmerson, and Barrett. Talk to Bruce Barrett. He's an attorney but works closely with a team of forensic accountants who do that sort of work all the time. Maybe you could work something out with them." He shrugs. "I'll text you their info."

"Thanks," I say.

He looks at me for a long moment, and if I could crawl into his mind, I know I'd see how much he wishes I would just let Cade be. Let the system take care of him. Stop worrying about him and instead focus on my life, our life. And yet I can't. He knows that. I know that.

"You look beautiful," he says, beaming at me after I've slipped on my dress, black with a lace bodice.

"And you look very handsome," I reply. The truth is, Ryan always looks handsome.

When we arrive at Serafina for the party, at least a dozen of our friends are already there. I see Tracy across the room with an attractive gray-haired man. I wave and walk over. Ryan stays by the entrance of the restaurant to talk to a colleague from his office who has a chic-looking brunette on his arm.

"Look at you," she says. "Love the dress!"

"Thanks," I reply, smiling. "This must be Trent."

"Yes," she says, turning to her date. "Trent, this is my best friend, Kailey."

"We finally meet," he says, extending his hand. His grip is firm, his eyes kind. I like him instantly.

"I hear you have a boat," I say. "A sailboat?"

"I used to sail," he says. "But then I turned forty and got lazy."

"Trent is being modest," Tracy says. "He has a beautiful yacht."

"Oh, fun," I say.

"If you have a free day before the wedding, I'll take you and your fiancé out on it to celebrate."

"We'd love that," I say, just as Ryan nestles beside me, wrapping his arm around my waist.

"I'm Ryan," he says to Trent. "Pleased to meet you."

"Trent," he says.

"We were just talking about his yacht," I say to Ryan. "He invited us to come out sometime."

"Wonderful," Ryan replies. "I grew up on boats. Someday I hope to talk this one into buying one of our own. Until then we'll live vicariously through you."

"Trent," I say, "do you happen to know the brand Princess?"

"Princess Yachts? Sure. That's a quality line. I have a Sunseeker, but Princess is just as well regarded."

Ryan waves at a work colleague who has just arrived and kisses my cheek. "Excuse me for a moment," he says. "Trent, so nice to meet you."

After he's gone, I continue. "If someone owned a Princess Yacht back in 1998, is there any way to track it?"

"Tracy told me you work for the newspaper," he says. "Investigative reporter?"

"Yes, but I'm more into social issues than aquatics," I say with a smile. "This is a personal project."

"Well," he says, "if the person bought it new, you could definitely find purchase data on it. I have a buddy who used to work in yacht sales. I could ask him."

"That would be wonderful," I say. "Thank you."

It's a lovely party, and all around people are smiling, drinking, laughing—the trifecta of joy. And for a moment, I sort of forget that it's my engagement party instead of a gathering of old friends. But then I hear the tap of a microphone, and the room silences.

"Is this thing on?" Ryan says.

Everyone laughs, and one of his work friends makes a wisecrack that I don't quite understand.

"Okay, now that I have your attention, you rowdy crew," Ryan jokes, "I'd like to make a toast: to my beautiful bride-to-be, Kailey."

I feel my cheeks get warm as the room's collective gaze turns to me. I smile, but it feels forced, and my cheeks feel tight, as if I'm straining my muscles.

"My beautiful girl," he says. "The day I met you, I was done. Arrow through the heart. I was yours. And I knew for a million reasons—your smile, your kindness, the way your nose crinkles a little when you're laughing, the way you know the difference between tarragon and thyme and any spice from A to Z."

I smile, remembering one of our first dates, when I made him dinner at my old apartment in Belltown and gave him a lesson on herbs and spices.

"I love more things about you than I could ever recite here. And mostly and especially, I love your spirit and your heart. And I'm so honored that you've agreed to spend your life with me." He clears his throat. "The road to this moment hasn't always been perfect. And you've endured more hardship than I have, hands down." He raises his glass. "So this toast is for you, Kailey, and to all the plans that didn't work out, all the perceived failures and falters and detours in the road. Because without them, this life we're living, this love we're feeling wouldn't be possible. Disappointment is really just a stepping stone on the path to better things, to the best thing." He pauses and wipes a tear from his eyes, then turns to me. "And, Kailey, for all the detours you have had, and I have had, you are the best destination. And I am so grateful that my path led me to you."

Everyone claps, and the room parts so that I can find my way up to Ryan. I give him a kiss, and I hope he doesn't notice that my lip is trembling. "Thank you," I say. "That was so beautiful."

"I meant every word," Ryan says before his brother walks up to him and pats him on the back.

I see Tracy ahead and I weave through the crowd to her, waving at Jan and one of my coworkers from the *Herald* across the room.

"Trent had to leave early to pick up his daughter," she says.

I tug at my dress, unable to look her in the eye.

"Kailey, I watched you during Ryan's speech. He was speaking from the heart tonight, but his words went right through you."

"I'm fine," I lie, trying to quell the quiver of my chin and lower lip.

"You're not, and I know it." She reaches for my arm. "Please, I'm your best friend. If you can't be honest with me, who can you be honest with? Kailey, you don't need to do this alone."

I nod.

"You can't marry him, Kailey."

"But I'm going to," I say, holding my head up higher and turning to look at Ryan in the distance: so handsome, so confident, so . . . everything. "Tracy, I love him. I really do."

"Yes," she says. "But, honey, you know as well as I do that sometimes love is not enough."

When I look up, Ryan is walking toward me. If he was ever worried about Cade, he's successfully dealt with his fears and chosen to trust me, and my inability to settle my feelings leaves my stomach in knots.

"Hi," he says to me, kissing my cheek before smiling at Tracy.

"We were just talking about how great your toast was," Tracy says, coming to my rescue.

"It was wonderful," I say, finding my voice.

The jazz band we hired returns to their instruments and begins playing. I don't recognize the tune at first, but then it hits me: "All of Me," that old song my grandmother used to love.

All of me, why not take all of me?

I blink back tears as Ryan pulls me closer. And I know, in that moment, that as hard as I have tried, I'll never be able to give him all of me.

twenty-eight

*D*ue to a lucky cancellation, I'm able to get an appointment to meet with Bruce Barrett, the attorney Ryan suggested, and at nine he greets Cade and me in the reception area of his office. He's a large man with gray hair and a Cheshire-cat smile. He wears a tweed suit and navy-blue tie, and when he shakes my hand his grip is so firm that it hurts a little. I assume this is why Cade seems uneasy.

"Thank you for meeting with us," I say.

"The pleasure is ours," he says, leading us down a small hallway to a conference room. On the table is a breakfast spread: stale bagels, sad-looking grapes and melon. The eggs look somewhat petrified.

"Help yourself," he says as another man, a bit younger and more serious-looking, walks in.

"It's okay," I say. "We already ate."

He nods. "This is Tom Lawton, one of our best forensic accountants. Tom leaves no stone unturned, I assure you.

"Now," he says, clasping his hands together, "you have quite a case on your hands. I've taken the liberty of briefing Tom, and he's done a little digging this morning—well, with what little time he had. We think you'll be pleased with what he's already been able to find." He opens a folder and slides a piece of paper toward us, and I lean forward to take it. Cade looks over, as if the words and numbers on the page are in hieroglyphics.

"Mr. McAllister," Bruce says, "when you disappeared, you were a rather rich man."

Cade looks at me, then back at Bruce skeptically.

"You owned half of Element Records," Bruce explained, "a car, your condo in Pioneer Square, and you had equity in two buildings downtown."

I nod. "But Element Records was on the verge of bankruptcy," I say. "The company was struggling."

He shakes his head, flashing his Cheshire smile again. "Maybe it was then. But that company went on to gross millions, all of which appears to have been folded into a newer company, belonging to a certain Mr. Keatley."

I shake my head. "So what happened, then? Where are Cade's savings? His share of the company—surely he can still access it."

"As it stands, no," he replies. "Mr. McAllister's savings are wiped out. His condo was absorbed by Element Records LLC, which was dissolved some time ago."

My heart beats faster. "So somebody took everything?"

"Everything," he says. "Plain and simple."

I shake my head again. "But how could they?"

"Easy," Bruce says. "Was Mr. Keatley's name on all the deeds, all the contracts? Did he have power of attorney? Could he withdraw funds?"

"Yes, I think so," I say. "He managed the company's finances. Cade was more of the creative side."

Bruce smiles again. "Then there you have it."

Tom, the ninja accountant, produces another document and shares a copy with us. "Mr. McAllister, we believe you are owed at least eight million dollars, possibly more, once we factor in the current market value of the condo and your personal possessions."

Cade's eyes are big. And I squeeze his hand under the table.

"I say this all with a caveat," he continues. "You are owed this money, but whether or not it *exists* anymore is anyone's guess. And it will be harder to prove criminal intent here, as this is a complex case. Cade's assets, including his condo and car, were intertwined with Element Records'. But there are people behind all of that, and I believe they need to be held accountable."

I hang on his every word.

"It took a little sleuthing," Tom continues, "but I found a series of transfers from the business account of Element Records to a private account."

"Any idea of the name on it?"

"Not yet, but we're committed to getting to the bottom of this."

"As are we," I say. "And I understand, based on our phone conversation, that you take twenty percent of whatever you can recover?"

"That's right," Bruce says.

"That will be fine," I say, looking at Cade for approval.

Bruce's eyes narrow. Any trace of his smile disappears as he leans in. "I need to caution you not to try to confront this business partner," he says. "We need the *element* of surprise to solve this case. No pun intended." He winks. "Best to catch them with their pants down, if you know what I mean."

"Well . . . I've already been in touch with him," I say a bit remorsefully.

"Does he know you're working with an attorney, an accountant?"

I shake my head.

"Good. Keep it that way." He looks at Cade, then at me. "And you need to protect yourself. When this much money is at stake, people can lose their minds and do unspeakable things. Money is an ugly beast." I feel a chill creep over me. "Just be safe," he says. "Don't go poking around where you shouldn't. Let us handle that."

Before we leave, Cade, who's been mostly silent through the meeting, extends his hand to Bruce, who receives it with a firm shake of the wrist. "Thank you," Cade says to him, "for helping me." He casts an assured look at me. "I'm ready to get my life back."

I drive Cade back to Harborview, and once he's settled into his two o'clock session I stop into Dr. Branson's office.

"Oh, Kailey," she says, looking up from her computer. "It's nice to see you." Behind her are a dozen or more framed artistic renderings of the brain.

I sink into a chair beside her desk. "He's doing so well," I say. "Today when I was driving him back from an appointment, he recited the Robert Frost poem I used to love."

She smiles. "Which one?"

"Nothing Gold Can Stay."

"Ah," she says. "One of my favorites, too. I was a literature major before I decided on premed." She closes her eyes as if to extract the words from one of the lobes of her brain. "So dawn goes down to day."

We recite the last line in unison. "Nothing gold can stay."

She smiles. "Such a beautiful stanza. I've always felt that it's a realistic view of life, though a tad pessimistic."

"Why so?"

"Nothing gold can stay," she says, releasing the words into the air again. "It's a commentary on how good things don't last. True, in some cases. Not all good things last, so when they're with us, they must be savored. But I'm not sure I entirely subscribe to that thinking. Ultimately, I believe good things *can,* and *do,* last."

"Do they?" I say skeptically. "I'm not sure. Maybe that's the whole concept of beautiful things. We can only have them for a moment." I think of flowers that bloom and wilt in the summer, leaves that turn brilliant shades of gold in autumn before shriveling and falling from their branches. Parents who die. Love that is lost. In the world, and my life, gold does not stay.

She shakes her head. "I wouldn't be practicing medicine and so focused on the way the brain can heal and regenerate if I believed that. Sure, nothing lasts forever, but gold can stay for a long time. And I'm in the business of helping it do just that."

"Well, you've almost made me a believer," I say with a smile. "You've done amazing things for Cade."

"It's remarkable, really, how far he's come in this short time," she says. "Brain science is the last frontier of medicine. We don't know why some patients respond to treatment as well as they do, or why others don't. But Cade is talking; his speech is fluid. His memories are returning, and according to his imaging, his brain shows signs of repair."

"I know," I reply. "It's almost like he's himself again. Almost."

Dr. Branson looks thoughtful. "And he may always be an 'almost.'"

I nod, thinking of the Cade I used to know—the man who charmed me from the moment I laid eyes on him, made me laugh at the drop of a hat or whisked me away to Big Sur on a moment's notice.

"I expect him to continue to improve," she says. "We'd normally like our patients to complete the full year program, but we're learning as we go, and Cade may do well blending back into life on his own. We probably should begin talking about his plans for finding work and housing, that sort of thing. Have you thought about what kind of job Cade might apply for?"

"Job?" I say.

"Yes, perhaps janitorial work, a restaurant position?"

It's hard to imagine Cade washing dishes at some restaurant or vacuuming the carpet at a dentist's office. "He used to run a multimillion-dollar company," I say.

"Yes, I understand," she says, unfazed. "But he may be happier doing . . . simpler work now."

"Right," I say, thinking about our meeting with the attorney earlier this morning and hoping that they'll be able to recover at least a portion of the funds that are owed to him.

"Well," she says, standing up. "I'm late for my afternoon session."

I follow her out to the hallway, and she turns to me once more with a smile. "Gold *can* stay," she says. "Don't forget that."

"Wow, I can't believe he's coming to the wedding," Ryan says later that night at the kitchen table, eyeing his phone.

"Who?" I ask, looking up from my plate of overcooked lasagna Ryan's mother made and left in the freezer. I neglected to preheat the oven, and the top got scorched.

"Josh Graham," he says. "An old friend from Yale. He just emailed me."

"You've never mentioned him before," I reply, scrunching my nose.

"Josh is a fraternity friend," he says. "He's living in New York now with a wife and two kids. He runs a hedge fund and is doing really well for himself."

I imagine the email from Josh Graham saying he'll be coming with a date, and I look away indifferently.

"Is something wrong, honey?" Ryan asks.

I sigh again. "I don't know," I say, tugging at my sweater, which suddenly feels itchy around the neckline. "I guess I'm wondering if we should have kept the guest list to only close friends and family."

"But when we discussed it, you didn't bring up any apprehensions about the size of the wedding. And Josh is a close friend."

"A close friend? I have never heard of him, and it sounds like you haven't seen him since college."

"Yes," he says a little defensively, "but we email and talk on the phone now and then. Besides, he's a great business contact." He turns back to his laptop, looking a bit wounded.

"Business contact?" I say. The words shoot out with a little more oomph than I planned. "So our wedding has become a networking event?"

"Kailey, you're overreacting."

I sigh. "Didn't you say that a bunch of your dad's colleagues are coming, too?"

"The Hartmans, yes," Ryan says. "But I've known them since I was a baby."

"All right, fine," I continue. "But your father said he wanted to reserve a table for his employees. Ryan, really? His *employees*?" I feel anxiety welling up in the pit of my stomach and rising to my chest.

He sighs. "What do you expect, Kailey? My parents are paying for the wedding." He gets up and walks to the kitchen, opens the fridge, and grabs a beer.

"I know," I say. "I'm sorry. I didn't mean to upset you."

My phone rings before Ryan can venture a response, and I'm relieved to have an excuse to stop talking about the wedding. Since the engagement party, every interaction has felt strained, every conversation stressful.

I recognize the number on my phone: Harborview. Dr. Branson, perhaps? I pick up. "Hello?"

"Hi, it's Cade."

"Hi," I say, turning to Ryan, who's typing something on his laptop.

"I'm sorry if I'm bothering you," he says.

I walk to the living room. "It's okay. What's going on?"

"I, I . . ."

"Cade, what is it?"

Ryan looks up from his laptop, and his eyes meet mine for a brief second before he turns away.

"I just . . . miss you, I guess," he says.

The words pierce my heart. I remember the first time he told me he missed me. A month after we started dating, he called me one evening and those three words slipped out of his mouth and slayed me, right there on my couch on a Thursday night. And there is his voice on the phone again. The world has shifted, and yet his words hit me as hard as they did so many years ago. And maybe even harder.

"Do you need me to come over?" I say, aware that Ryan is listening.

"If you can," he says. "If it's not too much trouble."

"Of course it's not," I say, glancing at the clock: seven-thirty. "I can be over by eight."

"That was Cade," I say to Ryan. "He's . . . struggling tonight. I'm going to go over and check on him."

Ryan grunts a reply but doesn't look up from his laptop.

"I won't be long," I say. "Just there and back."

I grab my keys and purse. Ryan doesn't say goodbye.

Seattle is glorious tonight. The skyline sparkles over Lake Union as I drive down I-5, and I am struck by how much I love this city, all of its angles, all of its character. I've been drawn to it from the moment Tracy and I rolled in with all of our earthly possessions in the back of her car. I fell for its rain-soaked streets, the briny smell of the sea, the sound of ferry horns on Elliott Bay, the music spilling out of restaurants and bars, a new talent, a new yet-to-be-discovered sound around every corner.

But so much of my love for Seattle is wrapped up in Cade. Every song. Every neighborhood. Every hole-in-the-wall café. We left our mark on the city together, and without those memories Seattle might as well be Chicago or Los Angeles or New York or any metropolis on the face of the planet. Cade is Seattle. And Seattle is Cade.

"Hi," I say to the security guard at the reception desk at Cade's building when I arrive. I strain to remember his name. My head is foggy tonight. Chris, I think. Yes, that's right.

"He'll be glad to see you," Chris says. "He's had a hard night."

"What happened?"

He leans closer to me. "Someone scared the living hell out of him."

"What do you mean, someone scared him?"

"He went out for a walk," Chris explains, "about four o'clock, and came back an hour later really shaken up."

"Is it okay for him to be out on his own?"

"Dr. Branson said it was okay for him to leave for walks," he says, pointing to the clipboard sign-out sheet. "See, she signed him out right here."

I nod. "What do you mean, he was 'shaken up'?"

"He said someone was chasing him, that someone wanted to hurt him."

"Do you think it was real or post-traumatic stress, as Dr. Branson described?"

Chris shrugs. "Beats me, but the guy seemed really frightened. He kept looking over his shoulders thinking someone was coming for him."

"That's terrible," I say. "No wonder he didn't want to be alone."

"Nice of you to come," Chris says as I head to the elevator. "Let me know if you need anything."

The elevator deposits me on the third floor, and when I knock on Cade's door he opens it immediately.

"Hi," I say, giving him a hug.

"Hi," he says, pulling me tight. I'm aware of his hands around my waist.

"I'm sorry," he says.

"Don't be," I reply. "I'm glad you called. Now tell me what happened. Someone was chasing you?"

"How do you know?"

"Chris told me."

He gives me a blank stare.

"The security guard."

"Oh yeah," he says. "Kailey, it's not safe out there for me."

"Sit down," I say. "What do you mean?"

"Someone was following me. I started walking faster, and he started walking faster. Then I began to run, and he began to run."

"Are you sure the person was following *you*?"

"Yeah," he says.

"Did you get a good look at who it was?"

"No," he says. "It was too dark."

"We have to protect you. Please, don't leave the building unless you're with someone. I don't know what's going on, or why these people want to hurt you, but, Cade, promise me you'll stay here and keep yourself safe until we can get to the bottom of this."

He nods. "I'm glad you're here. The world feels better when you're with me."

Before I can respond, Cade's phone rings. "I'll get it," I say.

"Hello?"

"Kailey?"

"Yes?"

"This is Chris at the front desk. There's a man here who says he needs to see you."

"A man? Who?"

"Says his name is Ryan."

Why is Ryan here?

"Ok," I say, "um, I'll come down."

"Actually," Chris says, "he's just stepped into the elevator. I tried to stop him, but he said he was your fiancé."

"Yes," I say. "He is. It's fine."

"I'll just be a moment," I say to Cade, heading out to the hallway. Ryan is stepping off the elevator. His face looks ashen.

"What are you doing here?" I ask.

"Nice to see you, too," he says.

"Ryan, what's this about?"

He throws up his arms. "What's this about? I think you know what this is about."

"Shhh," I say. "Please, he'll hear you."

"Kailey," he says, "at this point, I don't care if *he* hears me."

I look down at my feet.

"I'm done," Ryan says. "Done pretending that this little charade doesn't bother me, because it does. You're the woman I love, and I have had to sit back and watch you spend every spare minute, expend every ounce of your emotional energy, on this man, while all I get from you is the scraps. Kailey, I would be fine with the scraps if I knew you really loved me, if I was assured that you wanted to be with me in the way that I want to be with you." He shakes his head. "But I'm not assured. In fact, I think that as long as Cade is in the world, I'll never have your heart."

My eyes widen. "Ryan, you *wouldn't*."

His eyes search mine. "Wouldn't what?"

It has never crossed my mind, this ugly thought that hovers now, but then I've never seen Ryan's eyes flash with anger in this way. I've never seen such a passionate response from him. That, and he came home from work late tonight. My heart begins to thump loudly in my chest. "Tell me you wouldn't hurt Cade."

He shakes his head. "What are you talking about?"

"Someone was following Cade tonight. Someone wanted to hurt him."

He shakes his head again. "I can't believe this. Even now. Even when I'm standing here, pouring out my fears to you, all you can do is worry about *him*? Or worse, accuse *me* of trying to *hurt* him?"

I take a step toward him. "But I—"

"It's okay," he says, forcing a smile. "I know this is hard for you. And at the end of the day, I've only wanted to make life easier for you. I've only wanted you to be happy. And if you're happy with Cade, then you should be with him."

"Ryan, please. I—"

"Goodbye, Kailey. I love you. I always will. I'm sorry I . . . I'm sorry I'm not the one." He ducks into the elevator before I can beg him not to go.

I fall to my knees and weep.

A few minutes pass before I pick myself up. I wipe away the tears on my cheeks before I return to Cade's door and peer in. "Cade?" The apartment is empty.

"Cade!" I cry. I notice a note, written in his handwriting, on the coffee table. It reads:

My dearest Kailey,
You saved me, and the only way I can repay you is by not ruining
your life. It's time I said goodbye.
I will always love you, no matter how close or how far.

Cade

"No!" I cry. "Cade, no."

He must have slipped out and used the stairs to leave while I was talking to Ryan. *Did he hear everything? Is he upset?*

I don't wait for the elevator. Instead I bolt to the stairwell. My feet pound down the cement stairs, footsteps echoing off the walls. When I reach the first floor, I race to the reception desk. "Did Cade leave?"

Chris nods. "About five minutes ago."

I shake my head. "Why didn't you stop him?"

"We have a sign-in, sign-out system here, but we can only advise patients. At the end of the day, they have free will."

I nod, solemnly. "Did he say where he was going?"

"He didn't, just left heading that way." He points right, toward the city, and my heart sinks.

It's after ten before I drive home. I looked everywhere I could possibly think of for Cade, but this time, it seems, he is gone. Ryan too. His car isn't parked in front of the house, and when I step inside, there's a permanence to the air of loneliness I feel, as if an era has ended, just like that, without my even knowing it or asking for it. Just gone.

I walk to the kitchen and somehow know I won't find Ryan at the breakfast table in the morning. I can't even remember the last omelet I made him. Sunday? The Tuesday before last? Was it spinach and leek or mushroom? I think about all of our lasts. Our last kiss. The last time he danced with me in the living room, made love to me on a Saturday morning with birds chirping out the bedroom window. The last time we held hands or laughed together. I want to memorize the details, and mourn them.

And yet I still wonder if he could have been part of the reason Cade left tonight. Did Ryan frighten him? Could he have hurt him? Impossible. Or not? The world feels cruel and sad and confusing, as if everything I love has been reduced to a small pile of sand and I must try my best to hold it in my hands, wincing at every grain that slips between my fingers.

I'm startled by the sound of a knock at the door, and even more startled when I open it to find James standing on my doorstep. It's begun to rain, well, pour, and James's hair is wet. His bangs are plastered to his forehead. He looks disheveled, anxious.

"I'm sorry to bother you at home," he says. "You mentioned you lived in Wallingford, and, anyway, it wasn't hard to find your address online."

"I don't know what to say."

"Kailey, we need to talk," he says, his eyes sad and pleading.

At first I want to send him away. I don't trust him, and I'm not sure if there's much more to say. But something in his eyes tells me to invite him in, so I do.

"Sit down," I say, pointing to the couch. He does so in one exhausted heap, as if there are weights strapped to his shoulders. Dark circles hover under his eyes, and for the first time the once ageless James looks tired and weathered, like Old Man Time has finally caught up to him. He buries his head in his hands. "I don't know where to begin," he mutters.

My heart beats faster. I'm not sure what he will tell me, but I know it is going to be a long and painful story. "Just tell me what you need to tell me, James. Please."

He looks up and nods. "Cade and I always had a complicated relationship," he says. "You know that."

"I do."

He takes a deep breath. "Element Records was our baby. We both were so proud of it, and we both brought different strengths to the company." He looks up at the ceiling nostalgically as I reach for a tumbler and pour him a glass of Scotch. He takes it. "Cade had a gift, you know. This special ability to recognize talent. I always told him it was like a sixth sense. He could walk into a room and smell the next Nirvana. For a long time, it seemed like anything he touched turned to gold, and I naïvely thought that would continue forever. But that was foolish thinking. There's a cycle to everything. Ups and downs. And Cade fell into a downturn. At first it was just a band here and there. He'd sign a group and offer them an enormous advance, and they'd sell ten thousand albums instead of the one hundred thousand we planned on. We'd spend fifty grand on marketing an artist only to have her fizzle out with a mere two thousand records." He nods. "This kept happening. But Cade kept wanting to invest more and more. There was no end to his efforts, no stopgap. He kept promising that we were so close to the next big thing, that I should trust him and stop worrying so much."

"But you stopped trusting him."

"I did, in a lot of ways," James continues. "He seemed to have lost his edge, but not only that, he was drinking more. The booze, the pills. He was spinning out, Kailey."

"I know," I say. "I was there. But was it as bad as you make it out to be?"

"It was and it wasn't," he says. "I have to tell you something that I've carried with me for far too long."

"What is it?"

He rubs his forehead. "I could have helped him. I was his best friend. But I let my personal fears get in the way."

"Fears?"

"Alexis," he says. "She was in love with him."

"What?"

He nods. "You didn't know. No one did. But I knew. I felt it every time she was with me. She only wanted Cade. Everyone always wanted Cade. After a while, it took a toll on me. I always felt second-best." He sighs. "So when Cade started to spiral, I thought it was my moment to shine. I thought that by his failure, I would rise. That Alexis, everyone, would see that I was worthy." He looks down at his lap. "I was a fool."

"Wow," I say, recalling the way Alexis had looked at Cade. I'd mistaken love for admiration. Had he returned her feelings? I shudder. "I don't know what to say."

"You and I both know that Cade was troubled in those days," James continues. "The drinking. The erratic behavior. Would he have snapped out of it? Maybe. I don't know." He sighs. "But I had to do something. So I started taking the company in a new direction, signing pop artists, changing our focus a bit. When we forced him out, I didn't think it would ruin him. I thought he'd take some time to regroup, maybe even start his own offshoot label. Instead it was disastrous. If you think for a moment that I haven't lived with guilt all these years, you are mistaken."

I lean in closer on the couch. "James, what happened to him. You know, don't you?"

He nods gravely. "Things were getting better. I'd signed a few bands that were looking promising. We were going to turn a profit that year, or so it seemed. It was August, and I'd bought a boat with my savings. The *Stella May*."

"August first was the last day, until this fall, that I ever saw Cade," I say. I swallow hard. It was the day I was going to tell him about the baby. "You might have been feeling flush, but I was devastated."

"I know you were, which makes the next part of the story even harder to tell." James pauses. "Alexis and I wanted her maiden voyage to be extra special, so we hired a full crew, complete with waiters in tuxedos and bow ties. Just as we were setting out, Cade showed up at the marina. He was drunk, belligerent when he got on. I wished he hadn't come. He was angry, and he said some ugly things to Alexis that I don't know if she'll ever be able to purge from her mind." He pauses for a moment. "I tried to calm him, but we argued and it escalated. I'm not sure who took a swing first, but we ended up in a fight, right there on the docked boat. I was as bloodied as he was, but I landed a lucky punch. The impact opened a huge gash on his forehead."

"His scar," I say. "That explains it."

He nods. "There was so much blood. Alexis begged us to stop fighting. She always said we were like two brothers hashing out a lifelong grudge, but this time, both of us too stubborn to step back and apologize for our respective mistakes, we took it too far."

"Why didn't you call for help?"

His voice cracks then. "I wish I had, Kailey."

"But you didn't, and something happened."

"That's just the thing," he says with a sigh. "I ordered Cade off the boat. One of the waiters and I dragged him onto the dock and then we launched."

"A waiter in a bow tie?"

"Yes," James replies solemnly.

"You left him there bleeding?"

"My actions were cowardly, but I thought I had a good reason," he says. "Alexis was pregnant, Kailey. I'd just found out the day before. What if I was charged with assault? I was about to become a father, and I couldn't fathom any of it. I had to protect my family." He sighs. "Listen, he showed up on my boat and ruined my party. Besides, I didn't believe he was hurt that bad."

He looks at his hands as if they still have Cade's blood on them.

"You said he just had the gash on his forehead," I say. "But the medical report from 1998 mentioned possible brain trauma. How do you explain that?"

James shakes his head.

"I don't know, Kailey. Something else must have happened to him that night. I've been burdened with guilt for so long. When you walked in to my office that day and told me he was alive, I was shell-shocked. Cade was never someone who disappeared. He was always present. And when he wasn't, I assumed the worst."

I shake my head. "I don't know what to say, James."

"It wasn't me, Kailey."

My eyes widen. "If not you, then who?"

"I wish I could tell you."

"What about all the money, James? Did you take Cade's money? Cade was worth at least eight million when he disappeared that night. I've hired an attorney and a forensic accountant. They're going to try to recover what is rightfully his."

"As they should," James says, exhaling deeply. "Oh, Kailey. I'm in this so deep."

"What do you mean?"

He rubs his forehead. "The money's all there. Invested. I'll cooperate, of course."

"James, please, can you think of anyone who would want to hurt Cade?"

He shakes his head, then after a long moment his eyes suddenly flash with urgency. "Where is Cade right now?"

I shake my head gravely. "I don't know. Ryan, my fiancé, confronted me tonight about my feelings for Cade, then broke off our engagement. Cade heard everything and then . . . he left."

"We have to find him." His expression is worried, anxious.

twenty-nine

DECEMBER 22, 2008

"*W*here do you think he could be?" I say to James as we run to his car. "I've already checked downtown, his old apartment, the usual places."

"I have an idea," he says, suddenly perking up. "Let's head downtown."

I fasten my seatbelt, then dial Dr. Branson's cellphone. "Hi, it's Kailey," I say.

"Kailey, is everything all right?"

"No," I say. "It's Cade. He's missing." I explain Cade's fear of being chased by someone.

"It's frightening, yes," she says. "But it's unlikely that someone is after Cade. In fact, these types of bouts of acute anxiety are quite common among brain injury survivors. When the brain is healing, it's a lot like a broken record, trying to get to the next chorus, but instead it keeps hitting the same scratch and repeating past trauma, playing the same stanza over and over again."

"So you're saying Cade just dreamed it up?"

"In a sense," Dr. Branson continues. "But be certain that to him it is all very real."

I nod. "I'll find him and bring him back."

"Kailey, your love for him knows no bounds."

Goosebumps erupt on my arms. We've never spoken about my love for Cade, but she knows. Of course she knows.

"It doesn't," I say after a thoughtful pause.

Foot pressed hard on the gas pedal, James races to the on-ramp. My heart beats faster by the second. James takes the Stewart Street exit, then guns the engine. "The market," he says. "He's got to be there."

"Pike Place?"

"Yeah," he says. "Cade loved Pike Place."

Of course. Pike Place Market. The memories rush in, one after the next. The walks we took through the market after dark. The little wine shop he always stopped in at. The fishmonger he befriended over a shared love of turbot. The street violinist he tipped with a twenty every Friday afternoon. And then James and I look at each other and open our mouths in unison.

"The phone booth," we say together.

When we arrive at the market, James parks near the iconic copper pig at the entrance. It's dark, but the cobblestones, coated with a layer of fresh rainfall, glisten under the streetlights. A row of lit Christmas trees line the entrance, and a wreath hangs beneath the Pike Place sign.

James and I jump out of the car and run ahead. We look right, then left. It's been a while since I've been down here, and I know why. Too many memories. "Which way?" I ask James. Normally bustling with people, it's a ghost town now, aside from the hum of the sleepy pigeons in the rafters above us.

"Downstairs," he says, pointing ahead.

I remember now. Down a flight of stairs, around a dimly lit walkway, past that old tavern he used to love and the spice shop that perfumes the air with cinnamon and curry, and then the phone booth, cherry red, with TELEPHONE in black letters across the top. It's a genuine London import.

Of course, the phone booth. Cade swore he could think better here, so much so that he purchased an identical copy for his apartment in Pioneer Square in 1998.

The phone booth is just ahead, and though it's dark we can both make out a figure inside, slumped over and possibly sleeping.

"Cade!" I cry, running closer. I place my hand on the little iron doorknob, and he looks up. When our eyes meet his face brightens, but then he sees James and the smile that has begun to form disappears.

"Cade," I say, "don't be scared. I talked to James. We're here to help you."

He stands up cautiously and steps out of the phone booth, facing both of us.

"Sorry, man," James says, taking a step forward to Cade. "I wish things had turned out differently. I'll live with that for the rest of my life."

Cade nods. "I remember."

"I know you do," he says, breaking down. "I'm so sorry, for everything I did and didn't do. I'm going to make it right to you, I promise I will."

He's silenced by the sound of footsteps behind us, and when we turn around, a police officer approaches.

"Everything okay down here?" the officer asks, casting his gaze at me.

"We're making amends," I tell him before he nods and continues on his patrol. I want to believe that I'm speaking the truth.

Cade's mouth opens. I know he has more to say. "I remember what happened that night, after we fought."

Both of us hang on his every word.

"Somehow I found my way home," he continues. "I was sitting on a bench with Ivan."

"The man who lived outside your building," I exclaim. "You were so kind to him. You gave him a blanket once, and your leather jacket on New Year's Eve."

Cade nods. "Another man came around. He wanted money, but I had nothing in my pockets. Ivan was an old man. He was scared. I told him to come with me, that I would take him to a safe place. We started to walk away, and that's where my memory stops."

"Your final act in your former life was trying to help someone," I say. "That's the Cade I know."

"I'm no saint," Cade says. "And I need to take responsibility for my actions. I lost track of my life." He looks at me. "I lost track of my love."

I blink back tears.

"I want my life back," Cade continues, eyes tender with emotion. "I want to make up for all the time we lost."

"We will," I assure him.

James slips his hands into his pockets and looks at us, overwhelmed with emotion. "And I let my best friend down." He swallows hard. "All the money, the company. I'll pay back what was rightfully yours, man. I give you my word."

Cade nods. His body looks exhausted. But there's a spark in his eyes, a fire that I haven't seen since 1998. A spirit awakened? A life reclaimed? I am hopeful.

"Can you ever forgive me?" James asks, his voice cracking.

"I already have," Cade says, taking a step toward his friend. They embrace, and I wipe away a tear.

"In the first act of my new life, and yours," James says, swallowing hard, "let me see you two home safely. Can I start there?"

I look at Cade, then back at James. "Yes, please. Let's start there."

At the Harborview security desk, James waves goodbye. Cade takes my hand, and as we step out of the elevator, I feel lost and found at the same time, secure and scared.

"Stay with me tonight," he whispers into my ear as we cross the threshold to his studio. His touch is so electric that for a moment I almost step back. But I don't, and when he pulls me closer, I relent to him.

Here we are, together. His hospital apartment isn't home, nor is the Craftsman I jointly own in Wallingford with the man I was supposed to marry. But somehow I know that home is where Cade is. Maybe I've always known that.

It's completely dark, aside from the city light filtering in through the windows. Our Seattle. Someone in the high-rise apartment building across from the hospital has put up Christmas lights around their window, and I smile, remembering the year Cade and I hung lights around his staircase so long ago.

There is no music, but there is a melody. Ours. And as we sway, I think of how far Cade has come. It's been an uphill battle, this fight. And perhaps it always will be. Two steps forward, one step back. Memories held hostage. Mental fogginess. Years lost. Jumbled sentences. Confusion. I'm aware of it all, and I accept it all. Because I love this man. With every ounce of my being.

"Cade," I say, "I need to talk to you about something."

He touches my cheek lightly in response.

"I've written something about you, for the *Herald*—a piece about your story. But it's more than your story, it's a story for anyone on the streets, anyone who's found themselves down on their luck. Anyone whose life didn't turn out as planned." I pause. "I don't have to publish it. I—"

"Publish it," he says. "It's your story as much as mine." He kisses my neck, and his lips travel up to my chin, and my cheek. And then he pulls me close, the way he used to—arm on my waist, hand in my hair.

"Cade," I whisper. "There's something else. Something I've wanted to share with you for so long." Fresh tears stream from my eyes. "The last day I saw you, I wanted to tell you the news that . . ."

"What is it, my love?" he asks, talking to me the way he used to. He nestles his face into the crevice between my shoulder and chin.

"When we parted, that day at your place in Pioneer Square, I was going to tell you something, something very important."

"What?"

"I was pregnant," I say. "I'd just found out. I was going to tell you,

I wanted to, but then . . ." I wipe away my tears. "But then we had a fight, and then, well, you disappeared after that."

He reaches for my hand.

"I had a miscarriage," I cry. "It was horrible in every way, but mostly because you weren't there beside me."

He swallows hard and looks deep into my eyes, then holds me for a long time. His embrace says everything. *I'm sorry. I love you. I wish we could turn back time and have the life that was robbed from us.*

We don't speak. There are no words. Not a single one would do. There is only love, the force that has bound us together for all these years, even while separated.

My back arches as he kisses my neck again, and I press myself against him. I can't get close enough. I've never been able to get close enough to this man.

I think about this as he lifts my shirt up over my arms, revealing the inked *toujours* on my shoulder. I think about all the dreams I had for us. The children we would raise. The flowers we'd grow in our garden by the sea. The family photos we'd pose for, making silly faces or sweet ones, arms clutched together. Parties, laughter, and music, always music.

Cade lowers to his knees, fumbling with the button on my jeans, and as his lips touch my skin my body trembles.

"I never stopped loving you," I whisper.

"I have always loved you," he replies.

Always. My eyes fill with tears.

He lifts me into his arms, his bare chest and body pressing against mine, and when he sets me on the bed, we kiss as if it's our last day on earth. And perhaps it is. What do we, or anyone, know of tomorrow? If I've learned anything, it's that not only may tomorrow never come, but worse, that when the sun rises, the person who holds your heart may vanish, taking a piece of you with him. Here today, gone tomorrow, like a storied ship in the Bermuda Triangle, taken under. Sent asunder.

But now he's here; my love is here, and I'm breathing in his breath, his skin. His hands are exploring every inch of me. I gasp and cry out.

And when our bodies become one, I know that all I want, for the rest of my life, is this. All I want is this love. I want it every day. I want it morning and night. I want to breathe it in. I want to drown in it. And it strikes me how wonderful and tragic it is that in a sea of people just one can reach you so deeply.

As Cade's body rises and falls against mine, I close my eyes tightly and pray that he will never go. I pray that this love, so golden and true, will stay, this time and always.

thirty

"Look at that scene," I say to Cade, pointing out the window of the train. The French countryside is stunning, just as beautiful as I remember from my childhood on that magical trip I took with my grandparents. "Never in America would you see this kind of terrain."

He smiles and squeezes my hand as we pass a pasture dotted with a dozen fluffy white sheep. Behind them is a crumbling manor that even in disrepair looks dignified, like it has housed many banquet tables and bottles of fine wine in its history.

France. It's hard to believe we're here. Here together. And soon we'll get off the train in Normandy and take a car to the little stone house by the sea that we'll call home.

Shortly before I resigned from the *Herald* last year, I published my final article in the series on Pioneer Square. I loved going out that way, with an article that was both personal and hard-hitting at the same time. It told Cade's story, every nuance. And it also told mine. It wasn't nominated for any awards, but Jan loved it. Cade too. As did hundreds of readers who wrote in to say the same. Ryan never closed his deal for the Pioneer Square joint venture, a casualty of the recession, though he did contribute to getting Portland's KGW NewsChannel 8's HD Studio on the Square open on schedule. The homeless shelter by Cade's old apartment was staying put. We'd saved it together.

Our attorney, Bruce Barrett, with the cooperation of James and Alexis, successfully recovered more than ten million dollars, and when the bulk of it was wired to Cade's bank account, we decided to leave our beloved Seattle and start a new life.

"Normandy," each of us said simultaneously the moment Cade's affairs were settled. And so it was decided.

"Do you want anything?" Cade asks, standing up. "I thought I'd get a snack, maybe a bottle of water?" His speech is slower than it used to be. Life is slower for him, but I can't help but beam with pride at how far he's come, and Dr. Branson believes that with continued treatment he will only continue to improve.

"Sure, maybe a croissant?" I ask, smiling. It's as wonderful as it is frightening to see him acting more independently. On one hand, he needs to be independent to thrive; on the other, I worry. What if he wanders off? What if he forgets his whereabouts?

As he walks ahead to the dining car, I think about the life we'll have in France. I'll cook beautiful meals in our little kitchen, windows open, the air perfumed with the smell of the sea and the herbs growing in our little outdoor garden. Every other Wednesday, I'll accompany Cade to his appointments to see the neurologist in Paris, the best in France, according to Dr. Branson. And—I place my hand on my belly, where a new life is growing—we'll raise a child together. Our child. I only recently found out, and though I wanted to tell him the moment the test came out positive, I've decided to wait and surprise him when we're settled in our new home. Besides, I didn't want him to worry about me during the move.

I tug at the ring on my left hand. Platinum with a row of alternating sapphires and diamonds, it was Cade's grandmother's. Simple, at least compared to the enormous rock Ryan gave me, but I love it so. James found it in the drawer of Cade's desk at Element. He saved it all these years.

Telling Ryan I would marry Cade nearly ripped my heart in two. I couldn't bear to do it over the phone. He deserved to know, and I knew I had to tell him, rather than have him find out from one of our mutual friends. So I drove over to the house on a Thursday night. I found him sitting on the front porch, holding a glass of whiskey with a large square ice cube from the ice cube tray I got for him last Christmas. The roses we planted in the garden in front of the house had long since withered from lack of water. Ryan looked withered, too. I hated to see him that way.

"Hi," I said, taking a cautious few steps toward him.

"Hi," he said, eyes brightening for a tiny moment before drifting back down to the glass in his hands. He took a drink. The sound of the ice cube clinking against the glass permeated the great void between us.

"I just wanted to come over to say . . ."

"I know," he said. "You don't have to say it. You're marrying him." He nodded and took a long sip of his whiskey.

"Ryan, I'm so sorry," I said, tears welling up in the corners of my eyes.

He held my gaze, and for a moment I could see the life I might have had with him. The joy. The children. The dinners and brunches and partnership. It would have been a wonderful life, yes, but it would have been a life without Cade.

"The thing is, Kailey," Ryan said, his voice faltering a bit, "I don't know that I'll ever get over you." He sighed. "I will always love you, and it's out of this love for you that I can love you as you go."

"Oh, Ryan," I said, instinctively taking a step forward, then catching myself before I could wrap my arms around his neck the way I used to.

"I have to let you go," he continued, standing up. "So go."

All I could do was stare.

"Go," he pleaded through tears. "Go before I beg you to stay."

My eyes are misty as the French countryside whizzes past. But for all the sorrow in parting from Ryan, there was joy in joining my life with Cade's. Our ceremony was small and quick. Tracy and her boyfriend joined us at a little chapel on Bainbridge Island. Grandma came, too. Although we learned that Cade's aunt Fay had passed on, she was there in spirit. We felt that.

Cade looked so handsome in his suit, as handsome as he ever had. I wore a simple white satin dress that crisscrossed in the back, and I held a bouquet of lilies. It was perfect in every way. Well, nearly.

Just as we were leaving the church, I saw Ryan, leaning against his white BMW, once a familiar figure and now a ghost from my past. *Why had he come?* My heart lurched when our eyes met. *Had he been there for the ceremony? Did he watch from the back of the church and listen to the vows I exchanged with Cade?*

"Go talk to him," Cade said before we drove off, his face beaming with the kind of confidence only true love brings. "It's okay."

My eyes filled with tears as I looked up into my husband's eyes. "Really?"

"Of course," he said. "He took care of you when I couldn't."

It was true. Ryan had loved me dearly, loved me with every ounce of his being. I nodded and let go of Cade's hand to walk across the gravel parking lot to the street, where Ryan stood.

"Hi," I said, approaching him in my wedding dress, a far cry from the elaborate Vera Wang I had planned to wear on the day I was to marry Ryan. I was still holding my bouquet, and I could only imagine the pain he must have been feeling seeing me this way. A bride whose groom was not him.

"You look gorgeous," he said. "I always knew you'd be the most beautiful bride." He sighed. "I knew it, but I still had to see it with my own eyes."

I swallowed hard, fighting back tears. Part of me wanted to reach my hand to his cheek and trace the soft spot between his cheekbone and his eye the way I used to. But those days were over. He knew it. I knew it.

Instead I smiled. I told him I was sorry.

He nodded, then turned to me once more before getting into his car. "I hope he loves you the way I do," he said.

As Ryan drove away that day, I felt as if I could burst. For him, for me, for Cade.

"Thank you," Cade said when I walked back to the car.

"Thank you for what?" I asked, setting my bouquet on the backseat.

"Thank you for choosing me," he continued, the sound of Ryan's car peeling off still echoing.

I wiped away a tear, thinking about all the people we meet along the way, and that Beatles song "In My Life" that sums up the experience so perfectly. The thing is, in my life, I loved Cade more. I would always love him more, plain and simple.

Cade returns to his seat beside me on the train with a coffee and croissant, and I feel a surge of gratitude for the way life has turned out, for that long and winding road that has brought us back together.

The train lets us off in a small town. After we disembark, we pile our bags onto a cart, then flag down a nearby taxi to take us to the little home we've purchased and not yet seen in person.

"We should be about twenty minutes away," Cade says, holding out a map on his phone for the driver, who grunts something in French. I do my best to understand, but my high-school-level French fails me. There will be plenty of time to learn.

The sun will set soon, but if we're quick we might be able to see our new home in the last few minutes of daylight. Warm air rushes in the open windows of the taxi as the driver speeds along the winding road that hugs the shore. We pass through a small town, but in the miles after, the landscape is sparse, save for a few stone homes that look to have a certain wisdom gained only from presiding over the seaside for centuries.

My heart begins to race as the cypress-lined road—our road— winds right, then left. And then, through the trees, we emerge. Our house is just ahead. Its walls, constructed of stone the color of light sand, look strong but also soft, welcoming somehow. The door, painted a deep purple to match the thriving bushes of lavender on either side of the entryway, beckons.

We pay the driver and wheel our bags across the stone walkway, then stand together, hand in hand, in front of our new home.

"Home," Cade whispers to me. He takes my hand and leads me to the door, where he slips our key into the lock, then lifts me into his arms, carrying me over the threshold like our newlywed grandparents might have done so many years before us.

"Oh, Cade," I say as he sets me down. "It's perfect."

Together we wander the little house, throwing open the windows to let the sea air in. The cozy living room is dominated by a stone fireplace and connects to the kitchen. I run my hands along the well-loved butcher-block countertops and can hardly wait to fire up the old copper stove. I think of all the quiches and cassoulets cooked here over the decades, the centuries.

The larger of the two bedrooms could accommodate a few beds, or even several bunks, for our children, one, maybe two, and those of our friends. For now it will be a nursery. I feel a flutter deep inside when I imagine Cade holding our baby. I think of Tracy, too. Just last week she'd told me her news: engaged and pregnant with twins. I smile to myself. Life. How funny and wonderful it can be.

The other bedroom is smaller but charming, with big windows that face the sea. "Let's make this our bedroom," I say to Cade, who nods and lies back on the bed to test it out. I follow suit.

"Not bad," I say. Of course, the place will need some work. Fresh paint. Some new furniture. Curtains, linen preferably. But Cade is right, it already feels like a home. Our home.

We wander to the patio outside. It's so close to the beach that, courtesy of the wind, sand has collected in small drifts along the edge of the garden. "Look," I say, pointing to a terra-cotta pot beside the teak table and chairs. "A little lemon tree."

Waves crash softly against the shore. The sun is setting, and the fading light is tinged orange. I watch Cade. He can't seem to break his gaze from the ocean; it's like it calls to him. I reach for his hand nervously. "You have to be careful," I say. "You may have once been a champion swimmer in high school, but don't forget that you haven't yet relearned how to swim." I know I sound more like his mother than his lover, but his accident has instilled in me a protective nature that I will never, perhaps ever, be able to shake.

He smiles. "Baby, there are a million and seven things I need to relearn to do." He reaches for my hand. "I'll add that one to the list."

I return his smile.

"One day at a time," he says.

"Yes," I reply. And yet I want to protect him from the world.

"How far away do you think that beach is?"

"What beach?" I reply, confused.

He reaches for the locket hanging from the gold chain around my neck. "The one where your grandfather found this shell."

I point ahead. "I think it's a mile or two that way. But don't worry about it. We'll go check it out together once we're all settled."

He nods, and the two of us sit on the bench at the edge of the patio. I lean my head on his shoulder. No love is perfect. And I suspect there will always be something lonely about my love for Cade. Something regretful, even something sad. An ache never to be soothed. After all, we've climbed great heights to be here. A mountain, really. And we summited it together.

"We did it," I say, nestling my head in the crook of Cade's neck.

"We did," he replies with a smile, eyes fixed on the ocean.

He is mine, and I am his. And if you ask me how long I will love him, the answer is as long as there are stars in the sky; as long as there is sand on the shore.

Toujours.

author's note

Dear Reader,

In 1994, I was a sixteen-year-old with short platinum-blond hair, the keys to a green 1969 Volkswagen Beetle (which I'd bought for myself with babysitting money, for nine hundred dollars), and a box full of cassette tapes. I lived in a sleepy, rain-drenched suburb of Seattle, and on weekends, my friends and I would ride the ferry to the city, which musicians like Kurt Cobain and Eddie Vedder frequented. We'd sit in coffee shops, hang out at record stores, or—if our curfews would allow, and sometimes after a pleading, twenty-five-cent pay-phone call to our parents—hike up to Capitol Hill to see a band. Inspired by the iconic movie *Singles,* we wore a lot of thrift shop clothing—flannel shirts, vintage dresses, cardigans—dated boys in bands, and drank too many lattes. Our anthem was music, coffee, and freedom. It was our own kind of nirvana.

Time ticked on, however. I went to college and got a degree in journalism. I gave away my Doc Martens, and traded my guitar (which

I was never very good at) for a laptop. I got married, had babies, endured a painful divorce. But I always looked back to that time, that
scene. The music. The cafés. The rainy afternoons fueled by coffee and
bad poetry. The ivy-covered brick building in Pioneer Square I remember so well. Coming of age in the 1990s.

Today I'm sitting in my Seattle office on a sunny afternoon. I've
written seven novels (ten, if you count the books I threw away), and
I'm thinking about *Always,* my eighth novel. When I began work on
this book, I immediately felt an undeniable pull to Seattle during its
music heyday. I wanted to set a story on the streets, in the cafés, and
with the people I knew and loved (and still love) so much. Seattle in
the 1990s will always be in my heart, and I hope I've done it an
ounce of justice.

But while the backdrop of this story is born from the landscape of
my adolescence, there is more to the inspiration. One day, two years
ago, I was exiting a parking garage in downtown Seattle. The incline to
Seventh Avenue was steep, and as I pulled my car forward, I quickly
slammed on my brakes when I noticed a bearded homeless man slowly
walking across the sidewalk.

Our eyes met, and in that moment, I was struck by an unshakable
sense of familiarity—the unmistakable feeling that we had met years
before, in college. But how could that be? How could a man who was
premed end up homeless? How could a former life-of-the-party type
trade preppy clothes and a nice condo for rags and a sleeping bag on
the street?

He rounded the next block before I could roll down my window
and ask his name, and besides, I had my children with me. On the
drive home, I was haunted by that moment when our eyes met, and
haunted by a story that began to develop in my heart—Cade and
Kailey's.

What would I have done in Kailey's shoes? What would I do in the face of such a weighty and heart-wrenching choice? What would any of us do? I enjoyed wrestling with topics like this in the story, and realizing that as much heartbreak as I've seen in my own life, I do believe in love, and I always will.

Happy reading,
XO,
Sarah

acknowledgments

I wrote this novel in the aftermath of one of the most heart-wrenching times in my life. My world had been turned on its head in every way, and I was trying my best to make sense of it and find some semblance of joy moving forward. I am especially grateful to my friends and family for being patient with me, for believing in me, and for reminding me that there is a season for everything, and that I could weather the rainy season, and that there would be sunshine ahead again.

I owe a heartfelt thanks to my publishing team, too, for standing by as I simultaneously sorted out my life and worked on this novel. Thank you, Elisabeth Weed and Jenny Meyer, my longtime agents, for believing in me from day one and for believing in me still. Also, so much gratitude to the wonderful people at Random House and Ballantine, Shauna Summers, Jennifer Hershey, and the entire team, for your patience, kindness, and for getting behind this book in such a smart and exciting way.

Thank you to Denise Roy, Katie Hunger, Jane Green, Jane Porter, and so many others who helped me along the way with their wisdom, assistance, advice, and encouragement.

To my mom and dad, my wonderful family, the one-and-only Claire Bidwell Smith, and my crew of girlfriends, who have laughed and cried with me and held my hand through rocky times—thank you.

And to my three boys, Carson, Russell, and Colby—may you find love that is beautiful and true, and not waver until you do. And to Brandon: Thank you for loving me and for showing me how beautiful it is to love again.

Always

SARAH JIO

A READER'S GUIDE

THE MUSIC BEHIND
Always

Reflections from the Author

Like air and water, music has been an essential element in my life. Coming of age in Seattle in the early 1990s was, for me, magical. While I missed the beginning of the "grunge" scene, I was old enough to ride out the tail end of it—soaking up afternoons in coffeehouses with my high school friends, spending hours in record stores on Capitol Hill and evenings at recording studios with musician boyfriends, and staying out past my curfew (begging my parents' forgiveness) to see my favorite bands, praying I'd make the 11:30 P.M. ferry home to my sleepy hometown just off the island across from Seattle. This was an epic time for me, and I always—always—knew I'd return to it in my storytelling.

Of course, when writing this novel, I listened to music constantly, and those songs fueled me just as much as my characters' motivations did. Here is a bit more about the music behind the book, with some commentary from me:

Soundgarden: When I was fifteen, my best friend and I would spend our Saturdays catching the ferry, saltwater mist in our faces, then hightailing it up Seattle's infamous hills to our favorite downtown Seattle café, Sit and Spin. Sadly, this café/laundromat (cool combo, huh?) went out of business a few years ago, but oh, did we have our fun there. My favorite memory was seeing the guitarist from Soundgarden order a foamy latte, then sit down right beside us. I was too shy to introduce myself, but I always wish I would have, especially as I think his companion that morning was the late Chris Cornell, rest his soul.

Mazzy Star: I never saw this band in concert, but the song "Fade Into You" might as well have been the anthem for my youth. These beautiful lyrics haunted me as an adolescent, and they haunt me now. They always will. Another track that I love on the album *So Tonight That I Might See* is "Into Dust."

Nirvana: I was in eighth grade when my friend and locker partner pulled a *Nevermind* cassette tape out of her backpack and said, "This is so cool; you have to listen to it." A few years later, a smitten fan, I was returning from a school trip to Mexico and checking in with my parents at a pay phone on a sandy San Diego beach, when my mom told me that Kurt Cobain (Nirvana's founder, singer, and guitarist) was dead. Suicide. I nearly fell to my knees, along with hundreds of thousands of other fans who felt his music in their bones.

The Gin Blossoms: I don't know when, or how, the Gin Blossoms made their way to the very core of me. *Happy, nostalgic, fun, free*—these are the words I'd use to describe the music that became ingrained into so many of my memories. Kailey would probably tell you the same.

Joni Mitchell: It's a tragedy that I didn't discover her until my late twenties, as Joni's music has come to be so special to me. I could listen to "Both Sides Now" for the rest of my life on a desert island, and I listened to it so many times as I wrote this novel.

Smashing Pumpkins: When I was a teenager, this band's music ran through my veins. My friends and I always had them playing in our cars (mine, a green 1969 Volkswagen Beetle). "Today is the greatest," are lyrics that will stay with me for a lifetime. Even if life isn't perfect, there are so many wonderful reasons to be grateful for another sunrise and sunset. I sure am, and I think my characters are, too.

The Turtles: Remember that song "Happy Together"? My parents listened to it in the free-spirited California days of the 1970s, and I always loved hearing it come from the radio or a record player. Funnily enough, I ended up attending a comedy show in Seattle and just happened to be seated at the very same table as Howard Kaylan, the lead singer of the group. He was just as kind and engaging as you could hope him to be, and it was fun to write his music into the novel.

Fleetwood Mac: I love how, on one of their early dates, Cade tells Kailey that her dress is a little "Stevie Nicks." "Gypsy" is one of my favorite Fleetwood songs (that and "You Make Loving Fun"), and it will always make me think of Cade and Kailey. Truth be told, however, on one of our first few dates, the love of my life told me that my dress looked a little "Stevie Nicks." Of course, I had to put it in a novel.

There are so many more songs and musicians who influenced *Always,* but these are at the top of the list. I hope you will play their records or pull them up on Spotify and enjoy a listen while you're reading the story. You'll find a part of me and my characters in every note.

Thank you for reading—and listening.

Love,
Sarah xo

PHOTO: NINA SUBIN

SARAH JIO is the #1 international, *New York Times,* and *USA Today* bestselling author of eight novels. She is also a long-time journalist who has contributed to *Glamour, The New York Times, Redbook, Real Simple, O: The Oprah Magazine, Cooking Light, Woman's Day, Marie Claire, Self,* and many other outlets, including NPR's *Morning Edition,* appearing as a commentator. Jio lives in Seattle with her three young boys.

sarahjio.com
Facebook.com/sarahjioauthor
Twitter: @sarahjio
Instagram.com/sarahjio

Chat.
Comment.
Connect.

Visit our online book club community at
Facebook.com/RHReadersCircle

Chat
Meet fellow book lovers and discuss what you're reading.

Comment
Post reviews of books, ask—and answer—thought-provoking
questions, or give and receive book club ideas.

Connect
Find an author on tour, visit our author blog, or invite one of
our 150 available authors to chat with your group on the phone.

Explore
Also visit our site for discussion questions, excerpts, author
interviews, videos, free books, news on the latest releases,
and more.

Books are better with buddies.
Facebook.com/RHReadersCircle

RANDOM HOUSE

RANDOM HOUSE
READER'S CIRCLE ®